ANDREI NAVROZC

AWFUL BEAUTY

Confessions of a Coward

Among the lilacs grown wild,
This awful beauty never dies.

— BORIS PASTERNAK

ONE

THE PLAYER

1

God how they lied to us, how they all lied to us, how they lied and lied all those years on end. German professors, pince-nez and aquiline glance subjacent, preening in front of the rather more common kind of gilt-framed mirror, squeezing the luxuriant Fraulein's dimpled buttock, dictating a tract on feeling to this or that quietly greying mouse. Russian idealists, beard goatee-neat or else broom-bushy, waving their arms in the air against a landscape of anachronism veiled in gun smoke, ransoming conscripts in time for the final harvest, stuffing winter overcoats with explosives, kissing each other on the lips with a loud smack.

French bon-viveurs, they also had a few words to say on the matter, for eloquence is but elegance pursued by other means, desperately smitten, simply awash with sentiment, yet with an eye to the love-struck suitor's annuity all the same, or else where would the camellias of the title keep coming from, you little sillikins, camellias don't grow on trees, you know. Italian *conti*, which rhymes with *racconti* and just about everything else in the dictionary, scrimmaging behind sensuously undulating brocades, dripping potions into Venetian goblets, eviscerating rivals in duels, always coming back to Mary Mother of God and the Heavenly Host, but have

these Casanovas not misled us too, if only by never saying
anything worth remembering? English gentlemen with
rusty iron whiskers, dreadnought sideburns, mutton dressed
as lamb don't you think, delighted you could join us this
evening – but that's the funniest lot of all, really, though they
lied much less than the others, for the houndstooth-check,
wet-rot, broom-cupboard, oilcloth-plain reason that they had
been thrashed as children and had come to fear the introspective forever after. Hence the willow's suppleness in our sentimental guff, hence the presumptive mother's milk of all that
codswallop, hence the gun-room's grammar book: bunkum!

But now a winter rain beats against the windowpanes, and
a winter wind weeps and roars over the skylight of the roof,
very Crystal Palace that skylight, always makes me think of
Dostoevsky's *Notes from the Underground*, though what has
he, even he, had to say on the subject that is life-saving, what
cure has he bequeathed to me personally, what recipe for salvation from anguish, what salve for the all-but-bleeding
heart? Don't laugh, *Signori Conti*, don't laugh, gentlemen
with whiskers. *Vi giuro, non sapete niente di me.* Nor can you
possibly have been where I am now, apparently in a small flat
with a large cast-iron skylight handed down to the previous
owner by the England of confident rationalism and great expectations, but in reality deep within the sacred heart of a
possible ancestor of yours, one who fought in the Third Cru-
sade, one who, in the confusion of battle, was left bleeding,
vermilion rose after vermilion rose, into the thirsty roadside
dust of Arsuf after the defeat of Saladin at the hands of the
uncircumcised. You haven't been there. You've never been
burnt by the desert sun.

This is a fact, do you understand me? A noble fact. You can twist it this way and that, you can spit on it, you can heat it to 1000 degrees Centigrade, or dry-freeze it and have a go at it with a hammer, you can try to dissolve it in aqua regia, but a noble fact is an imperiously stainless substance, possessed of the hardness of diamond and the elasticity of rubber, and it will never change. Besides, is it really all that shocking, this inert, immutable, adamantine fact I've adduced here? Suppose I said that not one of you people out there has ever had an original thought. Would anybody fight back? Would anyone argue? No, you would probably answer something like, 'You're quite right. But let me tell you, I don't mind. I'm fine just the way I am. Now look at the time.'

Or suppose I said, now listen you fellows, I bet you £1000 you've never been in the same room with a woman of awful beauty. What would you say? You would object, but mildly, groping for words, hemming and hawing, loosening the neckties, very much doubting that the bet could ever be won, what with the vagueness and the little bit of an oxymoron in there, you can't be serious, such an infantile thing to say, and what can it possibly mean *awful beauty* for God's sake, and how can anybody ever agree on a definition? Sure, one man in a thousand would go for it, perhaps, naming some selectively carnivorous flytrap or prominently macrobiotic vedette, deciding to stick to his guns, to ride out the argument to the end, but what then? Being £1000 to the good is no substitute for inner conviction. And all I can hear you saying with any kind of aplomb is that roses are red.

I don't want to be harsh on people, but the emotional life of our epoch reminds me of central Moscow in the old Soviet days, a time when *there was everything*. There were billboards advertising cigarettes and the national lottery, there were competent doctors and crooked lawyers, there were chauffeur-driven limousines and children's mud-spattered bicycles, there were girl Fridays and thoughtful academics who knew their Hegel, there were men's double-breasted suits with impressively large lapels and dinner jackets with shiny satin ones, there were smooth-talking men and hard-to-charm, capricious women, there were eccentric artists and their intriguingly cavernous studios, there were shops selling seasonal game and live fish, farmers' markets, dry cleaners and delicatessens... There was even a kind of praline torte with three chocolate bears on top, one big and two small ones, called 'The Three Bears.' And guess what? *It was all a sham.*

I don't mean, of course, that it was a sham for those participating in it, for all the stage extras in the centrally-planned, century-long political production. It was their life-saving duty, after all, to convince themselves and each other that their experiences were perfectly real, and hence perfectly deserving of the real emotions that went with them. Yet knowing what one does, now and then one cannot suppress a rueful chuckle: 'Ah, Grandpa! I can't believe how you drooled over those military decorations! And you, Dad! How you fussed over those three bears on my birthday! Come on, admit it. You've been had, all of you, haven't you?'

Man lives by caprices, thought Dostoevsky. Yet the entire thrust of the epoch, which has now reached its culminating point, is against these insubstantial urges of the soul. None the less, outwardly the epoch still bows to them, it still feels the need to dissemble, it still cannot proclaim its materialism to be universally valid, obligatory, and inescapable. As the Muscovites had that trio of bears, cast in the finest dark soy mass by the omnipotent hand of the state, so too does the epoch feel obliged to offer its inmates a modicum of respiratory, gustatory illusion.

Hence we have bookshops, and books that resemble bricks of pressed straw. Hence we have music, which makes the young dance their Saturday nights away in communal ecstasy. (No, we have serious music too, of course, we have Covent Garden and divas with voluptuous bosoms and everything!) Hence we have struggling painters in quaintly unadorned studios, and fine doctors, and crooked lawyers... Hence the photographs of unapproachably blond actresses, of dietetically irreproachable models, of society women said to be beautiful on the covers of popular magazines, though what does it matter, from the vantage point of totalitarian rationalism which is the guiding spirit of the epoch, whether these women are very beautiful, or just beautiful enough, or plug ugly? Like the chocolate bears made of Communist soybeans, they are there to represent human caprice, and by implication the epoch's covenant with mankind for tolerating it. Otherwise there could be panic. Otherwise people might bolt.

Well, I did bolt.

2

There is something I want to say here, but obviously it eludes me. Is that because I am still distraught and cannot see straight for the tears? Yes, but also because there is a pall of impotence that invariably comes to lie on each and every one of my resolutions, no matter how urgent or desperate they are for me as a writer. Wishing though I do that the prospect of action could be somehow less daunting, I am not ashamed of this weakness of mine. No, I recognise that it is in the very nature of art, which, since the beginning of time, set itself impossible tasks and then wrung its hands bemoaning its glorious failures. I say glorious, of course, because our kind of impotence is capable of moving mountains – provided they are made out of molehills – at the speed of thought, and of sowing epochal confusion among entire populations more effectively than the guillotine. But it is impotence nonetheless, because the object of our striving, after all's said and done and the resin dust from ballet slippers has settled on the boards, is not *to create* but *to describe*. And this we cannot do.

Ah, it is a pang of recognition painful enough to make the artist weep from frustration. Why, of course you can be a god! It is easy enough to create a world of one's own, as children make people and animals from potatoes and matchsticks, as Van Gogh fashioned his universes and Tolstoy his resurrections. But in the final analysis, that's just stuff, you see. Stuff for sale. On the other hand, try being an adult, try being a man under the omnipotent God you believe in, try to stand there, on your puny, buckling legs, while holding up that massive Rococo mirror – a hundredweight of opulent carving and ponderous gilt – in which the unconfessable reflects the incontestable. It is thus that the artist comes to know the sublime weakness of which I speak.

I want to describe a moment. A single moment and a woman's face. That is all, I swear it. But no sooner do I put pen to paper than the weakness comes over me like a viscous dream, and I begin drowning, suffocating in its varicoloured possibilities, sweating at the prospect of getting lost in its endless, labyrinthine corridors. The eyelid of my mind's eye grows heavier, as though from a draught of some soporific infusion, and a general feeling of wooziness, as though one is wading through cotton wool, makes it difficult to choose words, to distinguish colours, to tell left from right and right from wrong, to inquire, to explain, to remember. I feel like a traveller freezing to death – like a man dying of exposure – complete with the chill, the stupor and the letting go. I see clearly the object I'm dying to describe, like a fleshless hologram suspended against a background of velvet blackness, but my parched lips cannot move except to mutter, like Dostoevsky's Prince Myshkin upon seeing the portrait of Nastasya Filippovna: 'Perfection!'

I know I have to write a book, this book, and when it is finished I will probably have to tear up the anaemic and barren manuscript, or burn it, howling with utterly undeserved humiliation. I don't want any stuff, you see, any stuff for sale. I just want the truth. I want the awful, inner, ultimate truth about that moment and about that face. I want to find the strength to lift up that heavy mirror, if only for a few seconds, and tilt it towards the past in such a way that all the phantasms of my own creation should vanish and God's own truth should be glimpsed where now there are only shadows and guile and invention, in other words, where now there is only art.

Art has already been done. In my native tongue I have written a cycle of poems with the same title as this book of prose, and I know that my name, and my reputation as an artist, is now inseparable from those quixotic spasms. Hence it pains me to think that the narrative in the pages that follow may be regarded as a work of *fiction*, a word which, honestly, is simply too labile to have ever gained a foothold in literary Russian. Why on earth should I want, in an inferior medium and in a language other than that of my childhood, to go over the same fearful ground? No, this book is not fiction. It isn't even a novel, really, except perhaps by association with those essays in lachrymose malevolence that Dostoevsky dictated off the fraying cuff in order to gouge the next bit of gambling money from his ever mistrustful publishers. Yet in those ravings of his I have seen the natural illuminations, the reflections of God's truth, strong and vivid enough to displace art in the ornate mirror.

Now, I want you to notice something. The symptoms of impotence – helplessness, numbness, prostration, torpor, voicelessness, ataxy – evident in the psychosomatic behaviour of the artist who has chosen to forsake his art in the cause of truth are identical to those of what is called love at first sight. Remember Marlowe's

> Where both deliberate, the love is slight;
> Who ever loved, that loved not at first sight?

Because once the artist has found the courage to look it straight in the face, the splendour of naked reality – God's reality, not the sequined blouse of one's own preposterous design draped over the wax shoulders of one's most recent invention – is immolating and immobilising. And so he stares and stammers. Cat got his tongue.

Olga, do you recognise me? Let me try saying it now without using my tongue.

3

'How much energy you expend to appear soulless,' I chided her one day. 'No more,' she replied with a glance at the disordered dressing table, taking her time between lines of coke, confident and elegant like eyebrows pencilled in by an ageing movie star, 'than do you to discover whether or not you have a soul.'

When I think of what separated us, oddly enough this is the first logical obstacle I see in my mind. God, who advanced the doctrine of the categorical imperative many centuries before Immanuel Kant, did not suppose that sadism and masochism – as these two of the myriad human caprices came to be known, initially in clinical literature and later in common parlance – were mainstream enough to warrant a footnote in the Scripture. Yet the commandment to do unto others as you would have them do unto you is absurd without the underlying assumption that a unified ethical system, which predates the commandment, has long been in place. Thus the idea that God so loved the world that he sacrificed his only son for its sake falls flat if one supposes that God loved his son no more than did Russia's Ivan IV, called The Terrible Man, or Iosif Dzhugashvili, called The Man of Steel, both of whom sent their sole-begotten sons to certain death, not for the world's sake but simply because they did not love them very much. The belief that Christ's own parent, Who Art in Heaven, was different, is what makes a Christian a Christian.

Both were Christians, of course, Ivan the reigning tsar and Stalin the runaway priest. But, albeit for dissimilar reasons, the fashion for love – in other words, for sentiment defined by a system of values that could just as easily apply to the relationship between man and woman as to the bond of father and son – touched neither. One was a local brute who reigned on the outskirts of Europe, far removed from the world of European fashion. The other was a totalitarian ruler who jettisoned European fashion, together with all its sentiments and pieties, in order to conquer Europe. Unlike Abraham, whose sole-begotten Isaac was a late and greatly beloved child, neither thought love was all that important in the general scheme of things.

If the father did not truly love the son, then the story told in the Gospels is either religious propaganda or worse, a global political provocation. Without that truth, there is no Christianity. Yet what is subject to proof in fairytales about princes and frogs is left unproven here, as if the mere assertion that God so loved the world were sufficient. Well, Shakespeare based the whole tragedy of King Lear on the inability of a love that is proven to give expression to itself. What, then, of a love that is *not* proven?

The miracles worked by Christ are witnessed and attested to in the Gospels with the exhaustive precision of a juridical proof, yet at the centre of it all, where the cornerstone of the Christian world view ought to be, there is nothing. Like Cordelia, God will not heave his heart into his mouth. But why should a believer have more trouble believing that the loaves fed the thousands, or that the lame took up their pallets and walked, than that the God who made such things

12

possible was a loving father?

Well, nobody would ever doubt a mother's love. The fashion for love must have begun with the veneration of the woman whom I addressed in my prayers, or else why would our most miraculous icons, for nearly a millennium the holy images of the Orthodox confession, be images of her? As I said, I had bolted. Then a year passed, then a month, then another, and this is what I found myself saying one day, as the rain came down and the wind beat on the windowpanes, while kneeling before the small icon on which, in faint Cyrillic ochre, was the appellation, HOLY: MOTHER OF GOD: JOY OF ALL THAT SORROW.

4

Holy Virgin, Mother of God, bearer of joy to those who sorrow, forgive a repentant sinner, and if you grant me this one wish, that she should now knock on my door and return to me with words of love, I promise to have myself newly baptised, and to lead her to be newly baptised in the same font, and to newly baptise any child that she will bear me, and to pray to you to the end of my days in gratitude for the miracle you have wrought for my sake.

And you know that what I want from her is this and only this, that she let me look at her face, and that she permit me to partake of her kindness, and that she allow me to be near her in happiness as in adversity, and that she may wish me to kiss her whenever she feels the pleasure of it. And I do not want from her any of the abominations of the flesh you have witnessed here, unless they will divert and cheer her, for like the child you yourself once were she may crave the satisfaction of her caprices without the sadness that sometimes overcomes those whose caprices have been satisfied.

I want this from her, and then I want to conceive with her a child, a female child whom long ago we decided to name Katya. You do understand my language, don't you? Then you remember the manifold diminutives of Ekaterina: Katerina, Katya, Katyusha, Katenka… Because this girl will surely be a perfect likeness of herself, though she will also be wholly mine, for my own blood as well as that of my beloved will flow in her veins, and then I can feed her, and wash her, and dress her with the conviction that she enshrines the soul of my beloved forever entwined with my own. And I will love her with that absolute purity of love that I have only ever known with my beloved, except with us the carnal does of course come in the way of the absolute. Yet for the sake of that heavenly absolute, which is your own habitation, built of your infinite love and infinite suffering as our houses are built of brick and wood, help me O Virgin!

I pray to you now and ever, show me that miracle. Never before have I asked anything of you, nor of your Son, nor of the Holy Saints, except once of a Catholic, Sant'Antonio, who helped me find the way to her when she was quite lost to me, when the gold wedding band she had mislaid long ago fell out of the bookshelf and grazed my recalcitrant hand. Please, I beg you, merciful Mother of God, show me that miracle. Let her walk in so that I may weep at her feet, even as I weep now before your sacred image.

5

She never came that day. There was no knock on the door.

My prayer went unanswered. Maybe it was the money.

Don't laugh. Alas, we were both real, she and I, and in the modern world where we lived, money aliments reality. She could not have knocked on my door if there had been no door; I could not have expected her to walk up the stairs if there had not been a staircase in the building; we could not have met and been together if money had not made us exponentially more real.

We met in the autumn. Olga was twenty-five, I was twenty years her senior, married, with a wife and a young son packed off to Italy. In London I was leading the dissolute life of a writer *manqué*, scattering my rich wife's money, drinking, whoring, gambling. No, I swear I wasn't a bad husband. Sometimes she even remembers me fondly, they still tell me. But marriage is a complicated thing, just like everything else that's been lied about for centuries, though there may well come a day when somebody will tell the truth about it. The point is, suddenly there was money to kill, and I even started a book about my gaming tribulations, entitled *Killing Money*. Like so much else in those days, it never happened.

We met in the autumn. The manifold diminutives of Olga are Olya, Olechka, Olenka, Olyusha, Olyunya… She told me to call her Valerie. She never told me her name. She had been living in London for just a few weeks, on a tourist visa and a secret stash of a few thousand dollars in crisp notes of uncertain provenance. Imagine what a figure I cut with her – bon-viveur, gambler, wastrel, taking her to restaurants, to nightclubs, to casinos, showering her with flowers and presents – the ridiculous figure of the married man in the perennial plumage of optimistic duplicity.

No, I lie. The truth is that from the moment we met I have not told her a lie. Because from the moment we met I have known that she is the first and last love of my life. This is why I shall never tell her a lie for as long as I live, and why what I write here can never be a lie, and why this book is about her.

Everything goes just the way it starts, it's been said. When I used to meet strangers, in London as in New York, or Paris, or Rome, I never confessed my origins to them, thinking that prudence was the better part of whatever folly I was about to commit in their company. To her I confessed it at once, hopeful that my frankness would be reciprocated. It was not. Not that day, not a week later, not two weeks later. I knew she was Russian, of course. When it comes to the Slav accent in English, I'm Professor Higgins, and woe betide the Moldovan croupier who claims Muscovite origins, and shame on the Polish waitress who intimates she's Swedish. I knew it, but I wanted her to admit it. And, for weeks on end, she wouldn't. We met, we went out together, we slept in fancy hotels. We spoke English. I joked often, and sometimes, when I struck it lucky, she laughed in reply. She asked carefully crafted questions. I answered them truthfully, volubly, exhaustively, with great gusto, and of course I explained many things she'd never thought of asking me about. But most of all I kept begging her to confess, and confess she wouldn't. Nor would she tell me her name.

Then a thought came to me. The zoologist Konrad Lorenz proved the existence of instinct by projecting the shadow of a harmless bird, and subsequently the shadow of a bird of prey, over newborn chicks, who rushed to the mother hen for aid as soon as they sensed the predator's presence. One night, as we sat together on the canopied bed of an out-of-the-way Chelsea hotel, I shut my eyes and asked myself: Why am I in love with her? Why am I in love specifically with her, why with her and nobody else but her, why in love for the first time in my life, why in love with a woman whose name I don't know? If I really feel this wonder, I should be able to guess her name this instant. I should be able to work a miracle.

Then I shut my eyes as tight as I could, until iridescent circles appeared somewhere within, and I saw banks of snow, iridescent in the blue gloaming. I saw the Baumann Garden in Moscow, and myself on a winter afternoon, just as amethyst twilight begins beading its rosary, and I saw myself bundled up in my warm winter coat, with snow boots of black felt, with a big woollen scarf around my neck and a big fur hat, with my nanny chatting to some other nanny with a girl in tow, the girl bundled up in her warm winter coat, with snow boots of white felt, with a big woollen scarf around her neck and a little white eiderdown hat, and I'm straining to look at the girl's scarf – all I can do is strain, really, because it is wintertime and drifts of snow are deep on the ground where the paths have not been cleared for walking, and I am so immobilised by my clothes that I can hardly move my head – and on her white woolen scarf is a golden wisp of hair, curling from under her hat into a loose spiral, coming from behind her earlobe, and I open my eyes, and with a start I say to her in Russian *Olga, your name is Olga.* And she answers *yes, yes it is, how did you know?* By instinct. And then I say *Olya, I love you. Look, I have worked a miracle.*

Olya, Olechka. No, you don't understand, my angel. I love you. And it is because I love you that I have worked the miracle. Or maybe it's the other way round, and it's because I have worked the miracle that I love you? Yes, that's how it all started.

6

There are many kinds of awareness that are better at building character than the sense that one's life has been wasted, but anyway I would be lying again if I said that I awoke one morning filled with the remorse and the dread one associates with wholesale repentance. No, in Venice I usually awoke with nothing more eye-opening than a hangover from the night before, Harry's Bar until midnight followed by cocktails on one of the terraces overlooking the Grand Canal, not infrequently my own, until three in the morning. My wife and I had fallen in with the *jeunesse dorée* of the lost city and found in their company that saccharine oblivion, that ersatz lotus, which is so often a welcome substitute for the real thing and is almost always preferable to the alternative.

The alternative, in my case, was the life of a writer, failing, rather like Venice, with the imperceptible slowness of soil subsidence. Unlike Venice, that other landscape lacked charm, its situation being a booming London of spivs and sushi, a place that during the preceding decade had evolved in such bizarre, yet curiously predictable, ways that the last of the illusions I had been harbouring – illusions about my own future in it, I mean – fell away with a crash one day, like a patch of waterlogged plaster.

I wanted to be a vendor of coloured air, of perfumed silences and kidskin paradoxes. I wanted salon acclaim, I wanted to have risqué exchanges with visiting Bolshoi ballerinas and a hypnotic effect on women of society. Did I want to be lionised? No, I don't think so, that would've meant too much responsibility and not enough languor. Perhaps leopardised, with reference to the moment in Lampedusa's *Il Gattopardo* when the princely name becomes a mere ornament, but most of all I wanted to be treated as a precious pet, a cat sacred to Isis, a soothsaying parrot, a serpent used in divination. In the event I wanted to become half-Rasputin, half-Rastignac, with the public role of a writer *manqué* and a secret hoard of unpublished manuscripts whose significance would not be revealed until my selectively lamented demise.

Every provincial duckling wants to become a Swann, and in social terms, having spent my formative years in the United States, I came to London as just that, a country bumpkin with one or two letters of introduction to the great and the good in the pocket of a Brooks Brothers jacket. The fact that my childhood and adolescence had been spent in Moscow, in a position of social eminence simply unimaginable in the West – for the harshest class system, in comparison with the infinite profusion of social castes in the Russia of my youth, is kindness itself, as well as an object lesson in near-egalitarian even-handedness – was neither here nor there, because while it may be true that it is the good heart and the clear head, not the dancing master and the French tutor, that teach us manners and invest us with dignity, it is equally true that a social butterfly, like an international call girl, needs to know the whole layout of the fancy hotel before he can feel at ease under the head concierge's gold-braided stare.

Anyway, even now I feel that it was not the butterfly's fault that his persona never really developed beyond the pupa stage. London had changed and was changing more rapidly with every passing season, becoming more and more like New York or Hong Kong – or, indeed, like the Moscow of today – than anyone present had the courage to say out loud. Suddenly the place no longer had room for pirouetting on the literary catwalk, for cutting a controversial figure, for being intellectually dashing and charmingly original. The big money rolled in, streamlining everything in its path, and it seemed that it was all on one and the same day that the duchess realised that her usual table had been given to a Ukrainian footballer, the venerable maitre d' had been re-placed by a blonde from New Zealand in an electric lime-green lycra top, and the restaurant's former owner sold his house in Holland Park to withdraw into the hedged tranquillity of a new life which he would now feel safe enough to risk losing in the stock market. And, as I recall it, on that same day it occurred to me with alarm-clock clarity that I would never arrive at the imago stage of my dream, that in a society so aggressively dominated by ducks, a swan would fare far worse than in the fairytale, where he is as yet unrevealed to them as the Proustian character he is for the sympathetic reader.

The snobbery of money is a glaring tautology. In a rigidly hierarchical society where a person's rank is a tribute to his ancestors' role in his nation's history, snobbery is as absurd as it is inutile. To remain in London, to endure the blandish-ments of my ego and the collapse of my vainglorious expectations, now against a background of such social attitudes as I would not have thought benign and tolerated under circumstances more propitious, this, I decided, I would not do. At that time, my wife had only a little money coming to her from her family in America, and I was making even less as a literary journalist, writing for two or three editors who still retained the autonomy – then vanishing as conspicuously from that sphere of London life as from all the rest – to shelter a Russian eccentric, a gifted poseur and a potential embarrassment, all in the name of the obsolescent notion that entertaining an audience with something other than entertainment was their Fleet Street duty.

For the business of culture, more neon-sign obviously with every publisher who went bust, was show business:

Cousin Teresa takes out Caesar,
Fido, Jock, and the big borzoi,

a lilting refrain and big-drum business on the last two syllables of borzoi, as Saki had it in one of his absurdly uncanny prophesies. But we owned a London townhouse that could be let, in that first year, for £160,000, and in a few months after the decision to flee had been made I found myself on the terrace of a house in Rome overlooking the papal fountain made famous by Fellini in *La Dolce Vita*, where I began writing a book about Italy and, of course, myself.

Yet my vanity would not be appeased by a scene so bucolic, nor a denouement so inconclusive.

7

Now is not the time to speak of what my wife must have felt, but let me drop a small hint. Vanity is voracious, and a frustrated vanity takes on a cannibalistic aspect, in that the subject's ego, craving objective validation, begins to devour whatever personality happens to be within easy reach, finding in its emotional responses at least momentary relief from the world's indifference. I am not ashamed to confess this now, nor did I lack the introspective curiosity to remark on it then, for the irrepressible reason that the doubly displaced persona of a Russian émigré intellectual posing as an English writer of blatantly outmoded predilections was more than adequate justification, or cover, for the alienation I was experiencing.

Moreover, it was clear to me that even an individual of known means, with a solid background and an easily discernible position in society – my antipode in every sense – would be justified in having feelings of alienation, jealousy and resentment had he the passion to examine his sad predicament without the disinterest born of habit. Who needs him? Who believes in his goodness, to say nothing of his wisdom? Who values him for the qualities he values in himself? Who will come to his daughter's wedding? Who will attend his funeral? These questions teem just below the surface, like so many tadpoles, in even the shallowest minds. In the deeper, darker recesses of a mind belonging to a self-confessed, self-obsessed intellectual – a fugitive from himself and hence a misfit, constitutionally unable to find consolation in tranquillity, order, or comfort – they could not but have grown into horned toads.

No, I was not in the least ashamed of my reactions. And, if the workings of vanity had been all of a piece, logically it would have followed that I chose to quit the scene the moment it became clear to me that I would never get anywhere no matter how hard I tried, that I rejected the world because it was bound to reject me, or perhaps had already done so without my knowledge. But the sad truth is that, like all strong emotions, vanity is a house divided against itself. And the more my virtuous *I* insisted that my vainglorious *I* must renounce the wicked, coarse, loveless world, the more my virtuous *I* secretly pined for that world's caresses. Like the rubbing of invisible salt into a secret wound, it was my obsession with renunciation that in the end made the renunciation – and consequently what had been conceived as a life of virtuous exile in Italy – so unendurable.

The wicked world's caresses, for which I secretly longed, were of course the caresses of women, wicked or otherwise. It is a truism that many, if not most, men are resigned to seeing, in the degree of attention shown them by women, the measure of their actual success in society, even in those not infrequent instances when such attention is neither sought nor appreciated. I would go further and claim that, for most men, such attention is a measure of nothing less than their immanence, and that women, considered collectively – not as a harem, by any means, but rather as the petroleum reserves of Venezuela might be considered, for instance, for the purposes of a specialised stock-market report – are a kind of living godhead, a cosmic pleroma of otherness, within which all men's striving is measured, weighed and recorded for eternity.

Thus every woman alive is a scintilla of that undulating

immensity of omniscient plasma shimmering with the tiger's-eye lustre of a sheer stocking, a single nerve ending resident in that lambent, unknowable, eternally feminine presence, and when the male with the pint of stout in his hand makes the female with the glass of wine laugh like a silver bell, he senses that his victory, small as it is, is the stuff of epos, indistinguishable in kind from that which drew Homer to Troy. A woman's glance, her smile and her laughter, when a man has succeeded in becoming their progenitor, are the proverbial good works which, while in themselves insufficient to cause the heavenly gate to open before him, are nonetheless indispensable to salvation from oblivion, prerequisite to that paradise of actual existence where the enclosed oasis of the embrace and the plashing fountain of the kiss are but propylaea on the way to the inner sanctum for the festive ceremony of inscription in the book of being. Not for nothing do feminists – who, like men, believe in the existence of such a paradise, with the crucial difference that men do not hope to see it established on earth – claim that when a man makes a woman laugh, he's already raping her.

I had been living by that cosmogony since my mistiest childhood days, mindful that when, at week-ends, parties of my parents' friends arrived at the dacha, dinner table conversation appeared to be conducted by the men with the sole aim of hearing it punctuated by the laughter of the women. Punctuated is a misleading word, however, because their banter was like a thin gold chain and the bursts of laughter like pendant gemstones, leaving no doubt in anyone's mind where the true value of the prized bauble lay. And round and round those conversations went, bringing the poet and the raconteur and the paradox monger and the buffoon and the magician and the mime and the idiot a step closer to nirvana with every unexpected twist and strange turn, as eyes sparkled, as gentle hands absentmindedly brushed away loose strands of hair from slightly flushed faces, as perfect little heads inclined in the ecstasy of merriment, as goddesses accepted with evident pleasure the mixed offerings of thought, word and intent.

8

Thus was I raised in a world of sedentary feats, in a cultural microcosm which deliberately undervalued experience. More than that, it treated experience as a kind of monstrous blemish upon the face of thought, a defect that was deemed the more ungainly for being the more noteworthy, unexpected, or rare. It was as though the threadbare commonness of climbing the Himalayas or roaming the world as a hired assassin was more glaring than that of shopping for bread and milk. Experiences alleged to be more substantive or adventurous, went the implicit argument, were more physical, and hence distracting, polluting, and generally unsuited to the mind. And the abiding aim was cultivation of the mind, which alone could aspire to the immortality of feminine condescension.

Russian culture as a whole chimed in with this. Our writers did travel far and wide, they fought in wars, they had bizarre love affairs and lost fortunes at cards; but just as Russia never produced a school of formal philosophy, it never produced the intellectual type of Hemingway, T. E.

Lawrence, or Somerset Maugham – wise to the world, allegedly, and proud of it. Our writers wanted to travel, in Andrei Platonov's phrase, into the depths of man. *Not* to Arabia.

In retrospect, I cannot but appreciate the inverted cynicism of that approach to reality. I cannot help admiring my parents and their circle for having isolated me so effectively, throughout the whole of my youth, from action, and solely by means of an education in the pleasures of contemplation. *Vita contemplativa* was the sum total of their own lives, and all along I had been able to feel that their solicitude was not hypocrisy but the increasingly scarce product of a unique and absorbing, though quite possibly moribund, cultural tradition.

And so it went on in my later life and travels, this obstinate, indiscriminate denial of experience at all costs. So long as the joys of *vita contemplativa* are unceasing, I kept on thinking, the world is my cloister. Well, not quite, perhaps, but then everybody knows that even the earliest monasteries were not mere repositories for the Sid Sawyers of the day. Still, in a decade in the United States I never once visited Europe, and during my subsequent years in Britain I never once ventured beyond the Mediterranean. That's a quarter-century of an upheld taboo, of obstinate self-confinement to an abstract ideal.

The Russian émigré grandmother of an erstwhile friend of mine, a Hohenlohe by birth, refused to come out of her house in Rio de Janeiro to look at Sputnik, which everybody said could be seen in the midnight sky: 'It's a Soviet provocation,' declared the princess. At the American university I attended, I was drawn to the study of the Gnostic writers, and of the Coptic language in which they raged against the created universe, after I had glimpsed a similar Russianness in the totality of their denial. They went even further, of course, because to them not only all experience of the material world, but its very source, matter itself, was of the devil.

Having grown up under totalitarianism, I could see their point; for, if everything in the universe is the work of a malevolent demiurge, can you really afford to gamble on the likelihood that even a single atom of it will bring certain joy to your anguished soul? On the other hand, I was no longer living under totalitarianism, or so it seemed; and, if matter was free, and governed by its own laws, including those of physics, then perhaps the girl next to me was truly my beloved, the sunset I was admiring in her company was real, and the taste of the veal chop with wild mushrooms at the inn near the Vermont border was not, in the end, a Soviet provocation.

Thus, in the apt phrase of recent coinage, I smoked but didn't inhale. Matter, our source of experience, might not be evil, but relying overmuch on the value of experience was contraindicated to the man who wanted to save his soul and be truly free. *All action is provocation.* Certainly, I reasoned, there must be an ethical fissure between good and bad actions, but it is since time immemorial shrouded in moral mist and, more important, dwarfed to nothingness by the much wider chasm that separates action from contemplation.

It was into this chasm that I fell one night all those years ago in London, when I walked through the doors of a gambling club in Curzon Street and looked into the mesmerising whorl of the spinning wheel. It was, and in the context I cannot possibly think of a word more laden with meaning, an experience. It was as though all the pent-up thirsts of a puritanical past stirred to life within a desiccated soul, and I felt like the old spinster who, never having tasted liquor before, liked it so much that she drank a whole bottle of brandy and died of alcohol poisoning the same evening.

The experiment in experience yielded an illuminating paradox. A life of contemplation teaches one many things; yet it is only when one is drawn, perhaps unwittingly or unwillingly, or by pure chance, into action, that one realises that what all these things add up to is an understanding of the world one has spent a lifetime contemplating, not of oneself. And, quite probably, a life of action is likely to spin out the selfsame paradox in reverse; so that an experienced, decisive, resourceful, hairy-chested, Scotch-drinking man of the world will be deeply conscious of his own weaknesses and strengths, of his own cowardice and bravery, but will then travel to Spain to fight on the wrong side, write a panegyric to Mao, or lose all his money on Wall Street.

This is how my descent – or possibly ascent, depending on whether or not some members of the audience are standing on their heads – into the world of experience began. I realised then, as I gazed into the spinning blackness before me, how little I knew myself. But hardly at all! I'm not sure if anyone but an inveterate gambler can fathom the horrible truth of what I'm about to say, but it is much easier for a rich man to enter the Kingdom of Heaven than it is for a poor man playing roulette at £5 a stake to put down £100 straight up on a number. It isn't important to know just *how* poor he is, for everyone at the tables is or will one day become poor, so long as it is clear that my apophthegm revolves around the notion of disproportionate risk.

So the paradox was that the contemplative life which I had led, and clung to until then, gave me much knowledge of the world but none of myself. And I submit that it is at least as important for a thinker to know that, say, the velvet revolutions in Russia and Eastern Europe were masterminded by the secret police as it is to know whether he, the thinker in question, is or isn't a yellow-bellied coward. And one of the ways of ascertaining whether one is a yellow-bellied coward is to see if, while playing relatively small stakes, one can suddenly feel the winning number with one's innards and stake everything in one's wallet on that miracle of intuition.

As a rule, one does nothing of the kind. One bobs and weaves, one dissembles. One prolongs the experience of risk, keeping the stakes low and thereby making a mockery of what the experience is all about. One fingers the chips. One feels the gnawing fear of losing all, of having to stop playing, of going home empty-handed. Of not being able to borrow more money. Of not being able to take a taxi. Of not having that cup of coffee in the morning. Of not having the fare for the bus to get to the bank. Of inconvenience. Of embarrassment. Of ghosts, of thoughts, of friends. Of oneself.

How often, recalling the day I met Olga, I would reproach myself in these terms. If I had stayed with her from that day forward – I kept thinking – if I had gambled everything, straightaway, blindly, on the manifest chance of possessing her, if I had staked whatever it was that vaingloriously I still thought I had achieved in my miserable life, I might have won big. She could have loved me back, and forever. What I did instead was madness in many people's considered opinion

– for, without doubt, there are many people in this world even more cowardly than myself – but in my own eyes it was more of the same sickening calculation. Unaccountably, I sought to qualify the experience of risk, thereby reducing it to an empty gesture, and what could have been a miracle in the life of a poet became an episode in the life of a gambler.

But is writing any different, I ask you? Does not even a serious writer – I'm speaking here of men of overwhelming purpose, not highbrow timeservers or glorified airport-novel hacks – choose the word he is about to put down on paper, like that slippery big chip on the green-baize layout, with a thought to the audience, with a nod to the reader, with a wink to the editor? Is he not easily seduced by the phantom certainties, the clever simplifications, the convenient shortcuts that offer themselves, and appear attractive or useful, along the way? Do the sparkling ornaments and the altogether delightful subterfuges of what is known as his *style* not lead him astray, to the continuing applause of those too dense to understand the substance of what he actually hopes to say? And can he, one life-wrecking day that comes but once in a man's rotten life, risk it all on a single spin of the wheel, and to hell with the ever-rising mortgage of the anaphora, the mousy hair of the schoolgirl simile, and the small change of the well-placed comma?

Thus conscience doth make cowards of us all, conscience in the broad sense of ratiocination, deliberation, calculation. It is said that when the game of roulette was first introduced in the eighteenth century, the risk factor of 36 had been intended to represent the mature age of the average adult, beyond which a person could not conceive a quantity with any

natural facility. This is still true. We still live in a world measured by the number of years in our lives, of teeth in our
mouths, of letters in our alphabets, of houses in our streets,
of days in our calendars, of cabochon emeralds in our
bracelets. The billions spent on national health care, distances between cities or planets, and the speeds of sound and
light are abstractions, which nobody in their right mind can
be expected to gamble on.

Thirty-six to one is another matter. Yet which of us can
say with any degree of conviction that, were eternal bliss
proffered to him at these odds – oh, any man playing £5 a
stake who has wagered £100 to win £3500 on a single number knows the meaning of the word *bliss*, believe me – that
he would seize the chance? That he would not hesitate, ever
mindful of the fact that hesitation is to risk what thinking
about call options is to kissing? That he would throw caution
to the wind, in other words, and follow the miracle? All right,
forget the example of the good writer. Were not the multitudes that had chosen to follow Christ commanded to do the
same in His day? Yet how few among them did what was
asked. *Twelve* disciples!

9

At some point in the Italian sojourn, a couple of years after
I had moved my family to Venice, when the book I was writing was nearly finished – not that I thought that finishing it
would ameliorate the agony of displacement and all the other
vainglorious frustrations that, lengthening like afternoon

shadows, had followed me into exile – our house in Knights-bridge was sold for £2.6 million and my wife began to receive an annuity from family trusts in America. Suddenly it seemed there was money to burn.

My gambling expeditions to London became more frequent. I found myself in the vaudeville role of the corrupt accountant, something along the lines of the character played by Philip Seymour Hoffman in the film *Owning Mahowny*, throwing crisp packets to the croupier with one hand while embracing an alleged beautician with the other, all with the nagging awareness that the experience, though addictive and satisfying in the way that satisfied addictions are, could not resolve the fundamental dilemma of non-existence that had been tormenting me ever since I quit London in fear and disgust, and had only redoubled in Italy. Then as later, nobody loved me for the reasons I wanted to be loved, and those few who loved me for other reasons failed to convince me that they knew me better than I knew myself, however little that was. Ever since my first forays in the London underworld, when I fell into the vortex of experience and became, in my own eyes, a phenomenal man, I wanted to be loved as the man, not as the noumenon I had been. More than ever before I craved the attention of women, but now I thought I could finally offer them the raw matter, the tangible substance, the physical body that was always strangely absent from the intellectual orgies in the dacha Elysium of my childhood, where the participants seemed to content themselves with mere intimations of immortality.

Now I wanted to grab that immortality with both hands, I wanted to break it open like a ripe pomegranate and let the purple juice run down my chest, I wanted to feast with virgins without paying for their compliance with the silver of wit, and it seemed to me that I finally had the experience – and all of a sudden the fortune – to make that happen. That the fortune had come to me by way of the pockets of my wife's parents – like the money spent on whiskey-sodas and rock'n'roll by the Neapolitan teenager in the Renato Carosone post-war hit *Tu vuò fà l'americano*, which comes 'direct from Mama's little handbag' – troubled me far less than the twitchy fear that it would not be ample enough to finance my dream of existence. The ethical implications of my conduct were of no significance next to the practical difficulties of achieving my aim, however inchoate it may now be supposed to have been, rather as might be imagined in the case of an overenthusiastic scientist who, pursuing some mirage of metempsychosis, thinks nothing of using his own children's flesh in his laboratory retorts. If the analogy seems random, one can always recall Tolstoy and his treatment of his family.

Let me be as unambiguous as good manners permit. In all of my previous life women slept with me because I amused them, which was how I thought the world worked. My discovery of experience made a gaping breach in that world view, which no amount of subsequent ratiocination could fill. If one could know so much about the world without knowing oneself, what guarantee was there that making a woman laugh is the right way of getting her to go to bed with you? Or to love you? Or both? It was as though a long shadow of misapprehension had lain across the first twenty or perhaps thirty years of my adult life, and then all at once the source of illumination shifted and nothing stood between me and the solace I craved.

I imagined it as unsmiling, this solace, perhaps even cruel, at least to others, with a glance that was cold and piercing rather than warm and caressing, yet all there for my taking, and not on the old basis of an act of condescension in exchange for a disquisition on Schopenhauer, but on the new basis of well, here I am, world, let's see if you can manage to lock up your women in time. The elephantine coarseness of this strain of thinking never gave me pause, for once one has worn the Armani suit of the rogue accountant on a spending spree, one is quite insensible to humiliation by less recognisable labels, midlife crisis among them. The shabby aesthetics of my newfound *vita activa* did not occupy me any more than the ethical vacuum in which the gambler makes his appointments with destiny, and if the devil had appeared before me in those days, offering to accept my vaunted intellect in part payment for the year's losses, I would have considered myself the luckiest of men. In a few weeks' time I would have been back on his doorstep, begging him to throw my sedated originality and what was left of my conscience into the bargain.

10

It should not be surprising that, for every set of hypocritical attitudes I describe myself adopting, I proffer a corresponding set of rational explanations known as an excuse. Hypocrisy would be a shaky colossus were it not girded by the steel of reason. But what gives the armature its resilience is a unique property exhibited by truth in the domain of emotion, namely, that a feeling can exist within us as itself and at the same time as its opposite. Every time the impassioned patriot betrays his country, every time his loving wife cheats on him with his best friend, and every time his clever son asks for a Coke while meaning to have a cookie, Aristotle's law of excluded middle is revealed as inoperative in the emotional sphere. Patriotism and treason, love and treachery, satiety and thirst are shown to have a common middle, and the *A* of extreme delicacy, for instance, may manifest itself in one and the same breath as the *not-A* of mendacious insolence. One asks for bread and is given stones, though in the wonderland which is human emotion this is neither uncommon nor necessarily a bad sign. For who among us, while hungering for the meat of eternal life, has not turned to locusts for sustenance?

All of this is relevant because I am about to claim that my blinding need to be loved by women as a man of experience rather than of intellect never obliterated the ideal of womanhood instilled in me from infancy, that is, of femininity as divine omniscience. Rather, the two opposites coexisted. The leonine *A* of my conquistadorial, swashbucklingly carnal cynicism lay side by side with the ovine *not-A*, the notion that one's *beloved*, to use the only term really suited to the romantic outlook, is but a container for one's tenderness, and that the purer the tenderness one pours into this magic vessel, the more intoxicating the sensation of one's own immanence one draws from it.

What complicated matters further was the plain fact that many women, equipped as they are with the intuition that proceeds, perhaps, directly from the godhead of their collective identity, are cognizant of what I would call the vampiric quality of male tenderness, particularly of the extreme, dove-pure and hopeless-romantic kind. For while tenderness is no bad thing, their intuition tells them, the manic intensity with which he who bestows it is intent on turning its recipient into a private wishing-well gives new meaning to the word exploitation. It becomes clear to them that, having once consented to the role of receptacle, the woman would henceforth have to content herself with life on the receiving end of the man's emotions, *all* his emotions. The primacy of her own emotional being would be abrogated, with more than a passing suggestion of gender reversal about the romantically hermaphroditic couple that the two of them would make, Heaven forbid, when together. No, *I* want to be the vampire, murmurs the woman in reply to such a proposition, *I* want to be the one who sucks *your* blood while pretending to kiss you on the neck with infinite tenderness.

What was I to do, then, given the conditioning of my childhood? The clever thing would have been to conceal my predilection beneath the facade of my new *vita activa*, using my newfound appetite for experience to mask the selfish craving for selfless giving. But since I now insisted on being loved for the qualities I thought I possessed – having been loved for so long so ineffectually for the qualities others thought I possessed – this seemed like a gigantic step backwards, an act of cowardly subterfuge, even a betrayal.

11

I remember arguing with my father, who insisted that Marilyn Monroe looked like any number of God's creatures at the checkout counters of suburban supermarkets. I was sixteen and of a dreamy disposition, a consequence of having passed my adolescence in the company of older women who found my conversation amusing enough to encourage certain liberties on my part, liberties whose constitutionality I would never have dared to advocate, certainly, in the absence of such naked abetment.

Invariably taken, in accordance with long established romantic custom, in hammocks, garden benches, and deserted verandas bestrewn with autumn leaves, those liberties were at first more like licences, conditional and limited in their scope to the study of the grantor's inorganic attributes, such as fabrics, hooks, seams, buttons, garters, zippers, hairpins and the like. Into this area of study I thrust myself with the zeal of a scholar admitted to a previously sealed archive, and before long became convinced that far from being what philosophers call accidents – qualities not essential to our conception of a phenomenon – the attributes in question were inalienable components of femininity, and hence of my own longings.

More precisely, I saw that they gave beauty stricter definition, larger form and more objective measurement. As the use of metre and rhyme can transform a page of clever *vers libre* into the dozen lines a condemned man will recite to himself in his last hour on earth, the couturier's art, in the old sense of guile or cunning, seemed to extend God's cleverness beyond the limits of the physical body with a preternatural, almost clairvoyant specificity. Doubtless these attributes could be described as accidents, but only in so far as the accidental – at least while chance continues to vie with order for mastery over our universe – is essential to our lives.

They chafed and pinched, these little numbers in the corsetière's sense rather in the Miltonic sense of strophes, but loosening and unfastening, even removing them, did not make them disappear. They left a fragrance all their own on nature's skin, and to follow the indentations made by some vicious fetter of French lace or an impertinent bretelle of less outlandish provenance was to fuse all of the senses in the olfactory, rather like an apprentice perfumer at the moment of making the great discovery which he simply *smells* will make his name as the leading nose of his generation. The base notes of sunlight, grass and perspiration never rose to the top to obliterate entirely the mysterious exhalations in this or that passionate embrace of material, and even a commercially produced scent, in theory brazen as a trumpet of the Apocalypse, was in practice too broad and shallow to overwhelm these stubborn whispers, which then worked as a kind of clandestine response to a mercilessly oppressive regime, a hidden culture of dissidence impervious to the ravages of political tyranny.

An undercurrent of these early compulsions connected Eros to civilisation, proceeding from the biblical fig leaf, moving on to the industrial revolution, and ending with the modern times, when the riches of the world appear to have but one demonstrable purpose, namely, fetishist adornment of the greatest possible number of women with the greatest degree of variety attainable. It is as though, for mankind, playing with dolls began as a diversion and ended as a profession, with the result that, in the more prosperous countries, it is hard to point to a field of endeavour or an area of industry whose rewards and profits do not have women's bodies or souls as eventual recipients and beneficiaries.

Years later, in London and Paris, in St Moritz and Ibiza, in Monaco and St Tropez, with the binocular voyeurism of a naturalist watching an old hypothesis stir to life in the hollow of a dead African ficus tree, I was to observe the whole process of transmutation of flower pollen – oil, gas, iron ore, armaments, land, semiconductors, textiles, sugar, cocaine, cocoa, coconut, cough syrup, whisky, brake fluid, pork bellies, grain, cement, tin, timber, music, books, paintings – into the mellifluous fodder of nightclubs and restaurants, brothels and modelling agencies, outdoor cafes and motor yachts, hotels and beaches, plastic surgeons and health spas, jewellers and couturiers. Once aware of the historically observable nexus, I became conscious of the essential ambiguity of my own attitude to the women I was undressing. Original sin may have been a terrible thing, but what's done is done, and the kaleidoscopic variegation of fig leaves, in the giant wardrobe which civilisation has since become, is long part of what makes Marilyn Monroe, like Eve a fallen blond goddess, deserving of love.

She was a random choice, of course, and perhaps my father was right, *sub specie aeternitatis*, when he denied her uniqueness. But this is not the point. The point is that, once original sin has been accepted as tragic and irredeemable, and all the tantalising accoutrements of civilisation as inescapable and real, it is only logical that a woman's beauty should strive for objectivity, seeking acclaim which is measurable in the number of ships launched, tickets sold, or fans registered on the website. Civilisation, one of whose functions is to define all it surveys, has found a way of quantifying beauty, and if more people go to see a film with Marilyn Monroe than with anyone else, then she is the most beautiful woman in Hollywood and therefore on earth. Not surprisingly, it is with her that the president of the United States wants to dally, because to dally with another, with one who is *not* Marilyn Monroe, is *not as good.* So in Manhattan, for instance, not living on the Upper East Side is *not as good,* and woe to the naive interloper who would claim that he wants an apartment in Greenwich Village rather than on Fifth Avenue because he prefers it, and not because, like everybody else, he can ill afford to buy what everybody else dreams of having.

Those who would pour scorn upon this mode of reasoning, calling it simplistic, should renounce the world and mortify their flesh in monastic confinement, because either one must live with the consequences of original sin – in which case the opinion that the girl in the Playboy centrefold is beautiful has all the objectivity of an algebraic formula – or else one must renounce civilisation as the work of the devil, in which case monastic withdrawal from the world is among the less hypocritical options. In acknowledging the closeness of nipple to lace, in recognising the obligation of thigh to garter, I had made my choice and could no longer, constitutionally or logically, turn a blind eye to the symbiosis of nature and nurture – of God and the devil – that is the woman in her dressing room.

If you must eat pork, goes a Muslim saying, you may as well let it get all over your beard. Every cultural precept I had imbibed since childhood wanted to steer me away from the public playground of thought and desire, to protect me against koinophilia. Originality was prized above everything, even when it was perceived to cross over into eccentricity and finally mental instability. If the cultural enclave of my youth had a role model, it was Prince Myshkin in *The Idiot*. It is significant that, although this madman is physically incapable of having relations with a woman, Dostoevsky makes not one but both of his heroines – contrasting halves that, together, embody the totality of womanhood – fall madly in love with him.

And yet some overpowering, centripetal force made a nonsense of all that centrifugal nudging, because – not unlike *The Idiot*'s author himself as he was in flesh and blood, I might add – what I longed to see in a woman was her aesthetic commonness, her appeal to everybody else besides myself, her net weight on the scales of civilisation and her pulling power at the box office. Like everybody else I wanted what everybody else wanted. A Marilyn. A centrefold, a doll, a mannequin.

12

I began by saying they all lied. What about? About love, for the most part, though sometimes it seems that those who *haven't* lied have only made lovers' lives more impossible. I'm not talking Dante and Petrarch here, just the last couple of hundred years, roughly since the French Revolution. It was then that the *deluge* of ugly fiction – anecdotally forecast by the regnant scapegoat – was first let loose upon a world of beautiful sentiment. 'Immediately there appeared in the heavens the cold star of reason,' wrote De Musset in 1836, 'and its rays, like those of the goddess of the night, shedding light without heat, enveloped the world in a livid shroud.' But the truth, the truth, where did the truth go?

Introducing Exhibit A, a fictive hunchback, who opens his veins in the bathtub only to discover that his blood is blue. Where does he turn for help? What can he do at this late hour? Whom can he sue? Elsewhere, in Exhibit B, a woman called Psyche turns to the mirror of ancient myth to observe that the loss of her lover has aged her overnight. She now looks the very image of her grandfather, the tin magnate who died intestate. What is *she* to do? Where is *her* answer?

Why not send her rushing off to a famous Brazilian plastic surgeon, who reshapes her face, and a few days later – *I will survive, I will survive!* – she's out dancing with a handsome stranger in a Rio nightclub. The hirsute youth touches her face, pulling on the fresh stitches, and her forehead comes off in his hands like a banana peel. That's Exhibit C, as introduced by the prosecution. The hirsute youth faints. What of *him?*

And what of the child abandoned by his parents, who becomes mute? Or turns into a pigeon? And what about the recent account of one problematic divorce, straight from the pages of a respectable newspaper, in the course of which the faithful wife discovered that her husband of ten years, armed with sweet excuses and an artificial penis, was all along a woman? And what of the Paris friend of mine, the dashing abstract painter who'd picked up a pretty girl in a restaurant?

God, that was a crazy story. Everything about the girl seemed perfect, the dashing abstract painter said, the face, the body. They had lunch together a few days later. Then he took her to a gallery opening, they went out to dinner, had drinks at the bar at the Plaza Athénée, and ended up at his place in the Avenue Montaigne. She went straight to the bedroom to undress, he said, while he lingered in his studio, and finally the two of them were naked in bed, where, during what was by no means their first ecstatic embrace of the night, he suddenly felt, and then saw, that her left hand was missing, amputated at the wrist after a childhood accident.

We understand neither people nor phenomena, not even those that are so close to us – our bodies, our children, our instincts – they are practically right under our Gogolian noses. For modern culture has never given us a unifying theory of modern experience. Those who have striven to tell the whole truth have left us with mere fragments, like the surviving pages of an incinerated manuscript or the shards of ancient pottery bearing witness to a forgotten civilisation. The rest have just lied their whole *oeuvre* away, mendacious as the proverbial gypsy selling an old horse to a young peasant.

Here's an original thought, as surreal as blue blood in the bathtub and as sorrowful as a whole troupe of young Werthers. When a man and a woman meet and fall in love, the one who loves more – more deeply, more passionately, more recklessly – is the certain loser. This is the person who suffers the love, endures its pain, and groans under its weight, until a still weaker, more impressionable, potentially more enamoured subject – in short, a fresh victim – relieves this person of that unbearable burden, which can then be passed on in its own turn, like an infectious disease or a karmic influence. Thus the principle of the survival of the fittest, once logically applied to the recent history of love, spells the eventual extinction of love.

But leaving love aside for the moment, even a sideways glance at its modern vestiges called *relationships* would uncover the hopeless process of natural selection. He just sits there, reading the newspapers, in a fez and embroidered slippers, and she brings him French toast with the double espresso macchiato in bed. He scolds her if the toast is underdone, he loves it when it's a little bit crispy, and she glows with shame and pleasure. He loves it that he doesn't love her, this silly little bitch, while she loves it that he, her omnipotent master, doesn't love her.

Or does he now – one can never be sure. Because at the office, when the administrative assistant in the unfolding story permits him a glimpse of her pearly lace stocking-top, £29.50 from branches of Fogal worldwide, the erstwhile Turkish pasha quivers and whimpers like a homeless orphan: why, he would bring *her* coffee in bed, he would paint her toenails for her, he would be scolded for household misdemeanours and glow with shame and pleasure in reply. But wait, what of the administrative assistant's boss's handsome driver, that strapping lad with a ruthless smile and a pocketful of the best coke in town? 'Her knees buckled every time Jake…' Ah, but of course she would make him French toast in the morning!

Yes, softcore pornography if you like, with a little Vaseline on the lens, though it is hardly my fault that the sphere of modern sentiment is better illuminated by Harlequin Romance than by any other light source at the disposal of the epoch. Without a culture to sustain it, love *in excelsis* has all but devoured itself, leaving it now to relationships to repeat the suicidal cycle, until the last simulacra of romance have passed away and are completely forgotten, nothing in their wake but the unadulterated rationalism of barnyard bestiality. Oh, but indulge me! Really, none of this is irrelevant to the story I tell.

13

No, again I lie. Yet the truth is that from the moment we met I have not told Olga a lie. Because from the moment we met I have known that she is the first and last love of my life. This is why what I write here can never be a lie, and why I must start again from the beginning.

Of course I knew exactly what she was, a Russian prostitute working London, brought here for the purpose by the Russian procuress whose client I had been for several years. By then I had spent time with dozens of Vita's girls, all products of the newly emergent St Petersburg netherworld. All were under strict orders not to reveal their nationality to clients and worked under preposterous, usually trisyllabic names taken from television soap operas which, like the soap operas themselves, they had come to regard, in the course of their brief but eventful lives, as unarguably beautiful: *Jessica, Monica, Veronica.* Housed in flats which Vita owned or sometimes leased, they were in Britain on student visas which they took good care not to overstay, heading home after six-month engagements of twelve-hour shifts seven days a week with something like £50,000, enough to buy an apartment and a car 'back in Peter.' Why an apartment and a car? Because these were the coveted tools of their trade, outright ownership of which made them independent of some of the greedier intermediaries. Your own place meant manumission from greedy madams, your own wheels meant less leverage for pimps and a head start on the competition.

Of course I never disclosed my origins to the girls I was seeing, while the wise old owl of a procuress accepted that I was Italian. The thrill this charade gave me was, I swear, the greater part of the reason for spending time and money in their company. It went well with my new persona of the phantom writer, of a man outwardly gorging himself on experience yet inwardly attuned to the ideals of the contemplative life. How often would I tiptoe to the bedroom door, to eavesdrop on a girl's conversation with the ubiquitous Vita and to hear the account, in a language the girl assumed the inmate of the bedroom did not understand, of what the Italian client had wanted and of what she had done to satisfy or to circumambulate his wishes. Little by little, with every exchange I overheard, it became clear to me that the madam was keeping a detailed dossier on each of her regulars, using the information to brief new girls between appointments. One mistake and my cover would have been blown once and for all.

Only once did I falter, with a girl of such sudden loveliness that after seeing her I ran to a jeweller friend in Old Bond Street and returned to find her later in the day, a diamond pendant with her initial in tiny sapphires in my outstretched hand. *She had told me her Christian name.* It happened like this. I was holding her in my arms, feeling the small of her back that was still dewy with the perspiration sometimes attendant upon a vividly imagined pleasure, when, bringing my lips to her ear, translucent like alabaster in the lamplight, but opaque, like pale coral, against the white of the pillow, I began whispering to her the words of a Russian poem. *Taut silks a woman's waist enclosing...* Aleksandr Blok, 1880-1921. Something like reciting Swinburne to an English prisoner in Siberia, I imagined, or Mickiewicz to a Pole in a German internment camp. Gradually I raised my voice, and fixed my eyes on hers.

They showed incomprehension. So strong was her belief that the visitor was a foreigner, so great her faith that the only reason for coming to London was the apartment and the car, so immovable her conviction that certain worlds never overlapped except in fairytales or dreams, that she could not immediately recognise the language as her own. Then, a stanza later, something snapped inside her, and a tear, a flawless three-carat round, slid down her cheek and seemed to roll on the parquet. 'You speak Russian,' she said in English, still only half-understanding. 'I *am* Russian, darling,' I answered, also in English. 'Are you mad? Does Vita know?' she whispered in reply, this time in Russian. 'No, and I'm going to trust you not to rat me out.' She nodded. 'My visa's up end of the week. Got my plane ticket back to Peter for day after tomorrow. Why would I tell 'er? I'm outta here,' or words more or less to this artless effect. And so I rushed out to Old Bond Street to find a suitable keepsake to seal the bargain.

And of course I came to see her again on the following
day, her last in London. For an hour or two we sat together
on the unmade bed, embracing and saying nothing in the language we had in common. She never betrayed me. That was
all she could have given me of herself, and it seemed more
precious than any gift I had ever received, more even than
the precision scales for analytical chemistry experiments my
father had given me for my eleventh birthday. In the gesta-
tion of the obsession which would later unmake and remake
me, she was John the Baptist. Her beauty was shallow, warm
and somnolent like the Jordan.

It was none of it the same with Valerie. When I first saw
her, at once the dream sequence from Hitchcock's *Vertigo*
flashed in my mind, not least because if the woman before
me can be said to have physically resembled anybody on
earth, it would be Kim Novak in the role of James Stewart's
tormentress. I realise that I am about to do a great disservice
to the truth of this narrative by attempting to describe Valerie, and for this reason the reference to the film is useful as
a failsafe surrogate. The dyed blond hair, brushed back from
the face to reveal a luminous forehead, gathered into a pony-
tail with a length of black velvet ribbon; the arched eyebrows,
wondrously enhanced by the trick of permanent maquillage;
the fearless lips, made even bolder with the aid of some
provincial beautician's syringe; the perfect nose by Praxiteles,
evidently her own; the ears, like two butterflies at rest,
pierced though naively earringless; the cheekbones, of the
kind for which the women of the Slavs were famed and
fetched high prices in the slave markets of the empire; the
neck, graceful like the inclined stem of a lily of the valley in

full bloom; the shoulders, ever so slightly broader than the hips, as if designed, providentially, to carry the weight that had been added, at many a man's expense, to Solomon's clusters of grapes on which the acuminate bosom was shamelessly modelled; the Biblical stomach, again from the Song of Songs, a sheaf of wheat set about with lilies; the naturally slim waist, as in Blok's *taut silks a woman's waist enclosing*, which, instead of rising acropetally, seemed freestanding in the confines of the Eiffel tracery that encircled it like delicate black scaffolding; the perfectly sketched legs, as though illuminated from within by the adherent opalescence of synthetic fibre, with slim ankles and pearl-pale feet in the black patent high-heeled sandals of the oldest profession; the fingernails, manicured malefic carmine, and the whole impression of the figure, rendered somewhat *outré* by the effect of the inorganic substance implanted beneath the thoracic tissue; yes, Valerie would have looked the part in the famous little gray suit by Edith Head *c.* 1959, but I could swear then and can swear still by my love that this was not the point, not nearly all of it at any rate. The point was that her eyes, of a cryptic, undecipherable, almost vacant blue, brought to mind the bloodthirsty steel of Damascus and the icy waters of the Gulf of Finland. They wounded and flooded, and it was while I just stood there, looking into them, that Hitchcock's graphic animations of hypnotism whirled through my mind.

Who is she that looketh forth as the morning, fair as the moon, clear as the sun, terrible as an army with banners? I have described her forehead as luminous, but the truth is that a powdery light streamed from her whole face, phosphorescing like the apparition of Lucifer from eyewitness accounts cited

in witch trials. Yet is not matter itself, as the Gnostics believed, of the devil? And does not the word 'devil,' perversely,
echo 'divine' and other such attributes of supreme beauty?
In the Romany language of the gypsies, closest to Sanskrit
and to the common Indo-European of our race, it means
'god.' True, the word 'love' means 'money' in Romany, but
surely that is nothing more than an amusing coincidence.

Of course it was only in the context of artifice that was
Valerie's face and body and her whole aspect that those eyes
of hers were free, as it were, to perform their mesmeric task.
The artifice isolated them from the volunteer, rather the way
a guardrail, or sometimes the elevation of a platform, keeps
the stripper out of the reach of her drunken and rowdy admirers, or as the moonlit night of the orchestra pit, teeming
with all manner of exotic fauna, distances the opera audience
from what would otherwise look like a lovers' quarrel in the
street of any small town in the south of Italy. I opened my
mouth to say something in English, but the initial consonant
stuck to the roof of my mouth and would not budge. *Taut
silks a woman's waist enclosing*, I tried to begin in Russian, but
the Edwardian cadence of this, already once dress-rehearsed,
utterance shamed me into silence, so tawdry and inappropri-
ate it suddenly seemed. *I am Russian* was all that came out,
and from that moment I never told her a lie.

14

At this juncture everybody is free to laugh and to tell me that
I'm an idiot, that if Valerie was anything like the woman I

have just described, then she was the very image of the type of Russian hooker in whom the streets of every city in Europe nowadays abound, a little prettier maybe, and then that exotic Lucifer bit, but certainly nothing to think about once the brothel door has slammed shut behind you. To write a book about the idiot's attachment to so unremarkable an object, to read a heavenly Beatrice into a comedy so earthbound, is a task beyond the power of any writer. Perhaps so, though the appellation of *idiot*, by reason of childhood predilections and cultural associations generally, flatters more than it offends; were I less of an idiot, I want to reply, I would now be writing letters offering personal loans to people who have money and travel insurance to people who hardly ever travel. But, apart from this exchange of insults, what I want to say in my defence is that my physical description of Valerie predates her transformation, aiming as it does to capture her in the weeks before the miracle that made her Olga. Since it cannot be said that outwardly this event changed her, and since asking a man in love to catalogue the charms of his beloved is an anecdotally absurd proposition, that physical description must remain the only one on offer. It is not entirely useless, in the sense that the cleverest attempts of natural scientists to breathe life into reconstructions of prehistoric reptiles would lack plausibility were it not for our familiarity with ordinary lizards.

Olya, do you remember that ferry we took in the Aeolian archipelago, from Panarea to Salina I think it was, and how you slept with your head in my lap, and how you ordered me not to be idle while you slept, but to busy myself with a catalogue raisonné of your enchantments, in descending order of the power they held over me? I still have it, on the faded menu of an unnamed trattoria, announcing that the fish is not farmed but brought in daily by local fishermen: non di allevamento ma giornalmente ci viene portato da pescatori locali. *Have you kept up your Italian? It took me the better part of the journey you slept through to put those few words in the right order, harder than any poem I'd ever written, and when I read you that list of 21 attributes you stretched like a cat, and then laughed, and then yawned, and then said: 'And what about my —?' You used a childish word, something like 'fanny' in English. And I obeyed, and amended as best I could the list I had made:*

1) Eyes, with eyelashes.

2) Forehead.

3) Hair.

4) Mouth.

5) What you call —.

6) Stomach, with navel.

7) Expanse between foregoing.

8) Breasts.

9) Waist.

10) Teeth.

11) Ears.

12) Hips.

13) Shoulders.

14) Hands, fingers and nails.

15) Ankles, feet, toes.

16) Elbows.

17) Wrists.

18) Knees.

19) Neck, with nape of the neck.

20) Nose.

21) Clavicles.

22) Calves.

So you see, I've forgotten nothing and paper doesn't lie. I remember how I felt watching you breathe in my lap, like a miser counting his gold florins, like Vita counting her accursed fifties with curtains well drawn! You were my fortune, my treasure. And then you stirred awake, and broke all around me like the Aeolian dawn, and stretched like a predator in its lair.

Anyway, there she was. In those first weeks I still had to pay the madam every time I wanted Valerie: every time I went to meet her in the little house tucked away in a South Kensington mews, every time I took her to dinner, every time she spent the night at the Chelsea hotel which served as my pied-à-terre in London. The stubbornness with which she at once began resisting my efforts to prove her a Russian from St Petersburg was without question maniacal. Yet it was also noble, fearless, fascinating, sometimes hilarious and always inexplicably sad; there was a touch of Soviet heroism about it, of soldiers who threw themselves on machine-gun emplacements, of spies who would not crack under torture, of prisoners who never asked, never begged, never confessed. Valerie was Finnish, and that was that.

One time I took her to dinner with my best friend and his wife, both Russian. The conversation, in broken English – hers, theirs, and in the end mine – was as futile an attempt at interrogation as anything in an antimafia magistrate's files, because no matter how audible or palpable the truth was, it was not itself until it had spoken and proclaimed itself as such, preferably not in Finnish, to the assembled multitudes. 'How come you look at my wife when he speaked about her to me?' 'I understand Russian words.' 'Why is this, Valerie?' 'We lived near border with Karelia, many people know Russian language there.' 'Can you say something for me in Finnish?' 'Yes, but I don't want.' 'Oh, please! Just little word.' 'Okay.' She quickly said a word, but whether or not it was the Finnish word for raspberries mashed with milk none of us knew.

Anyway, there she was, as yet innominate, standing before me in her costume of artifice like a lily painted white, with steel and ice in her eyes, with a smile as unnatural as the light of the lamp in the room filled with September sunlight, yet I remember being unafraid as I reached out to remove what little there was that stood in the way of my destiny. Perhaps if a gambler were blindfolded, he would lose the inhibitions that come with the territory. If the prophets of old had not known what to call their deity, perhaps they would not have feared him. The truth is that my hand did not tremble because she was nameless.

I asked to see her again that evening. Madame Vita, her suspicions aroused by the unprecedented request, drove her personally and dropped her at the hotel, which, the shrewd procuress's proprietary sense was already suggesting, would in the coming weeks become a profitable branch of her brothel. And so it became, until that night when the scales fell away from my eyes and I saw myself on that winter afternoon at the Baumann, iridescent in the gathering twilight, straining, straining desperately to look at the girl in the little eiderdown hat with the golden spiral of hair against the snow white of the scarf, and I said *Olga, your name is Olga*, and I saw awful beauty.

15

O yea, awful beauty! Once faced with it, we are cowards all of us, and only more so when ignorant of our cowardice. And we do get a glimpse of it sometimes, a fragmentary impression in the subjunctive, a furtive brush with destiny and a quicker parting of the ways, passing a woman in the street, seeing a face in the crowd, a profile in the window of a moving train. Then it seems to drift toward us, silently explosive, like a ball of spherical lightning, and each of those watchful moments is like a decade of inescapable dread, and when the confrontation is finally over, our pallid faces are left feeling scalded, like the powder burn from a shotgun fired at close range.

'Phwoar, what a scorcher,' say the men in hard hats, as if seared by a blast of hot air from the mouth of a smelting furnace. And yet the archetype of the unexpected confrontation they have undergone is not in the least sexual. I would go further and propose that it is more to do with sociology than with biology. It is the fairytale moment when, on a cold and rainy November morning, a splendid carriage overtakes the lone mendicant walking in the road, in a tattered military overcoat with his spare pair of boots about the neck on a string, and splashes him with mud from head to toe, the liveried coachman oblivious to the humiliation inflicted on the pauper, the smart passengers absorbed in their conversation, the poor sod accepting of his fate. Or not accepting of it, as the case may be, and I dare say that it would take a latter-day saint to wipe the mud from one's face with anything like genuine humility while whispering 'May the Lord be with you!' to the cruel world, a point made by Tolstoy in the

novella *Father Sergius*. For Tolstoy makes his hero, a nobleman turned anchorite, realise that the most violent carnal
temptation, like that embodied in the woman who arrives
with the express purpose of seducing him in his hermitage,
is as nothing compared to the social temptation of belonging,
a temptation he only masters in the novella's denouement by
accepting alms in the roadside dust, cap in hand and head
bowed, from a drunken party of his erstwhile peers.

Like great wealth or exalted rank, beauty is above all else
an endowment. Its spectre passes us by like the gilded carriage of the fairytale, humbling us and turning us into beg-
gars, filling us with resentment, making us question our fate,
our place in the world, other people's good luck and our own
misfortune. It makes us yearn for a revolution – either in the
existing social order, or within ourselves, or possibly both –
whereby some redress of the scorching injustice we have just
suffered will be had once the heads have started to roll,
whereby such a redistribution of beauty will take place that
the last shall be first, or at least not the very last, the ragged
poor, the ulcerous dispossessed, the mud-splattered lumpen-
proletariat. In short, once the ship with eight sails and fifty
cannons has vanished into the night,

> Und das Schiff mit acht Segeln
> Und mit fünfzig Kanonen
> Wird entschwinden mit mir.

Oh, but it is only a vain dream, Jenny the pirate girl's, from
the threepenny opera whose communist sympathising
author was awarded the Stalin Prize for Literature in the
year I was conceived.

It is a vain dream, I say, because Promethean heroes we are not: we are men, mortal cowards incapable of rebellion and unable to launch any such revolution, slaves of reason condemned to live and labour to the end of our days under the merciless yoke of furtively glimpsed beauty. We are condemned to munch all life long on our sweat-leavened bread, to accept the penny alms thrown to us by superior power, to grab at the straws of compromise that instantly snap under the weight of our indecisive embarrassment. *Ah, but my wife is pretty enough, and my mistress's breasts are round and firm, and the girl I once dated at university had hair almost like that, only much shorter.* We have no other recourse, it seems, but to keep on pretending that we have transvalued the values and to go on composing communist manifestos in our head, because our egos are in tatters and our amour-propre has been splattered with roadside mud, yet deep down we know perfectly well that the spectre wandering over Europe is not the spectre of communism, but of inequality – eternal, ineradicable, Olympian. And when we come face to face with awful beauty, we are reminded that all the Nietzsches and Marxes and Freuds in the world have not been able to lengthen a single hair on the woman's head, nor change the divine ratio between the width of her luminous forehead and the distance between her cold eyes; that the vain fantasy of a revolution is the loser's lot; that we are doomed to poverty, impotence and oblivion. Hence the powder burns on our pallid faces, hence the envy and the resentment, hence the pornography and the sexual crime, hence the art and the literature.

But then, of course, there is the Father Sergius way, artless and meek, accepting of the inequity in this earthly life and only seeking redress in the next, the beatific humility of a true believer in contrast to all the firebrand fantasies of a revolutionary leveller. The rare ones among us who are capable of reining in their vanity, and with it their mortal fear of beauty, in as uncompromising a way as that, would probably reflect that all human endowments – beauty, wit, wealth or rank – are but the soul's terrestrial burdens, and that just as it is difficult for a rich man to enter the Kingdom of Heaven, so too it must be for a man of great intellect or for a woman of great beauty. All that such a saint would feel for such a creature is pity, pity and a desire to help her to throw off the ankle chain of white gold binding her to the world of appearances.

Olga, as it happens, had a common Russian surname, meaning 'Of, belonging to, or from the household of Sergius.' But I – I was no Sergius.

16

Just imagine what scope I now had for indulging my vanity, and what a grand spectacle it made once those armoured divisions of long-suppressed pride poured into the Lebensraum of my victim's unconcealed social innocence. Who better than I could come up with the Russian word for chanterelle mushrooms – called *Pfifferlinge* in German, I remember one time in the Käfer tent at the Oktoberfest in Munich, they are much plumper than ours, darling, but then of course we tend to fry them until they are quite shrivelled and crispy, you know what the Italians call *croccante*, as crispy as the potatoes they are served with – smiling all the while the retiring smile of a retired conjurer? Who else could recall and describe the early collections of Valentino – and work in the reason for going to see him in Gstaad, and how the magus sat spellbound for a whole afternoon as I regaled him with the sad tale of the rise and fall of a Polish sculptor of genius, and how the magus then said, Giancarlo, tell them to hold my calls, *è una storia veramente affascinante!* – while shopping for a poppy-red cocktail dress in Sloane Street? And who besides me in her scant experience of Britain was intrepid enough to address the taxi driver as *driver* – no darling, only American tourists in London say *sir*, please, will you just trust me, that's what you call a royal duke but you don't need to tap on the partition because he's heard me, and that's the restaurant where we're going tonight on the far side of the square, you need to go down some steps, yes in a basement what's wrong with that, no there isn't any sign – and sophisticated enough to tell the driver to take the young lady to Harrods in a way that did not make it sound like she was an innocent and the despot wanted her slaughtered?

And was there anybody else in this town who could take her to lunch at Aspinall's and not just play roulette – God, I'm glad I can tell you this in Russian, because the croupiers would be laughing at me, but you know the whole point is what Pasternak once said about not telling defeat from victory, like the story of Dostoevsky's wife, Anna Grigoryevna, whom he married when she was his stenographer and he did not want to pay cash for her services because he needed it to gamble and he was always so unlucky, a real loser, but then he fell in love with her, she was about your age by the way, and she fell in love with him, and they lived happily ever after and he never gambled again, and then he wrote *The Idiot*, and when he died she never remarried and went on to create the whole Dostoevsky cult, you know, so who is the loser and who the winner? – but also to translate what the maitre d' whispered in Italian as she entered the dining room? 'Finally,' the maitre d' said, 'finally what we have here is a lady with class.'

Before long the territories of which her exterior was comprised, at least in the key regions abutting the border between East and West, were totally under my control. I bought her what I wanted her to wear, and if I chose for her a divine little suit whose grace depended on its maker's deployment of buttons, I could relish the prospect of unbuttoning them with complete equanimity, not as a supplicant but as a client. I found her books I thought she should read, and if I brought her Dumas' *Lady of the Camellias*, it was with the confidence that a modern woman's excursions into vice would only benefit from acquiring an historical background. It was the same with the food we ate and the wine we drank, the films we went to see and the music we chose to hear. I did not pause to reflect that, contrary to all of my vaunted resolutions, I was paying for her condescension not only with the newly minted gold of experience, but with the tarnished silver of intellect as well.

On the face of it, my vanity was in a more vulnerable position than ever, because for the first time in my life I did not know whether the woman laughed at my jokes, as she sometimes did, because they were genuinely amusing, or because in effect I was paying her wages. But I thought nothing of this. I knew her name, like the girl in the old English fairytale who guesses the name of the wood sprite Tom Tit Tot and in so doing binds him to herself for all eternity, with the crucial difference that the girl in the fairytale had overheard the sprite's name while he was singing to himself in the forest. I knew her name because I had worked a *real* miracle. I had been able to divine what number was up next. Now all I wanted was to put everything I had straight up on that number.

Meanwhile, even as the border regions of Olga's exterior appeared to welcome my advancing armies as liberators, her inner being remained a mysterious heartland all too suited for just the kind of guerrilla warfare that is known to reverse the outcome of initially successful campaigns. Of her own accord she said little. When she did speak, her pronouncements, judgements or opinions were as unanswerable as they were ambiguous, drawing their inspiration as they did from Russian folk wisdom. And not from our imaginative, bizarre, insolent, delightfully loopy sayings, such as *a sparrow that's been shot at won't be fooled by chaff* or *better to drink in the morning because this way the whole day is free*, but from the sort of folk pessimism that to this day passes for sagacity among people from the provinces who suddenly find themselves adrift in the urban confusion, be it the photographic studio of a St Petersburg pornographer or the dining room of Claridge's, proverbs like *a whip is no match against an axe* or *from honest labours no stone mansions*.

'Life is practical,' she would say. What did she mean? Did she mean that she was only with me for the fleeting opportunity I represented, for the money while some of it lasted? But if that were the case, surely she already knew me and my feelings well enough to realise that it was a mistake to admit it? Or could it be that she already knew me better than I knew myself, but at any rate well enough to know that nothing would fascinate me more than this very conundrum?

Intentional or not, the naked sparseness of her self-revelation had something of the effect of modern art, particularly the trend toward minimalism in contemporary design and architecture upon a spectator predisposed to it, in that it represented a triumph of mood over substance, of intent over content. As such, it had all the advantages of a revolution without, apparently, any of the revolution's bloodier drawbacks, as in those abortive honeymoons with enterprises of great pith and moment when the accidental participant can feel the elation of being part of the new order while still unperturbed by the midnight knock on his neighbour's door. Like all velvet revolutions, perhaps like all revolutions, it was of course a spellbinding fiction.

17

Some of her cryptic utterances I would file away unopened in my mind, like letters from a problematic correspondent or credit card bills that arrive after the fun has been had. Others tormented me for days on end, as Cordelia's laconism tormented her voluble father, but the more I pleaded with her for hints or clues to help me solve each consecutive puzzle she dropped in my royal lap, the more evanescent its content became, until it seemed that there had been nothing to solve in the first place, that the whole episode had been the fruit of an overactive imagination, whereupon the whole cycle of mystification and anxiety repeated itself. I saw with perfect clarity that some of the things she said were said by her with almost sadistic premeditation, with every intention to create the sort of confusion which my mind – philosophically open to cynicism, yet drawing its quotidian nourishment, as she was quick to realise, from a culture that had been pronounced dead long before her parents were born – would not be able to dispel. But seeing this did not weaken my appetite, my ambition to metabolise the experience of those first weeks. Why was she doing this? What was the motive?

I did not need to be told that the culture clash over which I saw myself presiding was prodigious. Numerous chasms between me and a Russian of her background ran deeper than any between me and the England on which I had given up so precipitously, for the simple reason that my youthful female compatriots working the leading cities of Europe in the guise of students, models or tourists existed at an even greater remove from the Russia of my childhood idyll than the sushi joints and white stretch limos of American London. The hookers had taken two steps in the same direction, as it were, in the time it had taken the spivs to take one. But there was another dimension to the differences between us, and this I was slow to understand.

I had long believed that it is only in the grooming, dressing, and exhibiting of its women that contemporary civilisation allows life to retain some of its lifelike complexity. The customs of medieval Europe, the costumes of the Orient, the viticulture of France and the dialects of Italy still survive in some measure, of course, but equally there is little doubt that, like the literature of nineteenth-century Russia or the gastronomy of eighteenth-century England, they are the light of already extinguished stars. The steamroller of progress, which is admittedly indispensable in the building of motorways and perhaps of hospitals, is far more often used by our civilisation as an instrument of simplification, which is to say of death. For a greater simplification of life than death is yet to be invented.

If the booming London of my *noli me tangere* nightmares and secret come-hither longings belonged to the vanguard of that reductionist tendency, then Vita's girls – and their sisters the rich world over – were the vanguard of the vanguard. They welcomed the chance to enter the harem of excitingly Eastern complexity offered to them as women by Western civilisation, while rejecting complexity in every other sphere with a compulsion that was automatic and unthinking, Jacobin, no, I want to say *Bolshevik*. If an Englishman voiced the view that the House of Lords ought to be reformed or abolished, they would say: 'Just shoot them all!' If a Frenchman made light of a waiter's oenological expertise, they would say: 'Who needs that pigswill anyway when what we like to drink is Kahlua?' And if a Russian were to read them a line of Aleksandr Blok, depending on what their logic and sense of tact suggested they would pull a long face or reach for the mobile phone.

As most of the girls were in their mid-twenties, they had been born in the same epoch to which I belonged. They had only just made it, in fact. They had been Octobrists, then Pioneers, some got as far the Komsomol: *I, insert name, join the ranks of communist youth and in the presence of my comrades solemnly pledge to be always honest, always faithful and always truthful.* They had worn the deliciously black-and-cocoa schoolgirl uniform, they had spent long winter evenings starching and ironing white collars and cuffs; they had been lectured, in that squeaky spinsterish voice Soviet schoolmarms had, about virtue, about dignity, about honour, about why poetry is a wonderful thing and all the reasons one should help old ladies cross the street; they had been beaten, or worse, by their alcoholic fathers, who recited to them the same sententious platitudes but more incoherently and angrily, their drunken rage often fuelled by memories of wives who had died or left them; and on and on did that culture drone, and nobody even knew whether that inescapable noise was European or Russian or Soviet or just plain old boring, and then suddenly it seemed the nightmare was over and a nightclub opened in the high street and there were no old ladies to help across it because they were afraid to leave the house and the boy next door bought himself a new Mercedes by helping a friend sell hashish around town and all the schoolteachers got pensioned off and nobody needed to pretend to like poetry anymore and anybody could buy a bottle of Kahlua liqueur for a couple of dollars and you could make a hundred dollars a night.

18

Somewhere in his history of Rome, Gibbon mentions that Attila the Hun used to boast of never having tasted bread in his whole life. To a nomadic chieftain, bread must have represented all the evils of agrarian bondage. Like alcohol to a member of the Temperance League, or heroin to most people today, it must have meant security at the cost of independence and happiness at the price of addiction. It must have seemed to Attila that when the entire meaning of a civilisation is bound up with the earth – with the cultivation of and trade in a commodity whose highest purpose is the filling of the bellies of the deserving – then that civilisation has nothing to offer to the lover of liberty. Similarly categorical judgements have come down to us from the era of the industrial revolution in England, and Marx himself may one day be remembered as a kind of nineteenth-century Attila, tilting quixotically at the satanic mills which progress had planted throughout Europe.

I, too, was a spiritual descendant of the proud king of the barbarians, albeit one who had partaken of soft bread and sampled the civilised pleasure of pulling down a noiseless zipper. A part of me raged against the modern world, one in which my primogeniture had been sold for potage long before I was born, one in which intellect got laughs but not preferment, one in which wit carved out a wormhole of a niche instead of securing a high eminence. Yet the other part of me, the part that had learnt to metabolise fine white bread, the part that had assimilated to the perversions of vintage Krug and fresh foie gras, the part that had mastered the classifications of the transparency of stockings and of the clarity of diamonds, the part, in short, that indentured me to the things of the world as they stood on the day I was born, that part proved the stronger. I realised that the culture before me was trading in a single commodity, called frustration, for the obvious reason that the creation of human desires, called progress, went hand in hand with the illusion of satisfying them, called business. But there was nothing I personally could do, it seemed, to break free, to gainsay, to cross myself thrice and spit on the ground in renunciation.

Like the peasants despised by Attila, I lived in perpetual bondage, sowing the seeds of my own discontent and reaping the whirlwind of universal indifference. I longed to eat the bread of civilisation, but the knowledge that it was leavened with the sweat of slaves kept me from trying to earn it. I dreamt of unfastening the world's garters, of rolling down, ever so slowly, its stockings of artificial silk, of inhaling the fragrance left on its skin by polyester-satin straps edged in mass-produced lace. Nothing doing. Like Sputnik over Rio, the world was passing me by. And then, suddenly, there they were, those Petersburg hetaerae, reclining upon Oriental ottomans in the temple of Occidental civilisation.

Their cynicism had a familiar complexion, one that I did not find even remotely disturbing. I too grew up with a viscerally felt disgust for Soviet pieties, for the hollow sentiments plagiarised by the ruling regime from the pages of Russian literature. The disgust was second nature to the intelligentsia of my parents' generation, to nonconformist poets like Joseph Brodsky, ironic and aloof, who chose to avoid all expression of emotion in their writing rather than to risk exhibiting correspondences with the risibly heartfelt fabrications of the dominant culture. The poetry, perhaps Russia's last, written in those years, was consequently like a Martian landscape, an intricate surface devoid of sentimentalism at the cost of being devoid of sentiment. To a scoffer like Brodsky, addressing his main squeeze as *beloved* – which, only a generation earlier, a poet of genius could have done –

was only a hair's breadth away from lauding the noble strike-worker who would not let the collapse of the mine distract him from producing the daily state norm of anthracite coal.

We shared a common ground, then, those girls and I. They had lost their faith in sentiment to Soviet propaganda, as effortlessly as they would lose their maidenhood to alcoholic fathers, retired policemen next door or aspiring pimps, while I had never acquired it, due to the peculiar limitations of my upbringing and subsequent development, any more than I had acquired an adequate understanding of myself or my motives.

Of course I found some of their banter shocking, yet it was also strangely exhilarating. Never before had I imagined that one day I would be there to overhear beautifully undressed women who, while speaking a perfectly ordinary Russian with one another on subjects as platitudinous as world peace, would inject so much venomous scepticism into a single sentence while punctuating it with oaths that would defeat a Paris *plongeur*. Here was an experience more down-and-out than Orwell's, headier than roulette, more tortuous than the ways of Whitehall or Fleet Street, richer in ambiguity than a failing writer's life in a palazzo on the Grand Canal. Its one disheartening aspect was that, unlike roulette, with its antisocial cult of risk, or Russian hermetic prosody, with its deification of surface, it was not even remotely autonomous, not at all a law unto itself. For its law was money, specifically the money lavished upon women by civilisation, and in this it undeniably belonged to the world and was part and parcel of where that great big thing was going in the proverbial hand basket.

Life, as Thomas Mann said without ever having been to Studio 54, distracts and degrades. How could I, of all people, judge them? How could I pronounce them guilty? They had fallen in with an underworld that measured success in money, because the more money a thief can steal the more successful he is as a thief, only to find themselves in the real world of the richest nations of Europe where the same criterion of success seemed to apply, because the more money a man makes the more successful he is as a man. And each and every one saw that whatever retrograde tendencies were at work in that real world as a challenge to the criterion, and whatever interesting things one may have wished to say about any of them, these tendencies were first and foremost retrograde: backward looking, weak, sentimental, arbitrary, defeatist, curmudgeonly, in short a spent force that was never particularly viable in the first place.

In their intuitive analysis, that force, like religion in the Marxist scheme of history, had only become great due to its ability to befuddle meek minds, to confuse issues by introducing into the human equation such Jesuitical unknowns as the soul, in short to prevaricate and to meddle. Money, as they would have put it, cut through the crap, extirpating in its savage path all the superfluous complexities of the human condition while being sensible enough to spare the *temenos* of civilisation, that sacred precinct of life's variety which the hetaerae made their home. 'You want company?' they asked men. 'Relax! All you need is money. You want pleasure? Pay. You want friendship, or spiritual renewal, or wisdom? Pay. Happiness? Just pay.' But if you were a woman, and you wanted to alter the natural colour of your hair, then all of a sudden just paying was not enough, because everybody knows money cannot buy happiness, and to arrive at the precise structure of the balayage and the exact tint of the hair you have always daydreamed about, perfect for Cannes, beachy yet pulled together, you needed to befriend hairdressers, read articles on the subject in specialist journals and fly to remote destinations – in other words, to do everything that, were the underlying subject of it anything other than your sexuality, would seem hopelessly retrograde and, at best, utterly useless.

But again, in this the world was at one with them, and every magazine, every newspaper and every television programme, every politician and every politician's wife, every scientist and every writer, every corporate tycoon, every teenage girl and every boy of whatever age, every bourgeois snail and every capitalist stone and every offshore tree seemed to mouth the same revolutionary slogan, *their* slogan: 'Down with complexity, long live beauty!' Life should be practical, they thought, life should be simple and uncomplicated, men and their ugly wives and their teenage children with spots should want things and pay to have them. We are the thing they want most, *beauty*, and that's how it should be, of course, yet we ourselves are exempt, in the sense that we are beautiful women and hence have the right not to know what we want, and to take our time deciding, and to primp and to dress up and to strut, and in general to behave like the French aristocracy on the eve of the Revolution, while everybody else should just relax, relax and enjoy and pay through the nose like all of Europe after 1789.

I was much too innocent then to recognise my own

hypocrisy, or perhaps schizophrenia, and a long, long time would pass before I was able to see through theirs.

TWO

CERTAIN
NUMBER'D
DAYS

... to undergo
This annual humbling certain number'd days.

— MILTON

1

To say that this book is about prostitution, personified by the reticent yet delectable Valerie, is like saying that *Death in Venice* is about the perils of eating unwashed fruit. This book is about the woman who was the first love of my life because she was its first unconditional desire. Was she the last? If ever I should pray as ardently for death to spare me as once I prayed that she should knock on my door, then let death be called my last love.

She was, I repeat, my first unconditional desire. Like a gambling man who does not deserve the name of gambler, in my quest of sensations or experiences, ideas or friendships, I had always taken special care to leave myself a way out of every emotional or intellectual situation, a return ticket home, a safety net of ambiguity. I had never had the compulsion to jump fully clothed into the blackness of the ice hole, and if I wrote something which somebody thought profound I could always use that opinion to counter somebody else's view that what I had written lacked grace; while if my shallowness, on the contrary, became an issue in dispute, I could easily adduce evidence of some other literary virtue to redeem what may or may not have been a worthless piece of work.

I was thus accepting of the perpetual schizophrenia of

being, as the Russians say, one of us among them and one of them among us. I was a Russian in England and the mysterious outsider in a company of Russians; an English writer in Italy and an Italian client of a Russian madam in London; a seriously married man, with an American heiress for a wife, among the high-living young *scapoli* of Venice and a roguish, wisecracking habitué ever on the prowl in the fleshpots of Mayfair; a political thinker among poets and a poet among journalists; a *jeune premier*, romancing strippers, waitresses and shopgirls, and a happy buffoon before the women of society; an idealist, a dreamer, a naif to business tycoons and a man of vast experience and sound judgement to painters or writers. In short, I had more loopholes in my *emploi* than I knew what do with.

Roulette was my introduction to the irreversible – and I believe it was that which had opened the gates to the absolute, in the sense that if you bet on one number and another comes out, no amount of clever substitution of terms can change the fact that you've lost – but still, roulette was only a table game and, though an experience, a substitute for *experience* only to the extent that a viral culture may be for the disease which the vaccination prevents. Roulette never slaked my thirst for experience, it merely showed that somewhere, beyond the confines of the gaming table, was a magic source of life's effervescence that one day could; and that if I carried on with my quest, one day I would press my cracked lips against the cold limestone of the surrounding basin bestrewn with olive leaves, small and green like the hundred-dollar bills Olga kept in her locked aluminium suitcase.

That day had come when I guessed her name. I was now

face to face with the fierce absolute, which leapt upon me from the passport photograph of herself that she allowed me to see on that evening in the hotel. This had been taken in Moscow with the view to obtaining a British entry visa at the consular office there. Her hair was still a natural auburn, she wore the ambitious student's wire-rim spectacles and the good girl's white blouse, but the eyes were her eyes and as I look at that photograph now my whole heart freezes as it froze then. *How awful your beauty, my beloved. How sad that photograph, my only link with what might have been your love.*

I finally had a look at her Russian passport, gorgeously rubber-stamped with EXEMPT FROM MILITARY SERVICE and other proscriptive, lilac-ink gobbledygook characteristic of official Soviet documents. I had a look at her expiring leave to remain in the United Kingdom, at her forged St Petersburg driving licence, and at everything else there was to see before a course of action could be agreed. *A course of action. How ashamed I am of these words now, my beloved. How unworthy they are of a gambler.*

For the first time in my life I was facing the absolute. It had fallen upon me like a real beast in a storybook jungle. It had been made flesh by our chance meeting, revealed by the miracle of divination, confirmed by the documents, rendered unconditional by the nostalgic chiaroscuro of the photograph. She was the one I had loved since that winter day at the Baumann. My love for her was as irreversible as life itself because it too had been there all along. There was no substitution of terms, no retreat, no loophole. If I lose her now, I will never exist. If I ever lose her, I am not a man. If I don't put everything I have on the number that's coming up, I'm unworthy of the name of gambler. If I can't win her, I don't deserve anybody's pity, least of all my own.

Place your bets now, ladies and gentlemen. I saw the hand in a loose sleeve of cheap black serge give a delicate nudge to the heavy, old-fashioned wheel, and in a blinking of an eye the ivory ball was in motion. Last bets, please. No more now, ladies and gentlemen. No more bets.

2

Easier said than done, of course. What had I to offer her? My good intentions? She knew too little of who I was to trust in their goodness, and had she known me better I rather doubt that trust would have won the day, since after all I was a liar, a hypocrite and a coward. Could I ask her to marry me? No, because I was already married. Could I offer her money? Yes, but then again, men generally did.

Olga, I should have said to you then, I have finally found you and I will never lose you. I am here and I will not leave your side, and if we have nowhere to live and nothing to eat then we will live nowhere together and go hungry together. If you cannot marry me and have the protection of my passport, then wait until I am free, but if you are deported before then I will follow you to the ends of the earth. Let me take you as you are, naked and afraid, and take me as I am, strong and hopeful, and let us put away our former selves, you a woman of the night, I a man about town. Let us be faithful to one another to the day we die, faithful in word and in deed and in thought. From this moment, I am staking my all on you. I am putting everything on the table. Now let fate decide.

I said nothing of the kind. It lacked, as it were, that delicious, seductive urbanity which had characterised my pay-as-you-go relationship with Valerie, and changing horses in midstream seemed such a reckless thing to do. It seemed more prudent to think up some ways of prolonging the moment, of drawing out the experience, of balancing out the risks and the possibilities. Continuing to play minimum bets, in what I thought was turning out to be a winning game anyway, seemed so much more reasonable than putting the lot on a single number. Suppose the number doesn't come up? Suppose she says, 'Oh, I see. Second birth, eh? As in Plato, where somebody, Phaedrus I think, says that there will come a time in every philosopher's life when he rejects wisdom and falls for beauty, beauty in which he sees naivety and grandeur and form but which, in reality, is only a state of intoxication. What, didn't think I knew my greats, just because I let you explain to me who Socrates was while I was eating that raspberry crème brûlée at Aspinall's? Big mistake, darling. One of your many. Meanwhile, you're poor and married and a cheat and a liar, and you want me to believe that this will all change and you want me to stick with you through the thick and thin and I have your word on it! Now, get me my clothes. I'm calling Vita.' Then I would lose. Then I would lose *her*.

So I began to temporise, but something inside me, some vertebrae of a former temperament, had already been broken. Fatally fractured, in particular, was the sense that this spin of the wheel was but one of many, and that, whatever miscalculation I was now making, a way of rectifying it would be found in future. Desperately I tried to avoid the miscalculation, bringing all my faculties to bear on the single judgment call I was about to make, and while what I came up with, as I said, may have been sheer madness in the eyes of those more cowardly than I, in retrospect I regard it as sheer cowardice.

I told her that I would get a divorce as quickly as possible. I told her that until then I would be giving her as much money as she was hoping to make in the mews house. That I would settle everything with Vita. That if remaining in Britain became an issue, I would arrange for her a fictitious marriage. That I would find her a flat, obtain the necessary references, arrange with the bank to open a current account. That I would spend almost all of my time in London. That I would find a way to get out of Venice. And that I would never tell her a lie as long as I lived.

Why do I keep reiterating that last vow I made? Even to this day? Because from the first moment of seeing Valerie's face, when I broke cover and croaked *I am Russian*, it was clear to me that awful beauty was owed awful truth; that only a full confession would manumit the slave to triviality; that without complete honesty I could never transmute the mundane into the everlasting, and persuade love to follow me wherever I went; that here was the nexus in which all the strands of my two lives, my sordid life until then and my afterlife, met, intertwined and could find transcendent meaning.

It was all true, and during the next few weeks she was able to see for herself that I kept my promises. But what of it? She was swapping one job for another. I had elevated the £300-an-hour hooker to the position of a £60,000-a-year mistress. Given that Vita's girls worked twelve-hour shifts, my act of romantic generosity represented something like a pay cut for anybody with a head for maths. She would have more time on her hands, of course, now that she didn't need to be constantly on call in the little mews house, whipping Hitler impersonators, somewhat incongruously, with a riding crop, staging lesbian shows with her friend Anya in front of impotent commodities traders from Chicago, or doing three-hour-long makeup sessions with her friend Elena before being carried off to nightclubs by the gilded youth of fledgling African nations. What would she do with all that free time now, one might have wondered.

Forgive me, Olya. Forgive my blindness and my cowardice, forgive my weakness. Believe me when I say to you that it is easier for a rich man to enter the Kingdom of Heaven than it is for a poor man playing roulette at £5 a stake to put £100 straight up on a number.

'Place your bets now, ladies and gentlemen.' The hand in the floppy sleeve of black serge gives a gentle push to the heavy, old-fashioned wheel, and in a blinking of an eye the little sphere is in motion. 'Last bets, please. No more now, ladies and gentlemen. No more bets.' Just then the figure of calculated risk elbows his way in from among the shadows of doubt, slapping a packet on the layout and yelling loud enough to waken the luckless dead, 'Zero and the neighbours by a hundred!' For the briefest of instants it looks like the shadows are receding.

'Zero,' announces the croupier, flicking the cellophane wrapper aside with a contemptuous grimace. 'What about my call bet?' whines the wiseguy. 'I'd said no more bets, Sir.' The reprimand of reason is ever the bugaboo for the faint of heart. 'By the time you called it, Sir, the ball was down.'

3

If the soul can be imagined to have a musculature, then it may be said to atrophy with systematic disuse. The ordinary course of life, with its typically apathetic round of tactful sub-terfuge, well-brought-up tergiversation, and good-mannered avoidance of the truth, together with all the supposedly neg-ative emotions to which truth-telling gives rise, makes our feelings lose their natural suppleness, and the reaction time of our senses – of injustice, of wonder, of beauty – becomes ever so slow, bringing to mind the dilemma of the artist whose cherries, fish and Muscat grapes putrefy before he can finish painting the still-life. Moral action, which anyway in-volves going against the grain of hypocrisy or at the very least of complacency, becomes an ugly race against time, a race in which, as the oedematous and half-hearted soul sur-mises, it is bound to be defeated. Thus mediated, our sensi-bilities lose immediacy and become mediocre.

Yet it was to that round of ordinary life that I was now bound to keep returning with Alitalia from Heathrow. Let scoffers say that a life of lazy afternoons in the £5000-a-summer *capanne* at the Lido, of amusing evenings at Harry's Bar, of seasonal bellinis and tintorettos at Florian in St Mark's Square, of speedboat excursions to the smaller islands, of occasional scribbling and perennial sloth, is not ordinary enough to merit all the highfalutin scorn I'm heap-ing upon it. Scoffers tend to keep away from roulette, which is why a gambling friend of mine used to say that, at least in countries where compulsory military service has been abol-ished, young people should be conscripted to the casinos for a minimum of two years.

What scoffers fail to realise is that whether one is accustomed to playing with chips worth £5 or those worth £1000, it is the love of the disproportionate risk one takes, not the fear for the money that leaves one's pockets, that sets the player's heart racing in victory as in defeat. For the law of gambling is that the stake one *loves* to wager is bigger than the stake one *fears* to lose. And thus, whether the prospect of anguish looms as an overdose of velouté in French restaurants, as a lifetime of penal servitude, as the nine-to-five job of photographing lingerie models — or, in the case at hand, as the torpor of an unloved life — it is certain that there are people in the world whose hearts will sink at the prospect.

No, I didn't want to go back to my Venice. I wanted Olga, who, being everything that this Venice of mine was not, was now my country, my home, my dignity, my poverty, my courage, my talent and my soul. 'I've returned to my city, familiar to tears,' wrote the martyred poet of her native Petersburg, 'to inflamed glands, to childhood's veins and fears.' She was my nostalgia and my redemption.

It was not only that I had long realised just how retarding, how spiritually fattening that round of existence was, even compared with what I had been able to glimpse at the tables over the years, to say nothing of the experience of the absolute, and of the absolution, that now lay open before me. It was also that, in returning to my old existence, even for a little while, I would have to confront all over again the dilemmas which I had been given the chance, miraculous it seemed, to cast away forever.

I knew I would have to ask myself whether the cunning

petard of the smugly detached dilettante, unless I defused it at once, might not explode in my face at a later date, of its own accord, when least expected, and with suicidal consequences; whether the tragic part of the superfluous man had not been played long enough in dramas written by my compatriots, with the result that an original mind now had little choice but to relegate it to the summer-stock realm of vaudeville; whether the delightful charade of belonging to a Gnostic sect of one was not, diabolically, a variation on the far more common theme of belonging to an elite, a classic of self-delusion among intellectual vagrants and decadent good-for-nothings of any epoch; and whether the sceptic's pernickety aestheticism, a black pearl against the metallic gray foil of the Venice lagoon, might not fail to attract even a modest bid were I ever to become so alarmingly self-critical as to try and put it in an auction of old illusions, Russian objects and flying carpets. Other, less elevated kinds of self-doubt would stir alongside these, but now is not the time to stick a pitchfork into the compost heap of matrimony.

What could I tell myself in reply? That Nietzsche described wounded vanity as the source of all tragedy? That the spectacle of man is made only more thrilling by the fireworks display of delusion and caprice, of vanity and egoism? That one's ego always lives at the expense of others; that one's own life charges as much as it can get away with to other people's accounts; that he who would shut his eyes to these truths has not taken a single step towards himself in the path of prudence? Alas, somebody else's paradoxes cannot heal one's own wounds, especially when these are self-inflicted. What I needed to resolve my previous life's contradictions was an iconoclasm all my own, and the supreme dilemma was that since an iconoclasm in the flesh was waiting for me in London I really felt I had no business sitting in Venice philosophising.

Yet there I had a wife of fifteen years, and a young son. There I had my Russian books, all my papers, whatever work I had. There I had the pleasant means of daily subsistence, however stupefying, and a social circle, however innumerate it was to count me a useful presence. There I had the leisure, the tranquillity and the charm of life in a world-renowned backwater, itself reposing gracefully in a time warp of almost-mythic remoteness, and all the alcohol I could possibly require to desensitise me against whatever crises of faith, whether in myself or in civilisation, that even a mortally wounded vanity might provoke of a winter evening.

And so I flew to Venice, leaving Olga behind. She now lived in a studio flat I had found for her in Chelsea, where the owner had chosen the cash advance of a couple of cellophane packets stamped 'Aspinall's' over elaborate references, banking or otherwise. Yes, she had finally run away from Vita, and was now bored, disorientated and totally alone, an illegal alien in yet another city where the generally accepted view and understood purpose of beautiful women who allegedly spoke only Finnish did not differ substantively from Vita's.

4

It was winter by then. Even in the temperate microclimate of the Venice lagoon, beggared days seemed to snatch at hopes as if they were rich tourists' purses. Foggy evenings clung to dreams like lint in overheated hotel rooms. Gelid waves gurgled funeral dirges under the bridges with bedlam persistence. I had mastered the skill of mobile phone messaging, transliterating the Russian of devotion and reassurance according to the Library of Congress system – an apostrophe for the soft-sign, *shch* for the squiggle that looks like a garden rake, *zh* for the first letter of the word meaning 'life' that was devised by St Cyril as a scarab-like monogram combining the initials of Jesus Christ – hoping, this way, to attach myself umbilically to the forty square metres of real estate enclosing my half-heart's sole desire.

I sent her a message every few minutes, and she would reply, infrequently and perfunctorily I always thought, employing no system of transliteration whatsoever, approximating the phonemes at random, every which way, but since every time my phone hummed I felt myself more loved than hurt, what did diligence matter? I had grammar and spelling for two, in the idiom of the pompous earl serenading young Phyllis in Gilbert and Sullivan's *Iolanthe*. And then, once, twice, a few times a day, we spoke.

The hurtful news for me, a hypocrite newly promoted to adulterer – a man who had never had an 'affair,' in any meaningful sense of the term, during his fifteen years of marriage, yet carried in his pocket a Smythson's notebook filled with dozens of women's names, many euphonious and almost all trisyllabic – was that the whole purport of mobile communications seemed to centre on the uncertainty of the communicating parties' situations, with the result that the telephone was now a device for lying, a devious prompter quick to suggest a word of untruth whenever it detected a moment of hesitation. Where was she. Where was I. Why was it so noisy. Where in Covent Garden. What is the Zattere, the Lido, the Giudecca. Why was it so quiet. When later. Which friend. Why was the other phone ringing. Why is there an echo.

Of course I promised that I would never tell her a lie and I never did, but when reduced to the two dimensions of a roaming call, maddeningly, almost bewitchingly, lying becomes a quantitative issue. *Relative*, as liars like to say. Thus I found myself playing down whatever pleasures fell to the share of a rich and careless rentier, describing – accurately or not, I could not quickly enough decide – my rump existence in Venice as absolutely hopeless, my erstwhile friends as amusing in strict proportion to how much they were able to divine my unhappiness, and my dinner parties as uneventful to the point of purulent morbidity. For her part, she tried to play down her opportunities and her temptations, her streetwise intuitions, and her provincial conjectures to the effect that real life, in all its remote and forbidden splendour, was going on elsewhere, beyond the fool's gold bars of the proverbial cage which she graciously accepted as gilded.

Quite obviously, the fundamental question in my mind was whether or not she would remain faithful to me in my absence, again in that *relative* dimension – in that real, liars' world where she was my lover and love – rather than in some azure dream of a celestial absolute, a dream that would be shattered by her turning a trick or two on the side. After all, that was the deal. That was how we'd left it. That was the bed I'd made. Because I was still married, of course, and when I went back to Venice she knew I would be sharing another bed, larger, softer, and more splendidly appointed than her own, with a woman she would probably never meet. So how was that unfair? How was it not morally symmetrical? Surely I could not dream of some absolute just because I was paying her, paying to free herself from Vita, from six months' vassalage, from the certainty of coming home to St Petersburg as a freelance... Bah! Dreaming such a dream would be morally more repugnant than anything I ever did, worse than any reality of prostitution. No, for my part I could only hope with all my might that the fundamental question in her mind was reciprocal. That it was to do with what was happening in that other bed, in that other woman's mind, in that other woman's dressing room.

When, in London, we spoke of these things between us, without the telephone's truth filter and the need to turn a silken purse into a sow's ear, she had been able to glean such facts about my other life as were now, more than likely, giving her pause. Partly I had shared these facts with her because I wanted to be absolutely truthful. This, as a newcomer to the absolute and, when it came to absolute truth-telling, only a clumsy novice, I interpreted as a permanent injunction to tell more than was asked, under whatever circumstances and on any subject. But equally I must have shared them with her to help create, or to sustain, the atmosphere of sophisticated urbanity in which the beginnings of our courtship were turning into what, to my mind at the time, was like a promising sequence of winning spins at roulette.

Olga knew, for instance, that I had met my wife when I was approaching thirty and she was seventeen, a pupil at a Connecticut boarding school where no person in his right mind should have allowed me to loiter. That this innocent, intelligent and impressionable girl belonged to a famous American family, made prominent by one or two billionaire industrialists it had borne a couple of generations earlier and not yet completely ruined by the ineptitude and stupidity of her parents. That for fifteen years I had been this girl's education, which she formalised by finishing Cambridge; her inspiration, which she directed into a promising career in political journalism; and her love, which she objectivised by bearing me a child. That meanwhile the girl had developed into a woman of acknowledged beauty and, furthermore, of the sort of beauty that she had every reason to believe I myself admired. That during the first decade of our life together I remained faithful to this young and attractive woman, faithful in thought as well as in deed. That during the last few years of that life, under my watchful and in all likelihood not indifferent eye, this woman spent over a quarter of a million pounds assembling a vast and unique collection of couture lingerie by the world's oldest extant corsetière in the Rue Cambon.

In Olga's own mind, what had she in her own gift that could now be juxtaposed with the evidence of a history of affection so vivid, of a symbiosis so colourful? Nothing, save my profession of my endless love, that and my proclamation of her awful beauty. Yet the first could be written off as an impulsive fantasist's fit of nostalgia; while the second, as every one of her milieu could have told her, was only interest-bearing if bankable. Of the nostalgia I shall say something presently. As for the suspicion – which Olga's professional circle in St Petersburg, with its shared belief that life is practical, would have cheered to the tune of way to go, girl, and applauded as appropriately streetwise – to the effect that my interest in her beauty was by no means unique and therefore unworthy of a life-changing reciprocity, there my fence-straddling, mobile-phone love, impotent as it was to assuage or overpower this suspicion, played the part of the fatal number that invariably determines the gambler's fate.

With me, from the very start of my gambling career, that number was 22. But I only mention this in passing.

5

Nostalgia, apart from it being the title of an excruciatingly long film of Tarkovsky's about a Russian who finds himself in Italy, had never entered my field of vision until I came to Rome. Nostalgia is a kind of envy, a subjunctive mood that takes hold of a man without a homeland whenever he is confronted with the evidence that such a thing as a homeland can still exist. I had never felt envious of the Americans, who lived, after all, in a place called the United States of America: their country was so clearly not their own, so obviously heterogeneous and open to any expedient, that it didn't even have a name, any more than the Union of Soviet Socialist Republics could be thought to have a name.

In England, when I first arrived there wearing my Brooks Brothers seersucker suit, I admit I felt something like a twinge, but that was soon subsumed by the anguished awareness of the country's escalating Americanisation, a mortifying vision of London becoming what it did later in fact become: culturally a Sunday supplement to the *New York*

Times, socially a projection of Studio 54, politically just another united state superglued onto the map of prosperity by partisan hypocrisy and puritan materialism. With the political process later given the name of globalisation proceeding apace, I was not surprised that wherever in Europe I turned – to Germany, to Holland, to the Scandinavian countries, even to Spain or France – my nostalgia never stirred, secure in the perception that at work in the immediate present or the near future of these places were the same social and political trends that stripped London of its uniqueness. Italy was different.

I would feel awkward dilating on politics in a book about beauty were it not for the curious fact that the only line of English verse that has ever reminded me of my life with Olga comes from a political poem by Yeats, 'Easter 1916':

> All changed, changed utterly
> A terrible beauty is born.

For beauty is not transcendent in the physical world, but is as much a part of it as hunger and cupidity and feeblemindedness, and it would be as odd of me to pretend that I saw Olga's beauty in a vacuum of time and space as it would be bizarre of her to pretend that she looked at me without the slightest regard as to what, in her Petersburg circle, was described by the accounting term which I would translate from the Russian as *paycapability.* Had it been so, this book would have been much easier to write, and a good deal shorter.

It was of course for political reasons that during the first two decades of my life in exile I was both unwilling and unable to return to Russia. On the face of it, only unwillingness remained during the third decade, but as everybody knows, the face of politics is deceit. Then as now, I saw that the vaunted changes in the complexion of the country were cosmetic, and that it was the free world, if anything, that had become less free by having accepted them as substantive, not the other way round. The transition of power from the old oligarchy that ruled my people under the red banner of communism to a new, less visible, less doctrinally handicapped clique made up of secret-police functionaries, better educated, smoother, younger, but just as ruthlessly bent on world domination except by more modern means, did nothing to soften the émigré heart. The opening up of my homeland to foreign investment, though as festive as any ribbon ceremony in a provincial town, and the latitudes thereafter granted to indigenous capitalism, with similar fanfare, were a poor substitute, in my mind or the mind of anyone familiar with the writings of John Stuart Mill, for civic evolution or any real prospect of an irrevocable bequest of civil liberties.

It was uncanny that the umbrella-like *ex gratia* collapsing of communism over there seemed to coincide with the summer-shower-sudden end of individualism over here, with the difference that what had been snapped shut over there was only an ideology, which the change in the weather had made inexpedient. Disheartening as that observation was, I thought that with matters as they stood I could not in good conscience return to Russia even for a visit.

Especially for a visit, rather. Then as now, nothing was more offensive to me than the prospect of seeing my native city, which my grandfather died a war hero defending, through the tinted glass of a safari vehicle window; nothing was more abhorrent than the vision of myself, American Express card in hand, making a favourable impression on a comely aborigine; nothing was more depressing than the thought of passing through the place where one most wanted to live and die as if it were any other on the tourist itinerary. Going to beg Cain for mercy, I remembered, was how Nabokov's martyr of a father and his fellow White émigrés of the 1920s described their weaker comrades' returning. Their weaker comrade I wasn't. That kind of weakness would be my last taboo.

Anyway, Italy was different. There my nostalgia awoke with the bitterness one imagines flooding the heart of a Dickensian orphan as he peers through the brightly illuminated windows of Christmastide prosperity, festooned with hoarfrost and holly, at that incarnation of happiness which, to the vagabond, is the happy family; yet I cannot conceal that, admixed to the green gall of the envy, was the homeless tramp's devil-may-care disdain for the ordered nicety of all that rotten candy-cane happiness, his proud illusion that had the home been his, such a home would have combined order with liberty, dignity with frivolity, wealth with insouciance, arithmetic with poetry.

Still, perhaps from some dim recollection of the satanic mess left in the wake of my compatriots' revolutionary attempts to square the vicious circle, envy predominated. I saw that before me lay an enchanted land, happy as any valley that ever welcomed a dreamer, where old men spoke by the fire in dialects not widely understood, such as the Ampezzano of the Dolomites, of things long forgotten elsewhere in Europe; where a girl from Verona, who knows, perhaps by the name of Juliet, kissed a boy her own age, instead of a fat old Saudi, because he too was Veronese and looked good on his motorbike, not because he sent a bottle of Cristal to her table and promised to get her a part in the Shakespeare film; where a man known by his neighbours to have raped a young woman was cut into so many pieces in front of my Palermo local, Piccolo Napoli, that he could not be identified by his remains; where, in the market in Venice, tomatoes from the island of Sant' Erasmo still had the taste of tomatoes, and the salt, from the salines of Marsala in Sicily, had not lost its savour; where fountains, garlanded with the grapes of marble figures like the head of Dionysus and illuminated like coral reefs in an underwater photo shoot, plashed all the night long for the glory of Rome; where all was well, and all was beautiful and in its place, and all was of the place.

How could I help being envious? Where was my own language but in the hands of old Soviet propagandists and Communist Party hacks? Or, scarcely better, in the mouths of new Russian businessmen and advertising slogan mongers, of people who did not know that *sandali*, Russian for sandals such as worn by American tourists in Rome, is not the same as *sandalii*, such as the *sandalia* worn by the ancient Romans? Where was my patrimony and my people, where was my laughing Giulietta who would kiss me good night on the lips because I too was a handsome Veronese, where was the table laid in my honour, my table encircled by a merry tabor of singing gypsies with their shouts of *pei-do-dna, pei-dodna!*, where vodka flowed like wine, where the dark-eyed beauty opposite slipped a luminous shoulder into the shade of the velvet shawl with the nonchalance of night veiling the moon with a random cloud? Nowhere. Just nowhere, baby.

And so it came to pass that I began to seek out Vita's girls. At least back in London, at Vita's establishment, there was always a festive table laid in my honour. At least there, without abasing myself before Cain, I could spy on the native rudiments, eavesdrop on native speech. At least there I could have the occasional glimpse of native beauty, with its culturally conditioned charm of gesture, freedom of movement and pleasure of being. There, clandestinely at least, I could once more be Russian. There, at least for a night, I could be something newer than myself.

6

Not everyone would agree that Olga's fictitious wedding in London, to a *bravo ragazzo* I'd engaged for the purpose in Sicily, was a grand affair. Franco arrived with three of his friends, all looking sharp in black suits, with florid buttonholes, freshly-shaved unshaven faces, and sparkly eyes in which oleaginous frankness veiled the yellowish glint of sulphurous wariness. Three of Olga's erstwhile colleagues, lent visual credibility by a real live Roman princess whom I had asked to take on the part of official witness, posed as bridesmaids. After the formalities were over, the merry party of ten, including the photographer – who would later get hitched to the princess – repaired to a restaurant in Shepherd Market, where the rest of the day was spent in drunken revelry interspersed with toasts to the bride, the groom and, playfully, the *cosa nostra* that was our arrangement.

My boys were not mafiosi, of course, because in Sicilia we no have such a thing as the mafia, though it may be noted that back home each and every one of them had a relative serving life in prison. I had invested an appreciable amount of money, something like £30,000, in the arrangement, which had to be watertight enough to withstand the rough seas of Home Office scrutiny, local gossip, and changing circumstances; it was only logical that I should have turned for help to people who understood that it is the deaf and the mute who live the longest. Fortunately, during my last couple of years in Italy, somewhat as a side effect of the same thirst that drove me to absent myself in London, I had met a few such people, *persone perbene* who had seen the inside of the old Ucciardone prison in downtown Palermo, and could now number some of them among my very best friends.

As extant photographs of the ceremony attest, I looked jubilant throughout. Looking at them again, it seems almost possible to disremember the waves of nausea that kept washing over my innards. Why was I doing this? Why was *she* doing this? The rational explanation was that, though I was leaving my family, legally the divorce would not come through for at least a year, if then, while Olga's leave to remain in Britain was expiring in a matter of days, and consequently any proposal of marriage on my part was, if anything, more fictitious than the fictitious marriage which I had flown in from Venice to arrange. *O timing, the gambler's nemesis. O time, the wheel within the wheel.*

Viscerally, however, that facile explanation did next to nothing by way of relief. Of course the wives of the Decembrists might not have had the documents, the clothes or the money to follow their husbands into exile, but that was what some of those women did. And in Siberia the time is mostly winter. Of course it was foolhardy for the man who had lost his children's school fees in the casino to stake his cab fare home on the last spin of the evening, but one could not help admiring his attitude. Acts of courage are for the most part ill-timed. Why, then, was I doing such an ugly timeserving thing? And why was *she* agreeing with me that such a cowardly thing must be done?

Yet the alternatives were for her to return to Russia, or to stay on in England illegally. I recoiled at one, she was dead set against the other. And so the inexorable exigencies of the material world, smoothly hospitable like a bank of escalators in a shopping mall, seemed to have borne us along toward compromise, up from street level and past the level of the absolute, where courage was to be had at the price of forbearance. I did in fact feel like a child who had lost his way in one of those malls, running from exaltation to nausea, from justification to rationalisation, from one sort of excuse to another, panicking, unable to find the right door or to recognise the situation for what it was, until the fluent, perpetually mobile purposefulness of the escalator beckoned, offering time for reflection and probable deliverance.

7

Don't talk so loud because it hurts my ears, Theseus. Don't say these things to me now because I'm going to sleep. Yes, I'm here by myself. No, you can't call me later. O my brethren, is not the whole his-

tory of a man's world, an Ariadne's thread of busy days leading to anguished evenings, contained in these sample
phrases? Is there a longing, and a corresponding sorrow, that
the myth does not convey? Is there a labyrinth more disorientating, or a voice more desirable than the one within?

Somewhere deep in the intricacies of my love was hiding
an objective falsehood. Though experienced unconditionally
for the first time in my life, that love, that miraculous love,
was being treated by me with the practicality that put a prostitute's client on a par with the prostitute and, as Hegel
would quip in punning German, *vice* versa. But if imagining
a coke dealer from the local Chelsea pub in bed with Olga
was, by the terms of our agreement on the importance of relative truth, vastly different from imagining her with a paying
customer, that vast difference was now being smothered by
the dialectic of lies she could not help spinning from London;
though, admittedly, those partial lies of hers were indistinguishable in both degree and in kind from the tactful truths
I was imparting to her from Venice. The trouble was that
while I had broken with my wife, just as I had promised Olga
I would, that coke-dealing Egyptian boy was still there, free
of charge. Friendly, young and dark-skinned, in her narrow
bed. That was the trouble, but to manhood cuckolded by culture, trouble is another word for art. Let me say a few words,
now in defence, of art.

Anybody who has ever watched a home video knows how
painfully uneventful is the passing of undirected time. No
matter what or who is the subject of the exposition – sex,
drugs, conversations, children, a softball game, an outdoor
barbecue – time in the raw is all but unbearable. It appears

that only through the faculty of art can one ever hope to grab hold of this amorphous mass of undifferentiated minutes and hours, give it meaning, and refine it into some fragment of life more or less deserving of the name.

Yet art is regarded as the domain of the irrational, the elemental and the hermetic, and is often held up in opposition to those domains where reason, order and clarity are believed to hold sway. That the art which made us and the world is no exception is clear from the fact that the universe bears hardly any resemblance to a Corinthian column or a leaf from *Principia Mathematica*. And seeing how steadfast this universe is in its refusal to get fitted up for the Procrustean organon of science, logic and symmetry, it is culture that has been given the task of balancing things. It is culture that is expected to act as an Apollonian damper on all that fiery Dionysian stubbornness.

Consider the plight of the jealous lover, in the half-century, say, from Dumas-*fils* to Proust. There is a man deeply conditioned by his culture, and there he stands, with his coat collar up, at twenty-two minutes past midnight, in a cobbled alleyway pertaining to some fashionable *arrondissement*, gazing with despair into the dimly lit window above, wherein a shadow, perhaps two shadows, may be glimpsed through imperfectly drawn curtains. And as the illuminated, but then of course inexorably darkening, window continues to frame, focus and edit his very life, so too does his culture frame, focus and edit his emotions, making them – yes, art.

Now, compare that to what some callow youth of a vice president, tanker freight derivatives, of a Hong Kong-based investment group would be doing today were he to find himself in the same fix, perhaps upon having taken up with a Hungarian stripper of infinite sophistication and charm. He would almost certainly begin by installing what is known in the trade as clandestine audio monitoring into her mobile phone, whereupon his life would become just what it has always been – yes, boring. Boring because artless, unrefined, inedited, a tiresome stream of contradictory details, episodes, insights, juxtapositions.

'But at least he would know the truth,' a myope may argue. Not at all, and I say this being a certified myope myself, a handicap I once tried to correct by availing myself of a pair of prescription spectacles. The spectacles did not make me see better, just differently. Every astronomer who has had occasion to use the most powerful telescopes in the world will agree with me that a man's eye for the truth is always bigger than his stomach.

'But she's two-timing him, that's the point!' the myope persists. Not at all. The point of having a motorcar may be to get somewhere in a hurry, but it has been calculated that the average American puts in 1600 hours a year to get 7500 miles out of his vehicle, less than the five miles an hour at which he could easily travel on his own two feet. So, even when evaluated statistically, truths are never as empirical as they first appear.

'But what you're saying, then,' flails the myope, 'is that he should be playing some kind of game, performing some pre-lusive ritual, some ludicrous obeisance to the culturally de-fined ideal of courtship? You're saying that, so long as he feels, hates and shivers under a streetlight – as if emotion were a haphazard rhyme, a sudden insight, a roll of the dice

– the cuckold is an artist?' I am, and if even the loser is never bored at the tables, it is because art defeats boredom. Besides, as I say, sometimes there is no other way of seeing the truth because, without art, truth may be simply invisible.

Did I see the truth of my predicament in these terms? In part, in outline, as through a glass darkly, but nothing would have been more alien to my state of mind at the time than meek sublimation. I saw the truth, but could not act upon it as a philosopher. I felt the truth, but could not touch it with my reason, which, roughly from that moment in my sentimental education, began to shrink, to recede, and with every passing day to yield more and more authority to the irrational in my character. I was like the spellbound seminarian in Gogol's *Viy*, mounted by the witch hell-bent on taking him out for a midnight ride, when his arms do not move, his mouth cannot produce a sound, and only his legs are as nimble as a Circassian stallion's.

Olya, this morning I leave for Palermo. I love you, loved you and will always love you as nobody's ever loved anyone, and some day you will understand this and believe me. But we must part because of all the lying. I have tried and failed to pull you up and out of it, and now I read my gross ineptitude as the only explanation of why everything must end. There is no other. I think it's absurd to propose marriage to a liar. But then you think it's equally absurd to wait for my proposal of marriage, for unspecified reasons: is it because you love another? Is it because some persons unknown forbid it? Who? The Russian security services? Godfather Part IV, back in Peter? Your evanescent aunt? I don't know.

When you told me yesterday that you didn't really believe I had guessed your name, that somebody must've told me, I plumbed the whole depth of my illusion. I saw the end. That I guessed your name, Olga, was a miracle wrought by the power of a dawning love, a love that would look just like you if it were imagined in the flesh. Was not Dawn your nickname at Vita's? You too could work a miracle by the power of that love, if you would only let me come back to you a whole husband, if you would only come to me as a wife. Not as before, evasive, cunning, asking nothing, believing nothing, confessing nothing like a good zek on his way to the punishment cell, but as a wife, as a dove, as the girl I've known since the childhood which we never had in our different ways, as the Olya I've loved since then. Whatever is lying in wait for you out there, whatever beast crouches in the post-Soviet undergrowth, whatever disturbs, confuses or frightens you, it would all be swept away at once like so many cobwebs, I promise.

Or else keep on living your lie, alone, alone or with a trusted accountant who drapes his jacket over the back of the chair before he removes his trousers, alone or with a tiny yapping poodle like Vita's. Then I will only love you at aged three, you and your tightly tied plait and the golden wisp that always keeps escaping... Olechka, what have you done?

8

That morning I fled to Palermo, where a flat in the care of friends stood empty, offering refuge to the errant husband who had cast away his family and respite to the distraught lover who would not cast away his pride. It was the end of March or the first week in April. Most Sicilians had not had the chance to wear their overcoats all winter, but now those of them who had were putting them away. All over the countryside jets of sheep's and goats' milk were hitting the zinc of the pails with the *zh-i-zzz* reminiscent of the Russian sound for *life*, the key word St Cyril branded with Christ's monogram. Everywhere people were busy eating cannoli, cutting open cassata pies, scooping pistachio ice cream onto glazed ceramic plates. They kept inviting me to lunch at the Charleston in Mondello, they were trying to drag me along to see the Greek temples at Syracuse, they were asking me to accept the coming of their African spring as if it were my own, as though I was one of them, as though my homeland had never had a spring, as though Olga had never existed. I kept myself locked in the flat. I never answered the door. Text messages were arriving from London.

How paralysed I was! Mute with frustration and anger, seething with thoughts of inadequacy, sociopathic, sodden, passing the nights in insomniac hallucination. I could not read or write. I listened to Russian music, songs of the White emigration, seeking inspiration and finding solace in the suffering of those who had lost my civil war before me – the war for the homeland, for the kindred and the ideal, for the coming of spring – a war in which, unfortunately, there always seemed to be two losing sides.

> Everything's now against us,
> as though we've never worn crosses,
> As though we're serpents of cold heathen blood…

And as though conjured up by the power of nostalgia, those text messages began arriving from London. She wanted me to telephone her. But telephone her I would not, because the few voices of reason I could still hear in my head were all in agreement that this was my chance to sort myself out, to press my case, to understand whether my nostalgia, my loneliness and my obsession had not been cruelly misdirected to an object destined to reject them as the body rejects a transplant of foreign tissue, or as water expels a wine cork.

Foreign tissue! God, was *I* an Englishman? Was I not a Russian like her? Did I not make the sign of the cross in the Orthodox way? Did I not guess her name? Was I so old, so boring, so inept? Did I not make her laugh, if only every so often? Have I not lived and breathed her image since the day we met? Has she not said she loved me? *Then why did she have to lie?* Why did she lie about the dark-skinned boy in her narrow bed? Why couldn't she tell me how much money she'd saved, why did she need to fabricate that ridiculous story about sending it all to the mythical aunt? Why did she have to tell me she'd finished university? As if I had any respect for diligence, or even wisdom, to say nothing of university degrees! For Heaven's sake, my role model was the epileptic autodidact Prince Myshkin. And why did she never admit that her commercially acclaimed double act with Anya was not entirely a foray into illusionism?

Speaking of illusionism. In the conundrum called Necker's cube, in which the simple geometrical figure of a cube, drawn by using twelve lines of equal length, is complicated by the addition of a fat black dot, an optical illusion is created, whereby the dot seems to jump like a flea from the centre of one face to a corner of another and then back again, bewildering the viewer. It is said that it is impossible to predict in which position any one viewer will first see the dot, but what is really magical about the workings of the conundrum is the inexplicable abruptness of the subsequent change of perspective. This, in fact, is often used to illustrate the mathematical theory of sudden change, introduced by the French mathematician René Thom under the name of catastrophe theory and applied to fields as diverse as economics and behavioural sciences.

Why did she lie? That was the rub, the rebus, the conundrum. Whereupon my reason suggested a way of solving it, an original methodology for getting to the bottom of things, which in retrospect seems of a piece with the inutile prurience of the Hong Kong banker spying on his Hungarian girlfriend. If I restricted myself to the text-message format of inquiry, I would manage to sidestep the disorientating labyrinth; I would not be beguiled by the siren's song; I would be insulated from Olga's bewitching presence, from everything distracting and seductive about her, from whatever stood between us and the essential contradiction I had uncovered.

Sex and money made up one face of the Necker's cube, love and beauty the other. One was the near side, attainable, terrestrial, impersonal; the other the far, celestial, unreachable side of all my longing. Reason was telling me it would be prudent to begin digging on the near side, where it all began; and then, once a foothold of fact has been established there, to occupy myself with higher, more remote, more esoteric varieties of truth. It never occurred to me to shout in reply that it was in the unreachable of heaven, in fact, where it all began, not in the gross clay of the civil war trenches I was being asked to crawl through on my stomach, to shout that love cannot not be won like a war and that, anyway, even wars are rarely won... No, like an idiot, I listened to reason and did its bidding. And then the dot jumped.

I reproduce Olga's messages in their entirety, just as her torturer wrote them down in an Italian school exercise book.

9

18:48. Forgive me my silence, I behaved childishly. 18:55. I only ever think of you since that day, I want you very much and my head is spinning from all these thoughts. 19:31. But what facts are those? That neither of us has feelings? You speak as a judge. What is the verdict, and can I appeal it? 19:35. I can't, no, no, I don't want anything else. What am I to do? 19:43. But you forgave me even when I conceded it was all over. 20:33. Have me, O how can you not want to have me? 21:09. If we are not together, then I take it as a sign, and begin being once more what I had been before I met you. From there I shall never return. 22:35. I will come to you be-decked in morning flowers, in warm rays of sunlight. Or you will come to me!

13:09. I cannot live without you, come to me. 13:42. Yes, there are two things I've never told you, but maybe it would be easier to confess them when I see you? 16:59. You hate me! It made me sick to have lied to you, do you believe me? 17:22. I refuse to do this in writing, I cannot find the right tone of voice. 17:41. For the sake of our love I will admit everything and repent of it. 17:47. Of course I feel that for you the main thing is to be purged of the lie, and for me also. But no, I never sent my aunt money, I just said that out of laziness, can you forgive me? 17:53. I never finished university, and that's the other thing I'm ashamed of not having told you.

17:57. No, not an adventuress, I was just stupid, I simply didn't realise how seriously you cared for me. 18:00. I'm ashamed to have fallen into the trap, forgive me for lying. 18:05. What torture! 18:20. I thought it's always better when the man does not know what the woman's actual circumstances are. But now I realise it's not my way. I've never asked for anything and I never will. 18:39. Such are the customs of the dependent. 18:40. Can't we talk on the phone? 18:57. Please take my call.

19:04. You can easily figure that out for yourself. Keep in mind I haven't worked since we've been together. You know how much the girls are making at Vita's, and what you've been giving me. 19:20. Why does a millionaire want to count my farthings? I told you I'd never ask you for anything. 19:23. What else, and how much longer will this torture continue? I'm so humiliated as it is. 19:28. My worst sin is lying about having sent money to my aunt. 19:30. I hate you. 19:51. You don't love me! You're torturing me just like you used to torture your wife. 20:03. All right, I have £60,000. 20:04. Next question?

20:36. You only want to come to me when I've answered all your questions, and then you'll disappear. Why must we go through this hell, if we can simply live in tomorrow? No, I will not write any letters. Speak to me on the phone. Goodbye. 21:04. Do you love me or do you hate me? Tell me, I implore you. 21:06. I don't want anyone but you. 22:06. I'm dying for it, what am I supposed to do? I want you in my bed, you know I can't go without it. 22:16. She doesn't like thinking, come and calm us both down. 1:23. Do you want your Olya? She is dying of lust, save her, or else that lust will consume them both, her and her little one together. 1:14. I've just come five times, maybe that'll help. It's now my favourite cocktail. Going to Anya's now. Good morning, my deathless ogre.

9:22. Are you awake? Come to me, darling, I'm longing for you, I can't not see you, my body is aching, my soul is in pain, I want to be with you. 9:43. I love you, today Anya's moving in with me for awhile, you understand I can't be alone. But that's another life and I only want it with you. 9:47. It was Anya's birthday yesterday. 9:51. Yes, with Anya. 9:59. No, the last time was with you, I can't imagine it with anyone else. 10:04. You are jealous! I'm laughing. All we did was share a bed. You're the only one I love. 10:40. Number 6, Flat 14, you know the street. 10:42. He is called Ramzi. Don't know his surname. 11:00. But it's a fact, I don't know it. 11:55. No, there was nobody else. 12:05. An hour to respond because I was in a place where there was no reception. 12:34. Your questions are only about money and sex!

12:54. Because I never believed your wife would let you go. 12:57. I want to surrender, I have the bends from withdrawal, get over here now. 13:18. When will it all end? 13:22. It was a childish attempt at self-defence, I'm ashamed of myself, I never thought this would happen. It's all because of my state of shock, my rigidity and my self-destructiveness. 13:28. You do understand me, but you haven't been able to see through me to the inner contradiction and I doubt you can help. 13:43. But that's my patrimony, my inheritance! My sad dowry. 13:46. I want both. First I want to be hurt, then caressed. 14:03. If only you had some idea of what that's like, screwing the first person who comes in the door! 23:06. I'm at Chinawhite club. 2:55. Going home now. 3:19. My salty treasure, I'm in bed.

10:22. Are you awake? I'm going to the gym – your athlete, your Young Communist idol, but anyway quite a decent girl if you really think about it. 17:00. At the hairdresser's. Tonight there's a party with lots of girls. 10:01. Good morning, my madness. I'm sorry I switched off the phone yesterday, we were in a nightclub. 10:46. I want to love only you. 10:59. You are my air and I want to love you without end. 11:41. I'm crying, I want to take you in my arms and cradle your head between my breasts and drain all the fears out of you because I love you. 12:12. How I long for paradise to return to our world of crazed lust! I'm home, I want to be with you. 13:22. Without you I lose the sense of my uniqueness.

10

How unlike Valerie does the woman writing these words sound, how unlike Olga in her *zek* fatigues, asking nothing, believing nothing, confessing nothing. Responsive, vulnerable, lacerated, whimsical, hopeful, sexual, all of a sudden she was all those things and many more besides, and yet somehow it all seemed an act and a sham. I lived with the sense that had I not blackmailed her into this display of emotional choreography, she would have remained as impassive and aloof as she had been on the day we parted, recumbent in an attitude of immovable, clenched-jaw hauteur which, though already as natural to her as the shell to the tortoise, had been enhanced by cocaine. It was as though she wanted to underscore, by the physical poise expressive of the attitude, that her essence was of the dawn, and that the heavenly mandate of awful beauty was to be rather than to act. Moreover, once one separated the wheat of emotion from the chaff of flirtation, it seemed clear that she was giving away nothing in all those ineluctable dawns of words, apart from her earlier un-willingness to reassure, her initial reluctance to play the game according to accepted casino rules.

She had told me nothing of substance that I had not known already, not about the money, not about the Egyptian boy, not about her friendship with Anya. And yet there was something to be proud of, something to appease a lover's wounded, swollen, enraged vanity, in that choreographic display of hers. I had always insisted that there is such a thing as a choreography of love, and that the very idea of courtship is a nullity unless the mutual courtesies of the courtiers, or of the courtesans for that matter, follow a pattern of moves as recognisable as that of chess pieces on the board. As a person who wants to fall asleep will first yawn, then sigh, then close his eyes, turn on his side, pull the blanket up to his chin, and at length find himself in Morpheus's embrace, so a person who wants to fall in love must immerse himself purposefully into the vastness of the element.

Strange that I should have insisted on that, I must admit, in a case where everything was from the beginning a topsy-turvy chaos, where consummation preceded courtship, where money so plainly had the upper hand, where the romantic parties were so absurdly mismatched, where nobody could tell whether chance came as the messenger of God or of the devil, where intellect was a house divided against itself and beauty a trial, a punishment and a reckoning. But then again, no stranger, I suppose, than the rest of my schizophrenic vac-illation with respect to the material world, my innate inability to reject it decisively or to embrace it once and for all.

Anyway, if the taste of packaged sucrose somewhat resembles that of the apples of paradise in the Koran, and the timely reassurance one is offered is almost as sweet as the timeless truth one craves to hear, then this must have been the reason why at some point during that fireworks display of sentiment I ran to the telephone and dialled Olga's number. The following morning I was on the plane to London, repeating to myself Milton's lines – not, I had the distinct foreboding, for the last time –

> Yet beauty, though injurious, hath strange power,
> After offence returning, to regain
> Love once possessed.

It took a doubting and hollow heart, I now see, to have read the diagnosis of dissembling into the composite text of those disjointed lamentations and pleas; worse, a heart cloven in two by inbred cynicism; or even a heart congenitally incapable of genuine feeling. All I know is that despite having taken the decision to return – if following an astrologer's advice, for example, is anything like taking a decision – I would now be lying if I said that I was boarding that plane with a heart cleansed of misgiving.

How could that ridiculous exercise of reason, that drowning test of witchery, have convinced me of anything? If the girl drowned, she was not a witch. Well, the girl did not drown, it seemed, all that happened was she got very cold and scared and wet, and her teeth were chattering, and there was not a Christian soul about to wrap her in a blanket, and yet I was just as much in love with her as before, so what was the use of the dreadful ordeal? What did it really prove? That I loved a witch? That I loved her *because* she was a witch? Or

113

that I loved her *despite* it? What did it matter? I was coming back to London, where the same girl as before, witch or no witch, was waiting for me to dress her.

Olechka, forgive me that too. What madness! What weakness! What presumption! What depths of ignorance of the human condition! Why was I, the old warlock, the trench-coated creep not averse to scouring school playgrounds, the self-invented dandy with a mind ravaged by hypocrisy and cynicism, a suitable magistrate to decide this case of alleged witchcraft, to act, as you wrote in your message, as your judge and pronounce your sentence of which there would be no appeal? To judge you, to judge my own life's only love? Why, one had to have contrived to convene a jury of twelve lynchers, inured to all human feeling, not to have seen through the laughable self-delusions of such a man, if man is what he must be called, appointing himself to preside over the deliberations of such a tribunal.

Olechka, I am trying to explain to you now where I had come from and where I was when you met me and, against your own better judgement and contrary to the advice of those who had won even less in life's lottery than yourself, decided to fall in love with me. Not as I fell in love with you, perhaps, not as a stone falls into a bottomless well, not as a soldier falls to his death into the unplumbed infinity of paradise, but as a young girl with a mottled and confused and unhappy past – without independent means, without valid documents, without any real expectations – can be expected to return the feelings of a suitor who is so desperately in love with her that he promises her the moon. It is not by way of justifying myself that I mention that I made good on the promise, drawing down the moon in instalments, as well as I could. I mention it because I once prided myself on being a gambler, and as a gambler I ought to have known that timing is everything. What

*good is betting on 26 and the neighbours of zero over and over
again, when it's 22 and the neighbours of 9 that keep coming up?
What good is another stack of chips, or two, or three, when you're
on a losing streak? What good is a part of the moon, or even the
sum of the parts, when what is asked of you in return, from where
on earth you are standing, is greater, more remote and less gras-
pable, than the whole?*

*Olya, my love, they're now saying that you never really existed.
They're saying that I've invented you. But we know the truth, you
and I. It is by your grace that I have been invented as I now am, in
part thanks to that unbaited, feminine, indeterminate trap of your
instinctive devising, equipped with a Sicilian spring, which I fell
into in Palermo. For you gave me nothing then, and for that I forever thank you. You made the son of man lump it, swallowing his
pride, his vanity, his amour-propre and his hubris for the sake of
seeing you once more, for the sake of laying his head upon your
artificially enhanced breasts, for the sake of your awful beauty. You
made the hypocrite realise that there was no limit to how low he
could stoop, that there was a time when even a worm had to rise
up and walk on the hind legs it had never grown, that there came
a time for the wolf to shed the sheep's tears. You, you never existed?
My darling, my love, it is those calculating cowards saying it who
have never existed and do not exist, and may the fires of their loveless hell consume their cold reason like a tin soldier.*

11

A new epoch began for me now, first in London and then
back again in Palermo, where I persuaded Olga to accompany

me once she had gathered all the documents required to clear passport control. It was the sole period of my life of which I was to remain unswervingly proud, because, of everything I had vouchsafed or accomplished, its representations and realities came the closest to that ideal of the absolute which man is commanded to pursue in life and only ever pursues in love. I had done with my smoke screens of urbanity and worldliness, with my vast collection of social crutches and antique loopholes, with my need to astound and to bedazzle. What remained was an uncompromising desire to please, to comfort and to reassure.

Every night she woke up screaming, and night after night I swore every oath I could find in Dahl's *Dictionary of the Living Russian Language* that the tenderness of my embraces would in the end prove more lasting than the stuff of her nightmares, that our present could rewrite her indelible past as Virgil rewrote the Italic song and Chopin the village dances of Mazovia, that all would be well. Weeks passed, then months. She tasted cassata, cannoli, pistachio ice-cream. She heard Callas sing in *La Traviata* on a long-playing record, and saw *La Cenerentola* from the royal box at the Teatro Massimo. We went out to the Aeolian Islands. *Ti vogliamo bene!* was writ large on every face, in a kind of siege of blond intransigence by mustachioed benevolence, and wherever she turned she saw only guileless pleasure, adumbrated by neither lust nor greed. By and by the nightmares began to shrivel. Then they dried up altogether.

She was becoming a fully fledged Leo, demanding and deserving of everyone's adoration. In July, her twenty-sixth birthday was celebrated with a gypsy-themed party at the

Verdura Gardens to which *tutta Palermo,* which is to say all the respectable people – those with at least one member of the family doing *l'ergastolo* somewhere in the Sicilian penitentiary system – came bearing gifts of bright-coloured shawls and home-made puddings. My gypsy friends Petya, Lilya and Pascal had flown in from Paris with their accordionists and violinists, to sing happy birthday in Russian and Romany. Her anxiety was being laid to rest, it seemed, in the same grave as my nostalgia, for finally my long-envied Italian happiness-mongers could see for themselves what Russian *bellezza* was like in a storm, if only a storm of music, and what it could do to allay a man's fear of nonexistence if given half a chance and a gypsy costume of black and red lace.

If the world were a physic garden, like the Verdura, and love something that made use of its specimens to heal hidden wounds, then I could easily say that during this period of my life with Olga I worked as hard as any young physician, glad of the long hours that left neither time nor energy for ordinary reflection, to say nothing of suspicion, jealousy or resentment. If the world were such a garden, I imagined myself collecting its verbena and its nightshade, its dandelion and its cumin, its styrax seed and its cloves, to piece together a cure for any future complications of my patient's condition, a malady I perceived as the insecurity of living with an immoral past in an amoral present. In this case one did not need to feel overly judgemental, or too deft a juggler of ethical criteria, to make the diagnosis: 'immoral' simply meant 'sleeping with all comers,' whereas 'amoral' meant 'no longer.'

But then summer came to an end and we headed back to England, where Olga had enrolled in a course of study at something or other called Fashion College, part of something else again, called the London Institute. She was going to study fashion, she said, because she liked fashion and because the people in fashion were young and beautiful, and what could I say to that? Could I say: *Beloved, in my despair I shall rend my outer garments, in deep mourning I shall blacken my fore-head with ashes? Or could I say: All fashion models are hookers by another name?* Could I ever say, with anything like a straight face: *Why youth?* And could I really cast away all shame and say, addressing beauty incarnate and beloved: *Why beauty?*

I had in my little black book the telephone number of an Indian woman, whose name is best undisclosed here, who to this day is perhaps the most distinguished madam in Europe. From her base in London she has established an international reputation for herself by her ability to negotiate a contract for the body of any woman in show business, television or fashion, any woman at all, at prices starting at £100,000 a week-end, excluding commission. I showed the number to Olga, dilating at some very great length on the fundamental venality of the world she was proposing to enter. Would you now spend a week-end with some towelhead of a stranger for £100,000, I asked.

'Of course,' she said. She said it with all the naturalness of a child's kiss, without so much as a shadow of a smile, with eyes rounded as though to underscore the spontaneity of her disbelief. But why, I insisted. What would you do with the money? And then, incredibly I thought, she fell to thinking. Minutes passed. 'Well, money is always useful to have,' at length she replied. The dot in the Necker cube jumped, and then jumped back again.

When Dostoevsky said that the soul of man is the battle-field where good and evil fight over beauty, he was being a little too apocalyptic. Doubtless the soul *is* a battlefield, but the armies clashing upon the verdure are many, and the combatants not all of them archangels. In this case, I was beginning to feel, the future of my love was inextricably linked to the outcome of the fight between two cultural forces contesting the dominion of Olga's soul, forces to which I now inwardly referred as 'mine' and 'theirs.'

Mine was the force of Europe's fin de siècle and its modern successors in interest, of Russian culture in its silver age, of childhood associations, of nostalgic fantasies, of decadence verging on innocence and innocence reminiscent of joy. Theirs was the force of the coming century, of ownerless, odourless money and all the Technicolor colour and glamour it bought, of the global metropolis and the fat-fingered spivs who had promised to pay the piper of Hamelin, of women as flat as deflated dolls and men as persuasive as the lies they threw in their rubber faces. Theirs ran on vanity; yet it would be dishonest to claim that mine did not, because, considered from the point of view of the actor, the act of reciting a line of Blok to a Russian prostitute is no less vain for being less convincing than the act of dangling the keys to a Ferrari in front of a Cinecittà soubrette at Jimmyz. Hence the antagonism between them could always be viewed simply as one man's struggle for greater refinement in his choice of vanity, or, even more dispassionately, as his search for the appreciably less vulgar, fancier, classier brand of the same weakness, which, for some capricious reason, he found more appealing – less common, as he himself would probably say – than the department-store, off-the-peg kind. So, was that all it amounted to, this great Dostoevskian struggle between good and evil, with beauty as booty, with the flashy Arab as the devil, with myself as Archangel Gabriel? To a tempest in a teacup over some hair-splitting distinction between varieties of braggadocio?

Yet this very fine distinction, I answered myself, is all that has ever really mattered to me; just in the way that the insubstantial gossamer web of culture is really a crucial safety net, holding human life aloft over the abyss that is the animal kingdom. We all know those terrible stories, scarifying like the engravings of instruments of torture from books *in folio* on the Inquisition in Spain, but actually just filthy emanations of prurient late-Victorian minds: female scorpionflies, 'extorting gifts of insect protein at least sixteen millimetres square' from their mates 'with the act of coitus lasting only as long as the meal to harness the male's material largesse to the female's egg production,' elephant seals sharing the bed with a whole lecherous safari of savanna baboons, stickleback fish, immunocompetent rats and tribes of the Orinoco... Surely life is not only this, or else why is it that of all the numberless animal species on earth, and in arrogant defiance of all that scholastic levelling, only women – O, those beautifully kissable women! – have lips made for kissing?

It would have been easy for a Darwinist to expose the mating strategy that underlay my love for Olga in a single sentence, though I doubt I was ever such a coward that he would have lived to finish it. My insistence on fin de siècle values, he would drone, was nothing but a ploy mimicking the male display of resources, intended to head off potential competition from males who were capable of such display in reality, so that by asking her to cling alongside me to the wreckage of old Europe, I was seeking to isolate her, as though on a raft in the open sea, from more suitable providers in the modern jungle... But truth to tell, Darwin-inspired reductionism never did get under my God-made skin, if only because childhood immunisation by Soviet propaganda made me impervious to claims of central-planning efficiency. In this I had the full intellectual support of my milieu, where a phenomenon was seen as fit to survive only in so far as it did *not* have an evolutionary, which is to say social, function; thus poems that never mentioned coalmining, youth, or world peace were its lips, so to speak, lips made for beauty's sake and aimless kissing, not for the greater power of the communist international or the female stickleback's egg production.

Be that as it may, all I can say is that one would have had to have a heart hard as a conker, or a brain pliant as Sicilian *primo sale* cheese, to have followed the argument through to this, or any other strange conclusion, upon hearing those words of Olga's. 'Of course,' she said. 'Money is always useful.' But then again, perhaps that was only a taunt, another in the famous series of instinctive jabs at genuine sentiment which, in the wilderness of Soviet fakery, she had brought herself up not to distinguish from fraudulent sentimentality? Good Lord, how my head ached from those conjectures, doubling up in loops, changing larval masks, slipping through my fingers like sand! For the first time I understood what Spenser was on about in *The Faerie Queene*, and just how impossible it really is to know anything, or to believe in anything save one's own love.

In the beginning of September we came back to London, there to live as man and wife in the newly acquired flat with the Victorian skylight that made me think of Crystal Palace. The same flat where, nine months later, I would be weeping over these confessions of impotence.

12

It is difficult to explain, in a way that wouldn't make even an ordinarily sentimental person cringe to hear it, but having entered my life as its first-ever absolute, my love was now becoming more and more horizonless, in the sense that there was now not one topographical mark in sight to orientate the sailor on the high seas, or somehow to calibrate the infinity he faced on all sides. I stay on this tack because, however brave the seaman, however prodigious his appetite for adventure and his thirst for experience, it may none the less be imagined that the occasional shiver will run down his spine at the realisation of a coveted dream in so perfect a way, though just why that will happen is shrouded in the morning mist of the simile. All I can say is that in Russian gypsy romances joy is ever commingled with sorrow, for the very good reason that joy, like a fair wind, is temporal, and always an accurate prophecy of imminent sorrow.

What made my obsession more uncontrollable with every passing day was a disturbing quality of Olga's physical presence for which there is no word in English, but which I can perhaps introduce, as Nabokov, famously, introduced his quirkily transliterated 'poshlust,' a species of posh lust for highfalutin kitsch. Transliterated the Nabokov way, the Russian word would come out as 'nannygladness,' I suppose, so long as one allowed that the main attribute of a loving nanny is that she can't take her eyes off her beloved charge; as for the gladness she feels, the root of the Russian word is to do with 'looking,' 'staring,' 'gazing,' not all that far from the 'smooth,' 'shiny,' 'glistening' sense of the English. A semantic long shot, admittedly, yet the constituent elements of the process of seeing beauty – the objective, looking at a woman across a crowded room, and the subjective, being stared at by some creep in a lustrous suit – conjoin nicely as the man gives the bit o' an eyeful the glad eye.

Anyway, Olga's beauty had that quality. In all the time I spent in her presence, I cannot ever recall observing a single mannerism, gesture, or expression that gave me pause and made me wonder, if only for a fleeting instant, whether I might not have another reason for pausing in future. Her face was like a body of phosphorescent water in which, losing all sense of time or purpose, one waded fully clothed. Her glance was never anything but direct and unswerving, her posture always faultless, her movements never lacked grace; if at times a vagueness, or a softness, appeared in her eyes, this did not make her glance any less confident; if at times a hesitance, even a timorousness, caused her lips to tremble slightly, this did not make her seem any less sure of herself.

The physical perfection – perhaps too indiscriminately regarded as suggestive of mental health – that she radiated was, moreover, equally palpable at every stage of dress and undress. Everything she wore became her. A high-heeled shoe would fit her like the groove made by a garden slug in a turnip fits the slug; a cheap polka-dot dress would make her waist seem orientally, geisha silken; a ribbon for tying back her hair would look like it was born, christened, confirmed, married, and buried in her hair.

When more than the requisite number of weeks passed without the visit to the hairdresser to have it dyed, and the dark, trailer-trash roots became more visible, that hair only suited her face the more, as though highlighting the syncretic nature of beauty. Dressing to go out in the evening, from stockings to makeup to the final flourish of scent sprayed into the air, always at the same invariant 45 degree angle as though to strike an invisible target in the vicinity of her neck, was an algorithm of movements so practised and precise it made the exacting ritual of the Russian Orthodox Church seem like a succession of drunken improvisations in comparison, yet she was always ready on time. When she undressed, her clothes seemed to leap from her body of their own accord and scatter all over the room like frightened mice, as if acknowledging that the house belonged to the owner who had flicked on the kitchen light even as the body belonged to the man for whose pleasure she was undressing. Whatever she touched, turned to emotion; whatever she whispered, to almost unbearable elation; whatever she wanted, to tears of lust. It was somehow a magical ingredient of her perfect self-possession that she never failed to lose that self-possession in bed, with the consequence that I could never look at her out of bed and believe that I had ever been an eyewitness to even a single moment of that self-possession deserting her.

Consequently she was unpossessable. Perhaps that is the

open secret of nannygladness, because, however strongly the nanny believes that her adorable charge is hers, deep down she must suspect that she is only the hired help, a chapter in the life, a developmental stage; that the child actually belongs to its own parents, to newfound friends, or to an eventual spouse, more permanently than to her; that in the long run it is made for bigger and better things than cutting out silhouettes of fir trees with her manicure scissors from green construction paper. Hence the nannyglad eyeful is the consummate product of a hysterically jealous eye, while nannygladness, as a way of seeing, is necessarily rife with frustration.

Nannygladness did not make Olga's beauty any less disturbing, for the same reason that the beguiling taste of vintage brandy does not lessen the narcotic effect of the alcohol it contains. If anything, it had the opposite effect, by amplifying both the Nietzschean exhilaration I felt in her presence and the concomitant animalism. It worked as an ever-active reminder of something I felt it important to be reminded, namely, that the woman before me was not my invention as a writer, that I had not gone out into the big bad world with a theory in my back pocket and collected the first specimen that seemed to fit it, that my acceptance of her past and my faith in our present were bespoke intellectual constructions, not prefabricated moulds. Her nannygladness was what stood between my seeing myself as a man in love and as a man in vaudeville, because such is the difference, more or less, between not being able to take your eyes off the woman you love and loving a woman because you once read a French novel whose heroine you suppose she resembles.

But then, as if these contradictory melodies were not in themselves discordant enough to wrongfoot me, there was the sound of her voice; that is to say, since a peroxide blonde is apt to use the voice box rather than the typewriter or pen and ink to project it, there was also her intellectual presence. And, as I have already pointed out, this was a trifle on the reedy side from the very beginning, meaning that from the very beginning the words she addressed to me, irrespective of whether we were alone or in the presence of others, were cast with the ambiguity of Old Testament prophesies on the one hand and the directness of a user's guides to a kitchen appliance on the other.

Her words to me were like so many shafts of mystery, sharp and from a certain point of view well crafted, sent forth by a blind archer in the direction of a target too large to miss. Of these, a great number found the aim they sought almost by default, piercing my heart with their myriad points that culminated in the wisdom that there's nobody can look into the future and, since everything's relative anyway, there isn't much point in trying. Life was as practical as ever, and money always useful.

13

Thus even as her physical presence brought me nothing but elemental joy, her presence in my life as a sentient and speaking being was an interminable trial. I would hardly be exaggerating if I said that, in all the time I had known her, I had not heard from her lips a single remark wholly intended to please, a single comment whose meaning was completely un-ambiguous, a single compliment meant to comfort, a single word of reassurance, a single fragment of a sentence that did not contain an ellipsis…There was but one exception. She did say she loved me. She said it often. I believed her then, and I believe it still.

She said it often, though not nearly as often as I wished, and in this too lay a staggering novelty. Never before, in all the dalliances or alliances of my past, had I had the occasion, or indeed felt the need, to ask a woman whether *she* loved *me*. For my part, acting on the proprietary instinct common to most people and in accordance, as it were, with established practice, I withheld the hallowed proclamation for as long as possible, sometimes bestowing it upon the presumably grate-ful recipient as a nobleman of old might make the gift of an old cloak to a favourite. But to wonder, to want to know, to wish to hear that proclamation in reply, was never in my thoughts. Now the desire to ask the question, to hear love af-firmed, to receive, became an itch, a mental tic, a thrilling and morbid preoccupation, like one of those loose milk-teeth we cannot keep from harrying, naive minds swarming with sixpence fairies, with our toddler tongues. Not for nothing, I now recalled, had my sainted mother, struck by what to her seemed like a certain aimlessness in my relations with women during some of the more restive years, warned me, in the words of a famous Russian proverb, that there would come a day for the wolf to shed the sheep's tears.

Apart from this one symbolic exception, in which, as in a droplet of real dew tipping the anther of a wax blossom, all the anxieties of a misspent life came into focus, as I said, my routine of existence, in the shadow of her elliptical thought by day and the merciless glare of her beauty by night, was as a matter of practical reality unbearable. Jealousy was easily excited, and never substantively quelled; conjecture ran wild, like a knight at the hands of an unthinking and inexperienced chess player; arguments erupted, burying the day's Pompeii of confidence under layers of silky ash; plans ran aground in open stretches of intransigent contrariness, whose shallows were unmapped and unpredictable; agendas appeared hidden, motives ulterior, silences interminable.

The mobile telephone, whose number at length I would persuade her to change, messaged the fleshpot latest from a world of which she was no longer part, yet whose ups and downs obviously interested her, in the way that the old-fashioned teletype tape connecting the lobby of a gentlemen's club with the stock exchange may continue to interest the longest-retired speculator among the habitués. Her new friends from what she called the world of fashion rang to invite her to parties, the object of which, as I, who had been on the other side of the divide for so long, could see with nauseating clarity, was to boost the number of available, tall, blond or at least tolerably buxom women in the purlieus of a potential investor in this or that dubious business venture, by no means always in the fashion industry, yet as a rule never hostile to the idea of smoothing its way forward with cocaine. Sometimes her old friends, such as the waiflike Anya, rang also, or simply appeared out of the blue to accompany her after school to destinations as innocuous, and every bit as implausible, as the alleged nature of the affection that evidently still bound them to one another.

Above the love nest, in the dim light of foreshortened days filtering through the cast-iron skylight, falsehood hung in the air like smog over a Victorian factory town. It seemed to me that she was lying about everything except that she loved me, but then the question arose of whether this one decisively important, truly pivotal fact was not a lie as well, for otherwise why would she have felt the need to shroud the rest of it in deception and silence? When finally we had quarrelled, I moved her out to the hotel where it all began.

Olga, I'm writing because you won't answer the telephone, and also because I feel I ought to write. Otherwise you may simply decide that I'm a schizophrenic, which is perhaps not far from the truth. But it is by no means the whole truth.

What happened? I think you've broken a taboo. It was the commandment of absolute honesty, honesty with oneself and with me. In retaliation, I broke another taboo. But, as children say with the truthfulness of innocence, you did it first.

Yet the question is broader than that, this much is clear. Which is what I meant by what I said, in the note I left on the door, 'This can't go on.' Had you not voiced the same sentiment during our last argument? You may answer that all you did was voice it, as you did not shout, smash crockery or throw anybody out of the house. True, but a taboo is a taboo, and each of us deals with its violation as the gods move him.

Forgive my selfishness, but it has a point. 'To win is easy,' we used to say in unison, 'to keep is the hard part.' Remember? We were always talking about me keeping you! And then I had this thought, a kind of revelation, and I assure you it came from nowhere, without so much as the vaguest shadow of smugness: 'Why? Why her? Why does the one who has won me so easily never bother to think of how to keep me?'

Listen for a minute. Love is a composite creature resembling a centaur, where you can hardly tell at which point the man ends and the horse begins. Sometimes it seems it is there, sometimes here, first higher, then lower down, but the relevant fact is, one is always astride the other, one rides and the other carries the rider. Well, the natural beauty of this whole conceit is that a man and a woman are endowed with different capabilities, and the great tragedy is that you haven't bothered to learn to use yours. In part the fault is mine. When all is well with us, I say nothing, I just look and look and look at you and I'm the happiest man alive, because as far as I'm concerned the mere act of your being – of my being in your presence – is more than any man can ask of fate. But all is not always well, and this is where a woman's capabilities become paramount in the delicate matter of the centaur, turning the man into a horse and herself into an experienced horsewoman, who knows how to use the spur without drawing blood.

I'm writing this in a tearing hurry. I'll write again, tomorrow and the day after if you wish, but I must have this letter delivered to you at once because I have the superstitious feeling that unless I do, it may be too late.

All I want to say now is that the main thing is to keep thinking, thinking about what's just happened between us, and not in a philistine way, not begrudgingly, but as though seeking an opportunity, an opening; thinking genuinely, by ripping open new, hitherto sealed, envelopes containing fresh answers. I don't want to be 'over' you, please realise this! But I don't want to be 'under' you by accident or coincidence, from folly or dishonesty, or for any other spurious reason, which – seeing that you do not use even a tenth of the capabilities in your gift to make me want to become what you wish me to be — is what threatens me, I think.

Let me remind you. Last Friday I told you in plain Russian that, come Sunday, I wanted to weep. Did you stop to think about what that meant? It was not, do believe me, a pat formula expressive of a lascivious dream, it went much deeper than that, it summoned something I thought you needed no less than I did to feel that at last a balance of power had been established. Well, where were thy arrows, Diana? To say that I love you is absurd. I love you more than I love my own brain, and this is the problem, because it is an example of the sort of weakness you are not exploiting to manage my love and to manipulate me.

14

It's four o'clock in the morning, and I've lost the plot a bit. And we have that party at Annabel's tomorrow night. Did you take that cocktail dress with you to the hotel? What about the shoes? Anyway, I continue. All these issues are somehow connected. For example, you write to me about wanting to study, about looking for work, about feminism and independence. Well, in the half-century of its aggressive existence, has feminism not discredited itself to the point that one can no longer say whether the pair of high heels to match your dress is a feminist, or an anti-feminist, statement?

If a woman works, in the sense of doing something she likes — because if not, it's a debilitating lot for a woman just as it's a dog's life for a man — then that's fine, and her high heels do nothing to undermine or contradict that. This is a cliché. But if a woman works, and they are missing from her wardrobe, or if she can't walk in them or doesn't see why the hell she should, then it's a disaster. A disaster for her, because, in Lady Macbeth's murderous phrase, she is unsexed. She has severed herself from mankind. Don't smile pre-emptively, please, murmuring something like 'Well, nobody walks in them better than I, that's for sure!' After all, it's only a random symbol.

Your excruciating beauty is not in doubt. I know it, but in some very mean way you know it too. Another problem! Because when we're alone, just the two of us, with a whole Sunday just round the corner, something extraordinary must proceed from you and occur between us, something that cannot and doesn't happen in the presence of strangers. But your beauty is terrible when we're alone and it is just as terrible when we're in public. This robs you blind, believe me, it robs you of so much of your power over me.

When we first began seeing each other, it was much less notice-able, in part because we hardly ever mixed with other people, you did not think about studying, you never mentioned work, and in part because you still had one foot in Vita's world. Now everything's changed, with the result that, supposedly, I have in my house an 'honest woman' with whom 'at night' I am to 'have sex,' while 'during working hours' I am 'to do my writing' and she is off 'to study.' You call this cutting-edge feminism? I call it creeping philis-tinism. Because the trick is not about how to combine a working life with a home life, any fool can do that, it's about how to never stop being the goddess of your beloved. Discipline him with your femininity, spur him on with your art, strangle him half to death with your beauty until he acknowledges seeing in you what nobody else has ever seen in a woman. Otherwise, all that remains is woman's work. Keeping up with the Joneses. The wife's cracked trough from the fairytale about the fisherman and the fish.

I know how difficult it must be for you to reconcile all these con-

tradictory accounts, those of my love, those of your future, those of our material survival, and all in such a short time. But just one effort, and everything will fall into place. This effort is to look at the world through the eyes of the man who loves you more than he loves his own brain, and it is precisely to help you make this effort that I demand from you what I give you, hundred-percent truthfulness in everything. At 99%, we don't even know what we ourselves are thinking, so how can one ever know what somebody else thinks? If everything is relative, then why X and not Y? Why 26 and not 22?

I told you that I wanted to weep. If you didn't have the tendency to relativize everything, wouldn't you have remembered that I always tell you the absolute truth, and paused to think about why that truth was significant? In your letter you say: 'I feel male.' But would a man ever be embarrassed to use his sex as a weapon, a tool, an instrument? No, a man wouldn't! And instead, you, a self-proclaimed man, want to have an intellectual tug of war with me... If it hadn't been for that, I would've lain at your feet.

Olya, there is a holy grail called modus vivendi, *which must be found. To help us find it, you must interest yourself afresh in the choreography of love, not as a dancer from the second cast in the guise of a* prima donna assoluta, *but as a repentant sinner in the guise of an aspiring saint. At present you know next to nothing of my innermost longings, not much more, at any rate, than some third-rate Vita could have told you in a three-sentence brief, and it fills me with despair that you don't seem to want to understand them better.*

It is as though you've accepted the world's compliment – she's awfully beautiful! – once and for all, and decided that, on that front at least, all is in your hands, that now you can worry about other things, about the side of yourself you call male. But, darling, that male side of you does not exist, and cannot emerge, until your own gender has affirmed itself by its own, feminine means. Unfortunately for both of us, living with a decadent writer – perverse, jealous, and desperately in love – is a more substantive challenge than flirting with a stockbroker across the table in a restaurant.

Here's an experiment I want to propose. Let us go to that Annabel's dinner tomorrow night. I'll collect you at the hotel around 8. Come with me as my date, not as my wife or my mistress. Afterwards I'll take you back to the hotel, and if I'm lucky you'll kiss me goodnight. Who knows, perhaps the distance thus gained between us will be the perspective that is now lacking, wherein new thoughts will arrange themselves, like Swan Lake corps de ballet, in neat rows of snow-white tutus.

Darling, love is in so many ways the choreography of love. I used to say that all the time, remember? You agreed with it only in the vaguest, most tentative way, and then we went ahead and started living together anyway. Like attending a ballet class for a summer and then demanding a principal part at Covent Garden! Do you even know me?! If so, I want to hear from you all about my own deafness and muteness, my own blindness and my own folly, with the same well-meaning sincerity with which I'm telling you of yours. I will not be offended, I promise. Apart from you, truth is my only fetish. Let me know if you're coming with me this evening. If not, I expect a reply.

15

Who is the hero? The man, Orpheus, doing everything in his power to find and to save as quickly as possible. Who is the heroine? The woman, Scheherazade, endlessly delaying the seminal moment of resolution and death. In this lies the paradox of gender reversal, for are there not men who long for artful postponement, or women who crave a brief but convincing moment of ecstasy? And at times it happens that one of these men can, like a woman, content himself with what one of these women, like a man, offers him: thus contented for a month, for two, he begins to yearn for a halt in the wilderness of alien pleasure, for a green oasis of his own natural inclinations. Perhaps this is the reason why women are so good at inventing or remembering various special dates, such as anniversaries or birthdays. Therein they find relief from the dissatisfactions of the routine, which they want to break up with sensual orgies, feast days, verdant oases. Well, the sort of man who longs for the infinite must have such a Valentine's day too.

Both genders lie within each of us, that much is certain. The art of love, which for some reason I like to think of as its choreography, involves our four ambivalent halves combining in no fewer than two dozen different ways, conspiring, kissing, holding hands, slipping little notes to each other, whispering in one another's ear on stage and off, promising the moon, flirting, fibbing… Their dance only seems like a pas de deux, *but it's always a* pas de quatre.

It sometimes happens that my two halves, often acting in concert, conspire with one of yours, and the three of them together lay siege to the other. Sometimes they chastise him the way a delinquent, caught in flagrante with a Beatles record under his jumper, was once upon a time chastised at the Young Communist League assembly after school. I have witnessed the scene on a number of occasions, when I, or sometimes my better half, tried to persuade you, or half you, of the whole truth of a proposition, and your better half wholeheartedly agreed. By contrast, the only times I recall myself agreeing with your arguments were the times when the whole of you spoke to the whole of me. Don't you see? This is crude, it is dramatically weak, it lacks plasticity. It's a frontal assault. It goes against the basic principles of choreography. All the dancers must be engaged, because if there are only two, then dammit, any member of the audience will feel he has the right to mutter, hell, I can do that myself, me and my Kitty, we're a regular Romeo and Juliet, she an' me.

There are moments when it seems to me that you are not at all a sexual being, that you fell into my arms by sheer chance, as a cuckoo's egg is said to fall in the nest of a songbird. For, whereas I'm quite unable to recount a single private thought of yours in which I might figure with any degree of plausibility, you know with absolute certainty what it means for me to think about you: you are the omphalos cosmou, *the navel of my universe, the dream and the awakening. Put another way, I haven't a single thought in my head that doesn't involve you, revolve around you, centre on you. And you? Remember, it was on that fateful Sunday last that you exclaimed, as we stood by the picture at the Victoria and Albert, 'Look how he is holding her!' In all the time I'd known you that was the closest I'd come to hating you. The man in the painting, you preferred him to me! And there were only two conclusions left to draw just then, either you're not a woman of feeling at all or you're not one when you're with me. Can that be, I now ask myself. And I answer yes, of course it can, you twit.*

Any movement of our organs — tongue, eyes, heart, lungs, hands, lips and all the unprintable rest of it — is a serious matter. 'What is set down with a pen,' goes the Russian proverb, 'can't be chopped out with an axe.' Rubbish, as any writer deserving of the name will tell you, of course it can be. A quick sigh, on the other hand, a furtive gesture, a fluttering of the eyelashes, to say nothing of all sorts of hardenings and shudderings in which ordinary life deals by the gross, those things, I say, no axe on earth is powerful or ruthless enough to obliterate. This is not, mind you, mere advice to a young lady in doubt from the agony aunts at Paranoid Schizophrenic Monthly, it is a summons to serious thought.

Think before it's too late, before we've had our Katya, while you're still young, while there's the time and the freedom to think any abstract thought you please. Think, because thought is neither illicit nor punishable, but immaterial and invisible, with the consequence that by using your brain you may well achieve everything you may not be able to achieve by using your body, entailing as that does everything irreversible and irretrievable in the material realm which is subject to the jealous laws of physics.

THREE

LAST BETS

1

Waffle, just waffle. Cerebral crutches under the branch of an apple tree laden with fruit, didactic supports groaning beneath the weight of irrational mystery, ineffectual solutions of a novice gardener perplexed by the sudden overabundance of emotional unknowns where he had expected the neat, obedient, laminated orchard on the cover of a horticultural magazine. What baffled was the apparent complexity of my dissatisfaction, because the one question most often whispered in my heart was so simple it could've been asked in five words and answered at the expense of a single daisy: 'Does she or doesn't she?'

It was all very well that she said she did. The theorem was succinct enough, just a word, really, a word and a question mark, but up on the blackboard the proof of it took the shape of a differential equation, of an apple orchard on the night in August when its moonlit ambages fill with tangled shadows and the sound of cracking boughs and crashing fruit; that sprawling proof, its roots deep in the question mark, was an arboraceous infinity, gnarled, unembraceable, insensible to ordinary ratiocination. The theorem, it seemed, could only be proved by some intense convolution, and that, at this juncture in the dream, was the role of coition. Hence the demands on Olga in the role of mistress.

'She was so little his mistress,' mused the protagonist of *D'entre les morts*, the novel on which Hitchcock based *Vertigo*. 'He thought he could do without that side of her so easily, even a little shocked that she could lend herself to such indecorous pleasures. What he loved in her was... it was difficult to explain... it was that she wasn't quite real.'

Yet on the face of it, and, one could only assume, from Olga's own point of view, she was every penny in the pound as real as the position in which she now found herself. She was, at least technically, free of her past; in her hotel suite of fair-to-middling luxury was a jewellery case full of Bond Street baubles; her wardrobe was bursting with ladylike clothes, expensive enough for any social occasion; she now owned a car, a snazzy cabriolet of silvery hue; her £60,000 in cash was still intact in her suitcase; her documents, her bank account, her status as a university student were all in order. But the situation's author, and the material fountainhead of that bounty, was an idiot, a fantasist, a maniac, who had fallen in love with her and made it his life's aim, apparently, to obtain the proof of her reciprocity by whatever means, possibly not excluding double-murder suicide. Who knew? Her favourite film was a piece of American made-for-television rubbish called *Gia*, a biopic of some lesbian model on heroin who cut a tragic swathe through middle-class hypocrisy with a supposedly plain-speaking but in reality merely foul mouth. Not for her the soul-searching nuances of *The Idiot*.

She could read insanity in every halting phrase of his verbose letters, she could see it in the affected boundlessness of his affections, she could sense it in the oddness of his manic pleas, erotic and otherwise. She hadn't been once or twice around the block for nothing. He had got it into his head that he wanted to learn to weep, as he had never, in all his life before her, been able to shed a tear, whether from physical pain or from embarrassment or frustration. The psychosexual overtones of the client's caprice were not lost on her, certainly, and some part of her knew that the surest way to give a client of this peculiar sort what he was bargaining for was to give him nothing at all. Nothing, that is to say, apart from sex, which, with the rest of the generation of women brought up on cinemascope, she believed was more in the nature of taking than of giving.

If that is indeed what Olga thought, she was right. I only saw the situation as real in so far as I believed that the proof of her love could be obtained. As for the rest, I couldn't care less. Much of the money I'd squirreled away was now gone, but I had a good credit rating and knew that I would be able to borrow whatever I needed to see the thing through, meaning until such clear proof as I craved was obtained. I dreamt of that moment as an accountant dreams of retirement, as a poet dreams of posterity, as a mother dreams of seeing her son conduct the Berlin Philharmonic or become president. More than an obsession, it was an occlusion, a shutting-out of thoughts and facts intent on irruption into the world of my pin-sized, yet absolutely blinding hope: to learn the truth, to know the truth of love.

'Do something,' went the accompanying prayer, 'do something to persuade me once and for all of the truth of your love, and then I will never shrink from anything, I will suffer hunger and cold and jealousy with equal indifference, I will become a part of you as immovable as the marble plinth is a part of the delicate figure of love it supports through sleet and snow, famine and pestilence, war and revolution, I will never ask anything of you again, of you or of the world around us.'

The occlusion was a kind of rigor mortis of calcifying faith and overindulged hope, a paralysis of the will that could only be cured by her, by an act of hers, by a miracle, by a tangible and irreversibly convincing covenant of love that she herself devised for the purpose. This last was the *sine qua non* of the proof, that without which it would collapse back into doubt and agony, and yet here I was, giving her these detailed, interminable instructions, these cerebral, didactic pointers in the art of feminine befuddlement, an art she had imbibed with her mother's milk and had been practising all of her adult life. Now, how absurd was that?

I wanted to conspire with her against myself, to teach her how to fool me better and longer, how to create the illusion of certitude in my feverish, possessive, jealous brain. But she knew better than I the art of being a woman, and she refused to be compromised by my absurd entreaties. She would say nothing except that she loved me, she would not sleep with me except in the way she liked, and that was that. Writhe, worm! Writhe in your insomnia-filled bed at night, in the frigidity of your social intercourse during the day, in the impotence of your writing in the morning. Writhe in the second-guessing, in the conjecturing, in the pleading. Writhe in the presence of your beloved and in her absence, in the contemplation of a skirt on a hanger and at the sight of a cigarette stubbed out in the ashtray. 'Why, she's hardly taken a puff...' Those of little faith need not apply for the job of saviour. Poor Orpheus! Yet still I persisted.

2

And this is why I'm so maniacally jealous, so fruitlessly controlling, so paranoically mistrustful. Because within myself I feel that, given a precise choreography based on a Roentgen image of my soul, I would be able to forgive and to permit you just about anything. When I look at myself with your eyes, I seem to myself a man without skin, absolutely transparent and therefore utterly defenceless. Imagine how afraid such a man is of being seen clear through, of being captivated, as it were, for free, of being taken prisoner for no good reason. He is like a chameleon with dysfunctional mimicry, and there he crouches, all white and transparent, against the asphalt blackness of the motorway. How can he not be afraid? How can he not be jealous? He knows that any time now she can capture him with her bare hands and that later there will be no escaping.

Olya, I've never breathed to anybody what I'm confessing to you now; this is more than a confession of something in my past, it is the laying bare of the most secret anguish of my present. In effect, while we're playing hide and seek with the house key, I'm handing you the key to my collar. But I repeat, in the absence of the experience of femininity of which I speak, that key will not close anything.

The other night, true to my resolution to travel in you as far as my legs would take me, I sat down to watch the film Gia. *If I were an Italian, I would rename it* Bugia, *but since we're Russians, I'll rename it* Lgia, *since the only reliable fact that emerges from the biography of its heroine is that she was an inveterate liar. Doubtless this is very much in the spirit of the epoch.*

The epoch is intent on simplifying, on streamlining, on ratio-nalising the production process, as factory managers in our country used to say. Complexity is an obstacle. The starched collar, the top hat, the corset and the crinoline, the Edwardian parasol, the silken turban of the East and the red-lacquer tramcar of the West are all, in the end, only hindrances, snags or kinks. They are complications representative of the complexity of life. By contrast, Gia's clothes, her thoughts, her manners, her way of dealing with the world about her, are all, as the phrase goes, plain as a boiled parsnip. In this context, even lesbianism becomes a life-draining simplification, to say nothing of drug addiction and prostitution.

God gave man an ego with a thousand mouths. To live as a human being, not as a microorganism, he must feed all these mouths, as a mother looks after all her children, for even if just one of them is neglected we call her a bad mother. The drug addict, who nourishes his ego through a single mouth, a single hole, a single aperture in the skin, is deserving of our opprobrium not because he is a sinner, but because his peccavi *lacks the variety we expect of life. The same with the prostitute, whose problem is the addiction to simplification endemic to her profession.*

Why am I telling you this? Ah, yes, lying. Well, lying is another of modern life's great rectifiers, made ever more respectable by democratic politics and the myriad associated hypocrisies now taken seriously by ordinary people even in private. So unlike the lie we lived in our country, which may have been colossal, but as you know, in private we none of us paid any attention to it at all. In private nobody ever believed Pravda. *Yet the truth of life is complex and strangely configured, it demands unwavering attention, it is awk-ward to transport or to transplant, it is ever so difficult to move from place to place without spilling, like the clear reflection of a star in the water held in the poet's cupped hands.*

It is a tangle of zigzags interconnecting points of being, alive as a silkworm in its cocoon. Lying kills it, steams it open, untangles the precious contents, spins out the silken thread, connects the dots with a straight line. It rectifies the living truth — deadening it in the process — combing it with hypotheses, smoothing and softening it with assumptions, packing it into theories. Such is the spirit of the epoch, and drugs and prostitution are but a pair of threads derived from what was once an organic whole.

Olya, it is an hour since we said our goodbyes in the hotel. You're not there now. Your mobile is switched off. What am I to suppose? I can suppose that you're out for a drive, smoking cigarettes, thinking, listening to music in the car. That you're in a bar somewhere, alone or with friends. That you're out with a man, not necessarily in a compromising situation, but all the same, maddeningly, in his company. Why am I free to make so wild a supposition? Because there's a cardinal difference in our past. I've never lied to you, and you have. And this is the spectre that haunts us.

When, in the earliest days of our intimacy, I was cohabiting with another woman, a woman other than you, you not only knew of it, you permitted it. This was, I thought, because I'd given you what we used to call the red button, and pressing it just once would have meant instant termination of that whole arrangement, which, I now understand, was despicably deceitful for everyone concerned except you, because at the time only you were in possession of the whole truth. Then finally you pressed the button, or maybe it was I who did, but anyway I was true to my word and left Venice forthwith. But you went on cohabiting with another man, a man other than me, a man of whom I knew nothing. You were lying, Olya.

You've often said to me that you aren't a liar, and I do believe you. I believe you absolutely, because really it can't be true that I've fallen in love with a falsehood, I, for whom Eros begins with Truth, I, who have never been with a woman who wasn't mine, if only for an hour. But the spectre is there, palpable as the historical reality of a famous battle, and to this day I'm haunted by it like a soldier by an old wound.

When in my Venice diary I read the entries concerning our telephone conversations last winter, I see how neatly the lie connected the dots. How you theorised about needing more space, about wanting more time, about having less pressure, and all for the sake of smoothing out the crumpled, tangled, perhaps unlaundered reality of seeing another man. That's how I read those pages now, anyway, and the spectre is still there, perhaps, only because you've never taken the trouble to explain its presence any differently.

'A sparrow that's been shot at won't be fooled by chaff,' you know the proverb. The horror is that, whenever we go through something like a parting of the ways, it all suddenly begins to seem like chaff. And the ways keep on parting. It's easy for you to say: 'Just trust me! Believe me! Have no fear!' But you've done nothing to allay the fear, nor said anything to explain what happened back then, when the wounded soldier, thinking he was at last coming home, found only a boarded-up house in a burnt-down village.

Of course we've repaired it all, we've glued it together time and again with saliva and tears and semen, but I've never had the feeling that you ever felt responsible, or suffered the tiniest pang of guilt, or looked back at the episode with anything like regret or any other emotion. How, then, can I 'just trust' you? Olya, trust you I do. But to just trust you is something altogether beyond my endurance. Forgive me my weakness.

3

One afternoon she rang the doorbell. It was one of those afternoons in October that people call golden, either because leaves turn that colour or because the sky looks like an overturned bowl of beaten gold. We had been together for over a year now, though the actual date of that first encounter in the mews house could only come to light were Vita's account books to fall into the hands of Scotland Yard. How apt, incidentally, that there was never an anniversary of our meeting to celebrate. It was as though it had never happened.

She brought me a bunch of roses, one of those sad affairs they sell at filling stations on the motorway, and I could not help thinking that this was the only gift she had ever given me. This is not a whine of self-pity, but a fact material to the narrative, as is the fact that since her first night in the hotel I had been taking care to smother her room in exotic efflorescence. So sudden, so unexpected was her coming, so uncharacteristic and naive her offering, so luminous her face and so dramatic the irruption of her beauty into what for a time had been her own home that I fell to my knees in a gesture of resignation. She did not bid me to rise. She had come to claim what was hers, my adoration, my love, my weakness, my flat with the Victorian skylight, and her demonic intuition was now seeing her unerringly through every step of the dance whose choreographer I had so vainly imagined I could become.

She told me that eventually she wanted a place of her own in London, but that in the meantime she was agreeable, not tonight but one of these days, maybe tomorrow or the day after, to moving back in and living with me again, so long as I understood her, accepted the plan, and consented to organise the mortgage and the deposit on a flat, somewhere near, maybe in Chelsea? As I said, what money I had was fast running out, but I still had a little left in the bank and could easily borrow more. Since the buyer had no verifiable income, I reckoned the deposit on a flat costing £300,000 would need to be about £60,000.

A room of one's own! Ever since Virginia Woolf, every slapper's promised land and declaration of independence. Of course I realised that the announcement, or demand, was something of a watershed in the story. True to her word and, more important, to my whole interpretation of her character, she had never asked me for anything before, accepting my gifts of diamond bracelets and evening gowns with the gratitude that was at worst begrudging and, at its somnolent best, recalled the suspiciousness of a well-bred cat sniffing at an unfamiliar houseguest's shoelaces. For this reason, but also because I had come to feel so untalented a choreographer, so indecisive a prince and so schizophrenic a lover in the fairytale, so many long months in the unfolding, I never got the impression that the announcement was really an ultimatum. Only a watershed of some kind, a leap into the unknown, perhaps a new leaf. And who was to say that every momentous change in our lives is necessarily for the worse?

I cannot remember what she was wearing, but I remember how the dress rustled when it fell to the floor, and how what had been left of the light, following the sun's bankruptcy in the precincts of the church spire beyond my window, illuminated the pearls on her neck. All these facts, thoughts, impressions seemed unconnected, haphazard, spontaneous, and yet it was as though an invisible thread was holding them together all the while. That pearl necklace was a parting gift from my wife to a woman she had never met, a woman who, she knew, was her lost husband's gamble, his drug and his whore.

O Olya, Olya, my beloved, my kin! You probably think that I just took it all as given, that the afternoon with you did not astonish me, but it did, it so astonished me that all my responses to the extraordinary and the miraculous were paralysed, frozen as with novocaine, and it's only now that I'm beginning to come round. It's three in the morning, and I'm writing this letter because why do I only ever write to you on days of pestilence and famine, why not write of a feast day like this. It was the first time, since the very beginning of our strange story, that with my own eyes I could see your ego step aside to make room for my love.

Believe me, I too much value this moment of truth — this window into you that suddenly raised its louvered blinds like eyelashes — to make emotional capital out of my insights, as happens sometimes in the life of a couple. I'm no blackmailer, you know, I yell only when it really hurts, not because I have some manipulative scheme fomenting in my brain. No emotional blackmail, darling. I want you, I want whatever you want and I want you to be happy with me always.

But for God's sake don't pull those blinds back down! Don't cede the eminence won at such cost, at the price of my sleepless nights and cold sweat! Not in the sense of 'Keep it up, good girl, I love it when women bring me flowers and then take their clothes off,' because I promised no blackmail, but in the sense that when I yell you must hear me and look through the window to see what's the matter.

You know, in the past, when we quarrelled, sometimes I would be seized by the overpowering feeling that you weren't alive. It seemed to me then that your hardness, your unyieldingness, your recalcitrance were qualities so singular they simply did not belong among the attributes of any living being, to say nothing of a person possessed of a soul. I believe that it's all behind us now, that the window's open, that the blinds can be rolled up whenever there is need, that the house is no longer blind, that inside one can see burning candles.

You're still a mystery to me, and a mystery you will remain twenty years hence, I believe, when Katya has men calling at the house at all hours. Believe? No, hope, but at any rate no longer need fear, as I had feared until today, though of course my jealousy will continue to escort your mystery wherever it goes. And here it's you who no longer need fear, because jealousy may be a terrible thing, but so long as the window is open and the candles lighted, one can be evermore jealous without breaking glasses or packing suitcases.

I have some of your snaps from the summer in front of me now. Olechka, how much I love you and how jealous I am! Even of this impertinent photographic paper, which has the insolence to reproduce your image while reducing it by a whole dimension, as though using the second-person pronoun without the person's permission. Well, there is a logical explanation: I love you with a jealous love, as the gods love their worshippers and command us to love their idols, especially when these show themselves capable of working miracles as great as your visitation here today.

Olya, something within me is crying a river from the love I feel for you, a love I have never known before, from the passion for your awful beauty, which has become for me the one infallible measure of objectivity for everything that happens on earth. The imprint of your body is still on the pillows, and I've been kissing it all night. If you truly love me as much as I thought you did today, then truly I'm immortal. Forgive me, my angel of resurrection, if I failed to formulate or acknowledge this as you left.

I kiss you on the always escaping wisp of your hair. Read this on the bus to school and don't blush.

4

Looking back at the years of my marriage, I feel like the man who for his whole life labours under the delusion that he is the victim of a jinx, that somebody has given him the evil eye, only to discover at some stage that it is *he* who has had the evil eye all along, and that everybody he has ever known is jinxed by *him*. Why was I begging Olga for even the occasional moment of clarity, why was I pleading with her to open even a single window onto her inward world, when, only months before, I had been playing the elusive manipulator in my wife's endlessly sincere love?

Why was I now bargaining for honesty, however tempered by the intractable mystery of femininity, why was I hankering after truth, however gracefully restrained by the bonds of beauty, when, in Venice, I had lived an out-and-out lie, deceiving all comers with the brazenness of a provincial gold-digger? It made me think of the story of the Italian adventuress, who, while in Palermo hunting a husband, a Sicilian grandee of one sort or another, had bitten into an unpeeled *ficcho d'india* to convince him that she had never seen prickly pears before and was consequently, as she had claimed upon their first acquaintance, a visitor from Bucharest. She was rushed to emergency to have the prickles removed.

The truth that made it all an out-and-out lie was that I had given Olga the imaginary red button, representing her complete control over the proposed liquidation of my marriage, though whether her reluctance to press it, and thus catapult me to London, for so many months, was predominantly the result of her indecisiveness or of my own duplicity I cannot say to this day with any degree of certainty. The one redeeming element of my conduct, in retrospect, was that, concurrently with handing my mistress the magic button, I told my wife the truth about her existence and the likely outcome of the humbling that the three of us were about to undergo. In fact, if anything, I was more frank in those conversations with my wife than I was with myself, because to her I openly admitted that this time round the odds of winning were so much smaller than what I had been used to in my previous life as a gambler.

Funny how that layout of green baize can stretch or shrink, like Balzac's swatch of chagrin skin representing earthly desire, depending on the way the evening is going. Every gambler knows that feeling, reminiscent of the tricks played by time: flying when you're having fun, stopping in its tracks when you're on death row waiting for a reprieve. At times it seems to the roulette player that there are no more than a dozen numbers to choose from, all winners, but no sooner does he begin losing than the layout expands, first growing to the size of a football field and then engulfing him in the endless undifferentiated monochrome of tropical forest whence even the bravest never return. It was from this perspective, from the point of view of the loser, that I told my wife the story of my life's gamble. She felt sorry for me.

An earthly love was what we had lived, she and I, and were I to write it one day, *Earthly Love* is the title I would give to a book about marriage. We had been enterprising lovers, we had been considerate friends, we had been interlocutors, idlers, sybarites, confidence artists and clowns together, but never had the smell of brimstone and myrrh wafted over the pillows in beds where we had slept, only lilac and lavender. Our love had achieved, I would say, everything that love is capable of achieving upon the earth's fertile plain that is neither the putrid chasm of hell nor the rarefied mountain air of heaven, and it took a monstrous ingrate of an Orpheus, determined to find a yet unknown Eurydice whom he had glimpsed but once in a childhood dream, to flood that arable plain with bitter tears and render it barren.

Strange to say now, but in the months that followed my declaration of intent my wife responded to the news of impending separation by seeking to transform herself into the wood nymph of her lover's inchoate dream. Consciously or not, she began to behave in ways that, to her, were more *Russian*: less rational, less emotionally straightforward, less predictable. It was like watching the little mermaid from Andersen's fairytale trying to walk on human legs in the name of a sailor's love.

She would become an elusive dryad even if it killed her. Consciously or not, she understood that I had created her as she was, and that in so doing her beloved creator, himself more or less a man, had shown himself quite incapable of making her a woman, not enough, at any rate, of a woman to keep him. Now that my declaration loosened the bond between us, she would find a remedy and make up for all the time she had lost.

On one occasion, when I was away in London, she packed her Vuitton trunks and checked into the Plaza Athénée, whose bar is famous for the exoticism of its nocturnal fauna, with the idea of spending a week in Paris behaving like a hooker without, however, necessarily becoming one. By coincidence, there in the bar she ran into an Egyptian I knew, a confidence man of sterling, or perhaps dollar, reputation who had swindled more than one woman out of her fortune, an aging American Jewess with a palazzo on the Grand Canal in Venice among his famous marks.

First the Egyptian mistook the provocatively dressed girl at the bar for a prostitute, which, for reasons quite unknown to him, she found deeply satisfying; then he proceeded to ridicule her preposterous claim that she was an American living on the Grand Canal in Venice, a countermine which by the simple trick of reciting her neighbours' names all the way down to Accademia she was able to defuse, again to her immense satisfaction; in the end, after having quietly obtained the pertinent though as often happens in such cases inaccurate information from the hotel concierge, he finally set about wooing her, thus making her satisfaction as complete as she might hope in the circumstances. Escapades of this kind quickly became my wife's preferred pastime, increasing her confidence in herself and showing her some of the ways of the world of which until then she had been rather less aware than I. Mystification became her roulette, her substitute for achievement and gateway to experience. In a certain roundabout way it also expressed her newfound *Russianness*.

By the time the bubble had burst she was quite ready to meet me on my home ground. Shortly before parting forever, we booked a week in a small hotel in the Austrian Alps, there to exchange lamentations and kisses, regrets and fears, reproaches and compliments, confessions and lies for what, at least I knew for certain, would be the last time. 'Listen,' I said, 'we both know what's happened. I've run across my Nastasya Filippovna, and the ending you can easily look up in an English translation of *The Idiot*.' 'I have,' she said. 'Well, in that case you realise that none of this is *a reflection on you as a person*, as they say in America. It's only a reflection on your femininity, on the sort of woman I've led you to become. In other words, on the part you've played in my interior mythology.' 'You're craving Nemesis,' she said. 'I want to do away with everything in my life that smacks of vaudeville, even if it means laying my head on the executioner's block. You know I've never cried. To a man of letters, there's nothing to cry about in vaudeville. This woman is going to teach me to cry.'

Defiantly she tossed her hair and walked over to the bureau in the corner of the room. A few minutes later she handed me a note on hotel writing paper, neatly folded into an envelope addressed to Olga. 'Beloved!' it began.

Beloved! My husband has told me about you and he is allowing me to write a few words to express the deep and genuine gratitude I feel towards you.

You have enabled him to bear somehow the nightmare life he has led with me, which I only now can see for what it was. How arrogant and vain and intolerable I have been! I was never kind to him

*in the slightest degree. For my own outrageous self-aggrandisement,
I exploited all his sweet and generous impulses. Now I suffer. Do
not misunderstand. I am not repenting in order to get him back. I
am jealous of you too, but I do not hate you: I admire you.*

You may think it a strange thing for me to say, but I want him
to be with you. *He needs you, and what is more he loves you. You
are beautiful and kind. You have made him happy for the first time
in a long time. Please accept from me the gift I am sending with
him. I hope you will understand how much I feel indebted to you
for saving him, and how much I myself love you for that.*

The gift was the necklace of sixteen-millimetre South Sea
pearls she had bought herself the year before. It had cost, I
knew, something like fifty thousand dollars, then about
£30,000. Apart from her engagement ring, it was far and
away the most valuable piece of jewellery she owned.

5

Turgenev has a famous novella entitled *First Love*, which everyone for some reason seems to read as a child, understanding nothing, remembering nothing, and retaining only the
flavour of adolescent sentimentality that its first few pages
contain. Yet to an adult its awful message would be more un-
ambiguous than anything in de Sade or von Sacher-Masoch.

As I string together in my mind the series of episodes
which had taken my wife from our family home in Venice to
that Kitzbühel hotel, I recall Turgenev's novella, with its
rough outer shell of unanswered yearning and its mother-
of-pearl interior of a secret and violent love. Where did it all

come from in her? From what quarter? From which genetic strain? Unable as I am to answer such questions about my own longings, or about my own view of love, I can only throw my hands up in the air and wail as pitifully as anybody's fallen hero.

To this day it is difficult to find an educated Russian who can so much as tolerate Freud, for much the same reason that one rarely runs into a Jewish Nazi. In many ways Freud, to us Russians, is a kind of Hitler figure, in the sense that the Viennese doctor stands athwart the irrationality for which our literature – with its central idea of the inviolate soul – is as famous as French cookery is for its sauces. And what have we Russians, really, apart from our literature? The notion that the human psyche – which our writers have made their supreme idol, their faith and their profession of faith – is an organ, open to rational scrutiny, subject to scientific laws and material intervention, is to us nothing short of a holocaust, a book-burning orgy, a wholesale destruction that looms before our culture and threatens our race.

In my own case, every disinterested attempt on my part to trace my own sexuality, indeed my conception of love, to my mother or father has ended in bemused failure. Physically my parents have always been fleshless, ever noumenal in their solicitude, incorporeal even in their affection. My father, to borrow the title of a Russian science-fiction novel from the 1920s, has lived his entire life as *The Head of Professor Dowell,* his intellectuality so complete it could have been fed through a plastic tube with a nutrient solution of liquefied ratiocinations. My mother, whose life's task seems to have amounted to ascertaining that I haven't got the flu, would likewise prove an unsuitable candidate for Freud's ministrations. Honestly, I never wanted to sleep with or kill either of them.

My grandmothers, on the other hand, wives of men I never knew, were another matter. Not in the sense that I wanted to sleep with them, or even kiss them particularly, but in the sense that, together, they represented the dual nature of womanhood which, later in life, I came to accept as part of something real and inescapable.

A small-town sophisticate who became a Moscow ladies' institute gold medallist and later a doctor of medicine, my father's mother, Dina, fell in love with my grandfather in large part because he was almost impossibly Russian, a writer and a drunkard. He volunteered in June 1941 and was killed in the first few days of the war. My father, who was twelve at the time, was brought up by Dina. Together they survived the evacuation of Moscow, the privations of wartime, and the pogrom of doctors averted only by Stalin's death. When I knew her, her hair was white as freshly fallen snow. There was something of an American Indian out of a Hollywood Western in her appearance and bearing, the hauteur, the sense of justice, the rabbinical rationality of her utterances.

Judging by the family album, it was a blond bombshell out of a Hollywood comedy that my mother's mother, Nadia, had been in her youth, though of course I never realised this as a child. The grandmother I knew was a peasant woman from Nizhny Novgorod, on the Volga, whose husband had died in jail, like so many husbands in those distant days, long before I was born. Her defining characteristic was a maniacal obstinacy, reminiscent of mules, buffalos, donkeys or whatever animals are still used for transport in developing countries.

She travelled with a rucksack, which she would not take off her shoulders for any reason; she believed in the curative properties of menthol and some lesser known derivatives of the *Labiatae* family so fervently that no doctor on earth could have convinced her that spearmint balm does not cure, say, tuberculosis, or cholera; she sighed a great deal, muttering something about us being delivered from perdition by the great mother who art the queen of heaven, and her own daughter's eloquence, excited by the prospect of at last having got her at the sewing machine, broke impotently upon those sighs like ocean waves against a desolate rock.

The dual mystery of these women, of Dina's attraction to her husband and of Nadia's to her putative lovers, is something I have always felt in my blood as one feels a trait, a compulsion, a vocation. Dina, a woman of science, a translucent alabaster pillar of reason, stability, loyalty; and Nadia, married at seventeen, capricious, stubborn as a mule, desirable, libidinous, inscrutable, incessantly cheating or appearing to cheat on my grandfather, incessantly driving him mad with jealousy. He once dynamited a small townhouse where he thought she was meeting one of her paramours. A mistake, apparently, because there were no casualties of the explosion, just a pile of rubble where the house had stood.

All right, I'll come to the point and blurt it out in plain English. My wife was one and Olga the other. Freud never said anything about grandmothers. Even so, I shudder to think that there may be nothing more to the story of awful beauty than this simple dichotomy, prizing my childhood apart like the cheeks of an unripe supermarket apricot.

6

'And so? Did she accept it?' is what people might want to know at this juncture. Of course she did, despite the murmured warning of a girlfriend from St Petersburg – then in London on a whirlwind tour for which the hospital-size box of disposable rubber gloves prominent on the dining table was, unaccountably, a requisite – to the effect that such gifts, especially of pearls, could bring bad luck anyway, but that this fancy number in particular must have had a spell put on it with the express purpose of psychic ruination.

That girlfriend from St Petersburg, I must note, had her share of quietly held yet stubbornly argued theories. Another of these was that some fabulously wealthy men, presumably of Russian origin – though this mattered less than the presumption that the filthy rich men in question were filthy, rich, and of course men – were on the loose in Europe, *staging things* for their entertainment, whereby innocent bystanders, unbeknown to themselves, would be suborned to these men's private theatre. 'So you'd think you were late for the bus,' she would say with a shudder, 'but it was them who'd paid the driver not to open the doors. Or you'd be refused an entry visa somewhere, but it was something that had all been planned in advance, you see? We'll never know. What I think is, we could all be involved.' I easily identified the hand of Grandmother Nadia in the crazy quilting of mundane reality, and that of the Gnostic demiurge in the universal principle of the unpaid extra.

Anyway, I remember Olga's obstinate silence, head tilted thoughtfully to the side, as she heeded the warning. What was she thinking? *Was* she thinking? I wanted to propose that we rub the pearl necklace with spearmint balm, but bit my tongue just in time. That was then. Now, a year later, the necklace seemed auspicious enough, because money had to be raised to put down the deposit on her new flat and the lucky charm could be taken back to the jeweller who had sold it. Since my separation from my wife, however, our account there had not been paid, and the jeweller withheld half the proceeds to cover the indebtedness, with the result that I returned home with a cheque for £15,000. I had another £15,000 in my current account, and now, from the suitcase of silvery aluminium where she kept her wages of sin under lock and key, Olga produced the remaining £30,000 in cash. This she handed to me to pay into the bank, as the solicitor handling the purchase had made it clear that, in these troubled times, money sources in all such transactions are subject to scrutiny. Laundering a prostitute's cash through a gambler's bank account seemed like an irresistibly elegant solution.

I dwell on these events in such detail because the arithmetic of filthy lucre, which inevitably underlay a certain portion of our relations (though the arithmetic, or perhaps the calculus, capable of ascertaining just how great that portion was at any given moment with any degree of certainty still awaits its *Method of Fluxions*), was to play the stochastic joker in the final unravelling of my life. Like the queen of spades for Pushkin's Hermann, money opened up with a smile of good fortune and ended by flashing the loser a mischievous wink.

When my wife and I lived in genteel poverty, as at first we did, money never seemed to matter; when more of it came our way, and we began to spend more, it still did not matter;

finally, when something like wealth befell us, and I took to squandering it in brothels and casinos, it mattered only in so far as it went, and whether it went too fast. Now, for the first time in my life, I was taking money seriously. I now perceived it as a metaphysical presence, an agency of hope and dejection, a conductor of chance and love. Welcome to the real world, one might say. Life is practical.

There is something I want you to know, I wanted to write to my wife and one day I did, an empty, miserable day like any other, with the rain coming down and the wind beating on the windowpanes in my Crystal Palace of a mortuary, with the blinds drawn low to obscure the Victorian view of the church spire that had been stuck into the swollen, oedematous sky like a steel syringe. *There is something I want you to know. Of course, one can never tell whether hearing things, for the person listening, is less or more important than saying them, for the person who's doing the talking. But that, as you know, is generally the problem with literature.*

Perhaps you are so alienated, by now, both from the distant past of hope and the more recent past of disillusionment, that you will read this letter, if you read it at all, with dismay tempered only by boredom. Because what I want you to know is to do with the circumstances of our parting in the hotel in Austria, circumstances which the passing of time and your own efforts may by now have erased from your memory.

By sending her the necklace, you tried, without fully understanding it yourself, to break the circle of malice that hangs over the head of love; I say 'circle' because the malice in question is karmic, auroral, eternally returning; it is a sadomasochistic orgy of give-and-take, a zero-sum game where the many different aspects of personality of those taking part collide and jostle each other to gorge themselves on emotion. As in all gambling, in this game the loser and the winner are one, in the sense that even as he is winning, the winner knows that he is losing something – a chance for another life, perhaps, or luck in some other enterprise – while the loser, losing, feels that he is being in some way redeemed.

Maybe there is a man, out there somewhere, as imaginative, as clever, as sensitive and sensuous as I, who at the same time has the discipline of mind to stay out of this neurotic abyss and not even look down into the wishing well; but I have not met him. The point is, if love of the sort I mean, the kind one glimpses at the bottom of the well, is necessarily unilateral and results in great suffering – which I believe it is – then the circle of malice over the head of that love is unbreakable. I would compare it with the Darwinian chain, where every predator is somebody's prey, and no amount of Christian or other moralising will change the fact that sometimes it is the hawk who will be hungry and sometimes the sparrow, and that sometimes a man will want to impress a woman by shooting the hawk out of the sky though she will one day betray him and the hawk will have died for nothing.

But beauty remains, and – ineffectual, perhaps, in the light of what has just been said – that farewell gesture of yours was an expression of everlasting beauty. I say this despite the fact that I was a participant in the gesture, even, in theory, something of its designer or architect, and this, I might expect, would have ruined it for me, soiled it and made it sordid or, in retrospect, risible. But this has not happened. The more time passes, the more the moment of beauty occludes all the years of the life that had come before it; it iridesces in the darkness of my room at twilight; it is so much like the necklace itself, shy pink, as though blushing with unrealised de-

sire; and not a day passes without my thinking of it, as now, through tears. You don't know my tears. I'm certain you've never seen them. They are almost as large as those pearls. I have wept more of them in the last few months than you would ever think possible, knowing me as you do.

Of course the gesture was ineffectual, have no doubt of that. Man lives for caprices, as Dostoevsky was first to say out loud, pursuing them with an ardour that is as destructive as it is self-destructive, indeed very much like a gambler in the state of what the Russians call azart, *meaning intoxication by hazard. To say, 'Oh, that's just self-indulgence, why don't you just act differently?' is like saying 'Oh, you can go without food, why do you have to eat every day?' The truth is you can't, not after a certain point, and every one of us as well as everyone around us must, to a greater or lesser extent, bear the cost of the way we are made and are. The circle cannot be broken, because we're all different and 'what's good for a Russian, to a German is death.' Are tears* good? *In the eyes of one who has never wept, they may be. Is betrayal* good? *To one who has never been betrayed, it can be an experience on a par with anything religion ever offered to man. Is pain, great enough to want to end it by sticking your head in the oven,* good? *It can be, especially if the alternative — that vegetative, undifferentiated state of passive, compliant satisfaction in which most people have been living and dying since the beginning of time — seems much, much worse. No, the circle cannot be broken.*

But beauty remains, and I will think of your gesture always.

7

Meanwhile, even as I totted up columns of figures by night and telephoned mortgage brokers by day, the world at large was fast encroaching on what little certainty I had been able to invent for myself – on that fond hope, fragile as the nutshells in which in the olden days, at Christmas time, Russian girls used to set alight bits of church candle, floating them in a basin of water to divine their future bridegrooms. The more consciously Olga and I acted as a married couple, and the more conscientiously we treated our obligations to society, the less the world seemed to want to accept the arrangement as a fait accompli.

Dark hints, delicately veiled warnings and sweet-and-sour Chinese smiles now came my way oftener than dinner invitations, despite the fact that I had been careful to withhold particulars of Olga's biography from even the closest acquaintances. Some, like my Russian friend Irina, would not be placated by the imaginative ways in which I filled the resulting lacunae, and one particular midnight discussion, with many an accusation ('She's just using you! No fool like an old fool! A hunchback is only righted by the grave!') and counteraccusation ('Philistine! Petty-minded bourgeoise! Korobochka!'), seemed to have slammed the door on our friendship for all time. Shortly thereafter, just to spite the likes of Irina, for £1000 I procured a Moscow University diploma in Olga's name from a black-market outfit in Russia specialising in original documents. She had become an honours graduate with a degree in comparative cultural studies.

But all of this was scarcely worse than what I had expected all along, that slightly sordid mise-en-scène with which most divorcing men besotted by youthful concubines must contend in the society of their friends, fair-weather as well as true. What was socially unendurable was watching total strangers make observations, calculate chances and place bets on the sanity of one half of the couple and on the reputation of the other, with the result that most mass divertissements, such as large dinners or charity balls, began to seem a nuisance best avoided.

Yet, to borrow an idiom of Franco-Italian melodrama, the ogre had on his hands a young bride full of joie de vivre, and the notion of keeping her willowy waist away from the sweaty palms of rich men and the narrowed eyes of their ugly wives by locking her up in an attic seemed a little too old-fashioned to pass muster in the aforesaid London of spivs and sushi. Besides, Olga's own social life – in the course of which she mixed with people on the safe side, as now she sometimes condescended to reassure me, of the divide between freelance vice and bohemian virtue – afforded countless opportunities for the placing of palms on her waist or of bets on her reputation, and to my mind it hardly made a difference for the better that much of the wagering was done behind my back.

I tried to balance fun and fairness with jealousy and revulsion as best I could, though the *divertimenti* I laboured so asininely hard to devise rarely worked out as well as intended. On one occasion, after she had expressed a fleeting interest in seeing the Houses of Parliament, I arranged for an acquaintance of mine, a minister in the last Conservative government, to take us to dinner in Lords, an experience common enough from a certain cynical point of view, perhaps, yet one which the force of my reverence for the vanishing institution would, I hoped, lift into the realm of the exotic. In the taxicab on our way to Westminster we passed a drinks party spilling into the Brompton Road, with the usual cast of erythematous men in funny hats and erysipelatous women in dresses several sizes too small, brandishing glasses of gooseberry-green wine amid talk of the Turner Prize. 'Look,' she said, pointing, and in the strobe light of fugitive street lamps I almost thought her lower lip trembled slightly in disappointment, 'why aren't we invited to *that?*'

Another of these occasions ended in an incident that was to have lasting consequences. I had booked a lavish weekend in a hotel long renowned, as it were, for the swankiness of its funkiness. We were to meet in the bar for drinks at six. Unusually, unaccountably, it almost seemed epochally, she was late, and as I sat there with a sinking heart, watching the clock and trying to reach her by telephone, two women entered the bar speaking an exquisite, Muscovite, effervescent Russian. I introduced myself, making a lightning-quick reference to the plight of the anguished lover whose assignation is delayed. One of the two, a languorous blonde in her late thirties with a gold Orthodox crucifix nestling, like the dove of the holy spirit, in the carnal plenitude of a low décolletage, gave me her hand and told me her name was Vera. She was an artist. The other woman, who had read one of my books and knew my father, worked for the Russian edition of an American fashion magazine which had recently published an article on Vera's paintings.

I did not recognise Vera and she did not let on that we had met a decade earlier, not once but twice in the space of a week, at the house of a mutual friend, when she had first moved to London from Paris. I saw she was beautiful then, beautiful beyond my filthiest imaginings, though the only image of those encounters that survived in my memory was her three-storey, spoon-measured, molasses-slow descent down a spiral staircase which I lapped up from the top of the stairwell in dreamy stupefaction. In Paris she had been a student at the Beaux Arts, a catwalk model, and of course something of a courtesan, though in retrospect I must add that, while much of her life story would never come to light, what little of it did emerge had emerged as an amalgam of bizarre and mostly contradictory inventions. The important thing here is to remember that, ten years before the events I describe, I was never an adulterer even in thought, and the brief glimpse of Vera at her most tousled and lissom was the one and only instance I could ever recall of the sensation of having been awestruck by femininity with the force of an oncoming train.

Now, ten years later, I neither recognised her nor acknowledged that femininity; not because she had changed or because it had faded, but because the pretty little speech of mine about the anguished lover whose assignation goes awry *was* an accurate description of my predicament, and had Vera entered that hotel bar stark naked, or costumed as a lion tamer or a French maid, it would have remained that just the same. She was, in my eyes, a shadow. Her friend was a shadow. All people were shadows, at best individual sexless presences at my feet, whose play upon the sand could be an amusing diversion for my beloved, and at worst a collective waxworks of irritating reminders that none of them *was* my beloved. As a woman Vera saw this at once, and was later to tell me, at great length and from every conceivable perspective, how deeply my visible aloofness on that evening had wounded her.

When finally Olga deigned to appear, at twenty-two minutes past seven, proprieties were observed, as the Muscovite pair ooh'ed and ah'ed over her beauty and I laughed heartily in the background like a Smyrna merchant whose ship had at last come in, though she quickly made it clear that she had not come there to talk to *women* whom *I* had met and was in the process of exchanging telephone numbers with, whereupon we said our good-byes and went in to dinner. Hesitantly I put it to her that, given that fashion was her chosen métier, she could do worse that befriend the editor of a leading fashion magazine. 'Hm,' she said. She was tense all through dinner.

8

Yes, the world at large was encroaching on what little I had, flooding, as though with the *acqua alta* of entanglements, misunderstandings and tracasseries of every description – what in the Venetian dialect they call *intrighi*, literally 'intrigues' – my tiny island in the lagoon, even as the money that held back the rising tide like a containing wall was being washed away. It was as if Venice had never let me go.

On the twenty-second of November... Forgive me this drama-queen ellipsis, but everyone knows by now that there would have to be a 22 in it somewhere. How often had that accursed cipher plagued me in roulette. How Olga had changed the Aeolian catalogue of twenty-one enchantments to make room for another. How I had watched the digital clock of my mobile, waiting for her, until the minutes became that number. How her telephone messages used to arrive, invariably it had seemed, at twenty-two past the hour. 'It just isn't your lucky number,' my wife had told me with genuine sympathy as we were parting in Kitzbühel. 'So why are you staking your life on it?'

The twenty-first was a Friday, and an old friend of mine had asked us to come as his guests to an expensive charity ball being held at a London hotel that evening. At first I hesitated, but then reasoned that at his table we would be under his social protection, and in the end we accepted. I don't think I had ever felt so awkward and uncomfortable at a cocktail party in all my life, having to greet people I had not seen for months, or maybe years, who eyed the woman on my arm as though she were a caged animal in the pet shop and gained time by asking random questions to which I stammered in fruitless answer, wiping rivulets of sweat running down my face with the sleeve of my dinner jacket. Like cleanliness, next to godliness in the view of those assembled in the room, worldliness had forsaken me. At length dinner was announced and we could go to our table.

There are men on this earth who, when they go in for ceremony, do so in a way so exaggerated and contrived that with all the good will in the world one cannot suppress the emerging realisation that they are actually swine in the guise of men, that manners, for them, are no more than the price of admission to human society, and that, given half a chance, instead of unfolding their napkins with a theatrical flourish, they would gnaw at the viands in the serving platter with their bare teeth. One of these men, unmistakeably of the type which the Italians call *porcone*, had been seated to Olga's right.

I spied at once with my jealous eye that he was finding it difficult to sit up straight in his chair and eat his food, which would have involved looking south, or converse with her, due west, when, were he to look southwest, he would be able to look down her cleavage, adumbrated, no more, though certainly no less, than the black-tie occasion required, by wisps of transparent chiffon, and since turning his chair by the requisite number of degrees to the west would have caused consternation on the part of other diners, he had come up with an ingenious stratagem. Whenever Olga made to leave the table, he would anticipate her, rising to show his good manners and to look down her dress at the same time. Who knows, perhaps the now somewhat moribund custom of men rising from the table in synchrony with women began once upon a time as just a sleazy stratagem of this kind. As I say, the inner swine came forth not in the observance of the custom, but in the exaggeration of it. He *anticipated* her.

This is not a discourse on manners, but an accurate record of the impressions that pulsed through my brain as the evening began. It was now the twenty-second, and the swine in human disguise had just asked if *we*, that is to say *Olga and I*, would come to Beirut as his guests at Christmas. Now, I must say something about the disguise.

Our hospitable host, I knew, had been a minister in the first government formed in the Lebanon after her occupation by Syria, and was now once again in the Cabinet. I knew he was married to the daughter of a Syrian kingpin, a woman who had made his political fortune, as well as his fortune in convertible liras and piastres, and I also knew that although

Olga had only the vaguest idea where on the map any of these exciting places might be found, she had a perfectly adequate idea of what a rich and powerful man in his sixties could do for a single girl if he decided he really liked her cleavage. Why, at Vita's establishment girls used to kneel for months in silent prayer, an attitude not unsuited to their other, more specific duties, waiting for the cat of fate to drag in a mouse so plump, and suddenly there it was, hers for the asking. How could she refuse the hospitable stranger her telephone number, or maybe *our* number? Good manners dictated that she give them both.

And so the twenty-second went on, now in the small hours, until the tables began to empty and people started to leave. At that juncture, I remember, what lacerated me were not so much the usual feelings of jealousy and possessiveness as the dawning conviction that while the man to my distant right was obviously a liar and a fool, and my beloved just as much of a liar and an even bigger fool for believing him, my earthly life, now and always and forever after, depended on whether or not, and how, their falsehoods met and their foolishnesses meshed, and if it weren't for this Arab *porcone* propositioning her tonight, there would be another just like him tomorrow, or the night after, or the day after that.

For beauty, as all Vita's girls knew, was an endowment. And awful beauty was an endowment beyond worldly riches, beyond South Sea pearls and Colombian emeralds, beyond dollars in Jamaica and sterling in Jersey, beyond factories, beyond land, beyond reason. Such beauty swept all before it with its witch's besom, and woe to him who would try to arrest its flight and grasp at it with any of the ineffectual contrivances which men, like so many self-made Fausts, use to keep Gretchens at their spinning-wheels.

That endowment was Olga's blessing, perhaps. Perhaps it was my curse. Then again, perhaps it was the other way round. But one thing was certain, and so long as I remained with her, or she with me, I would be a prisoner of the awful objective which her beauty embodied with such pitiless and uncompromising universality. I would have no will but the will to whisper *Olga, your name is Olga*. I would know no freedom save the freedom to pray to the god of love. And the coward in me looked over his shoulder and ran.

He ran for his life. I remember nothing of that rainy November morning apart from the protracted and nauseating scene which ended in her tears and her final departure, as this time round I had insisted, to a destination unknown to me and in all likelihood to herself. By then I had burned the Arab's visiting card, together with some of the bedclothes it happened to fall among. *It was all over.* I was now perfectly free.

The jailor had not given chase. It was eight in the morning. All day I sat there in my flat, in mute contemplation of the prospect of eternal liberty which, more than any abject servitude, more than any bondage I'd ever known, now yawned before me like the maw of blackest despair, and there I sat, motionless, all the day and all the following night. *All over with whatsername.* It had all been an awful mistake. It hurt worse than anything, but still I didn't cry. Again she hadn't been able to make me. And he who weeps last, laughs best.

The nightmare was over. On Sunday morning I stirred to life, walked over to the telephone and dialled Vera on her mobile.

9

The pesky mobile, which she had quite forgotten to switch off the night before, rang that Sunday morning while Vera was in church, at the Russian Orthodox Cathedral in Knightsbridge, and as she so sweetly put it when she arrived at my flat a few minutes later, she couldn't find a taxi and had to run from Ennismore Gardens undressing on the way – there, could I see, she was nearly done now. This, rather Bloomsbury on a bad day, start to a liaison did not put me off in the slightest, but then again, given the situation, I cannot think of anything which might have done.

My every greying hair, my every aching muscle, my exhausted body's every nerve, vein and pore seemed to be shouting in unison that it was all over. More than a year of backbreaking, Sisyphean labour in the name of an *idea* – for this is how I saw it now – whether it be the idealisation of Olga, or the nostalgic avenging of the White cause, or the project of standing my own family history on its head, had come to an ignominious end. I had tried, single-handedly, to turn the course of modern culture back on itself, to win the battle for beauty in the heart of one woman. But the sower's seed had fallen on stony ground. The idealist had not been able to get away with the cash box.

Ah, but wait a minute, that was the funny part. I had in my account £30,000 of Olga's money, in addition to the jeweller's cheque for the necklace. Like the callow youth who swindled the hooker who had robbed him of his roulette winnings in 'The Facts of Life,' an early story by Somerset Maugham, in this unexpectedly practical sense I had beaten the odds and came out, if not actually to the good, at least with some of what Vita's girls used to call 'paycapability' intact. To be sure, I had by then blown nearly ten times that amount, having got it into my stupid head to support and entertain her in a style to which she was unaccustomed – she was accustomed to stashing money away – but still, the money left sitting in the account was something more than an ironic vignette that fate had worked into the final act of the melodrama. It was a link, a cord not severed. *How come she never said anything? What was she thinking? Had she forgotten about the money?*

No, I had no room in my mind for such questions just then. Purge, purge everything! Leave not a bridge unburned, and don't look back no matter what. Shut your eyes, buy oblivion as you once bought hope, rent it if you must, but don't try to make sense of anything. Shut your eyes. Don't look back.

Vera had a remarkably textured voice, about eighty percent Barguzin sable and the rest ophidian slither, and the first thing I had her do after she got dressed was to breathe a long message in English into my answering machine, to the effect that *we* were not able to *come to the phone* at the moment, but that sooner or later *one of us* would *probably* return the call. I made her record it over and over again, until the result met with whatever vengeful specifications I had in mind, and in the end the message sounded as if dictated by a rattlesnake luxuriating upon an ermine stole.

The second thing was to book two tickets to Palermo, where the flat in the *centro storico* had already proven its worth, I thought, as a treatment centre for the lovelorn. Vera dropped everything. She never even went home to change her clothes. I'd get her whatever she needed, I pleaded, just come with me to the airport. I need your help to drown myself in Mondello Bay.

10

The old me should not have bothered with the witticism, because he had drowned already. I had passed away. Like a melting ice cube, or a drop of water volatilizing into a single Slavic sibilant on a hot skillet, a love that commits suicide does not always die in pitiful convulsions, reproachful agony or anguished screams. Its dying is a transition to another state, which, though irreversible, may look so peaceful it almost seems hopeful. And the desire embodied by Vera — which means *faith* in Russian — must have been that an altogether new me would now live, breathe and be defined by something other than the love that was lost.

She told me she had been in love with me from the day she met me, from the day I watched her descend those endless stairs. And? And what of it? I asked myself. And why shouldn't she have fallen in love with me? She was an *intelligentnaya moskvichka*, a woman of my parents' and my own intellectual and social circle, a Moscow sophisticate, a classy dame. She was like all those women who would attend dinner parties at our dacha, women who laughed at our rarefied jokes, women who were paid witticisms for kisses and considered it a good bargain. *Taut silks a woman's waist enclosing…* Well, here was somebody who would recognise the line and recite the next, somebody who knew the poem to the end, somebody who, if

she were to interrupt me, would only be interrupting to ex-
claim that nothing on earth is more beautiful than Blok...

> At some dark hour of morning,
> Or else a dream is rushing past?
> Taut silks a woman's waist enclosing
> I glimpse through misty window glass.

Too late, too late. I had outgrown all that. Nostalgia, for
me, had become wrapped up with what the French call *nostalgie de la boue*. No sooner did we arrive in Palermo than I
began dredging Vera's past for what needed to be found in
the gutter.

Thankfully, my dragnet came up full every time I cast it.
She had spent time in a Swiss prison, fitted up for arms smug-
gling by the Russian lover she ditched, a gangster who had
hidden a submachine gun previously used in a bank robbery
in the boot of the car she was driving from Paris to Zurich.
He wanted to *punish* her, she whispered with what seemed like
a shudder of pleasure, stubbing out a cigarette, her graceful
forearm silhouetted against the fragrant darkness of fallen
clothes in the deliquescent half-light of winter. There she had
been *tortured*, beaten *savagely* by her fellow inmates, *taunted*
by prison staff. Only the intercession of another former lover,
a Frenchman highly placed in the government, secured her
release some months later, when the charges against her were
dropped and the case quashed, *naturally*.

Frustrated at the failure of his plan, the Russian waited
outside her house one evening, to *frighten* her, she stressed,
nervously adjusting a slipping strap of white satin, by pump-
ing two bullets into her *body*. Her body I already knew, but

she pointed out the faint scars. One bullet went clean through a perfectly shaped thigh, which gallantly I bent down to kiss until it would stop hurting, the other grazed her head, and *naturally* the man was subsequently arrested and just as naturally soon released. And naturally he was still out there, holding up money vans, robbing banks, bringing over the boys from Irkutsk for the really big jobs. And naturally he was still in love with her, desperately, murderously, like Verlaine with Rimbaud.

Talk of the *nostalgie de la boue*, of new scope for vanity, of the eternal cycle wherein every predator is somebody's prey. I had expropriated that big thief's loot, taken the one thing in the world dearer to him than a Brinks van with anodised steel doors blown open, and done it without a shot fired, with no effort whatever, totally by chance. Bad jailbird put his money on 9, 14, 18, 22, 29, scrawny foureyes went with his luck on zero and the neighbours, and the ball dropped and I won Vera. I was the way I was, and she had fallen to *me*, despite his potato sacks full of Swiss francs, fallen for me just as he had fallen for her, naturally, murderously:

> Howdy, little Murka, howdy, li'l kitten,
> Howdy, li'l Murka, and goodbye!
> You've ratted out our hideout,
> An' for this betrayal you mus' die,

as thieves used to sing in the penal colony in the Urals where my grandfather spent nearly two years in the 1930s while working on his play, a slice of low life entitled *The Return*, written almost entirely in criminal flash.

To disbelieve Vera about all this would have been to doubt

her very name. It would have been a slap in the face of fate, an ungrateful, ill-tempered abjuration of chance. Her life story, as she told it, was so glamorous and thrilling one felt like reaching for the caramelised popcorn one moment and getting out the handkerchief the next, and yet some empirical evidence could be gleaned to show that it was all true, that paint-splattered easels and vintage champagne and gun clips and catwalk intrigue and false passports and murderous lovers and midnight trains and bars of hashish and exposed nipples and whatnot else had been among its constituents, since I, for one, could still tell the difference between the insatiate and the insensate, between Parisian haute couture and dirzi prêt-à-porter, between an inspired sensualist, for whom the album sepia beauty of Blok meant more than her luxuriant own, and a diplomaed fool of the literary camp-following kind.

Mind you, I had been wrong about things before. But now at least I was back on familiar ground.

11

This may be as good a moment as any to remember that inspired sensuality of Vera's, indeed to commemorate it. It was as infinite as any human quality I had ever tried to measure; certainly it was greater than the literary talent of any writer I had personally ever met; greater, perhaps, than the musical talent of most musicians now performing. It was a kind of genius.

Odd as this may sound, at least to Western ears, at the source of the sensuality that was Vera's genius lay her faith.

She was Russian Orthodox, of course, and an impassioned believer. An ancestor of hers was the Metropolitan of Japan, ministering to the White refugees who had fled there from the Bolsheviks, and she even had a sixteenth of Japanese blood in her veins, by no means an extraneous genetic component if Oriental indulgence happens to be your bailiwick. Yet she was no geisha. She was a purely Russian type of woman, much described in our literature and recognised in the West under the cognitive label *nunnery whore*, the type whose driving force is the oscillation between the nun's ecstasy of being forgiven and the whore's enthusiasm in doing something to be forgiven for. So she'd pray, she'd listen to Gregorian chants, she'd interpret the word of the Gospel for mine and her own spiritual benefit. But the next moment, before I could say *Newly arisen from my slumbers, to Thee, O Lord that loveth, I appeal,* I'd see her undulating out of something so insubstantial it really wouldn't have mattered if she'd kept it on.

My considered opinion was that nearly everything in her, from the sable fur of her voice to the rosy tip of a snake's tongue between her teeth, had been placed, squarely and unambiguously like the punctilios of an Olympic athlete's daily regimen, at the service of her peculiar genius, with the result that the cumulative effect of her presence was somewhat in the nature of a beauty treatment, beginning with an exfoliating facial and ending with a pampering massage. It softened and stupefied, like the hashish she preferred to cocaine, it turned a man's conscience into a zombie and his memory into a lotus eater. It was the oblivious Lethe itself, the very river I had jumped into when I died. It was a balm, a palliative and an antidote.

The evening we had arrived in Palermo, my mobile rang and I, quite lost by then in the harbour fog, couldn't be bothered to answer it. Vera got it. 'Olga? Ah, but she is not here, *mon ange,*' I heard her telling the caller in miniver-edged Franglais, 'it is with me you must content yourself today. At the ball at the Dorchester?.. *Mais certainement,* yes of course I was there, don't you remember me? I have waist-length hair... Yes, you silly man, of course blonde! *Naturally.* Everything of my *body* is natural... In English you say double D, no?' I ran to the bathroom, where I had not reached the toilet before collapsing on the floor in a fit of retching. The vomit was an embryonic yellow tinged with gray, like the yolk of undeveloped eggs one sometimes finds inside a boiled chicken.

When I had emerged from the bathroom, scarcely less than half an hour later, Vera was still on the telephone, alternatively twirling a lock of hair with the insouciance of a seasoned professional and using the free hand to caress the luckily bullet-proof marble of her inner thigh, which lay half-exhumed in dunes of peachy batiste. 'To visit you in Paris? At the Hotel Raphael? I don't know *what* he will say, darling...' Then she saw me there, standing by the bed, pale as death. Quickly she nodded, as if to say she understood that the joke had gone far enough. 'Where is he? He's right here, next to me in the bed. *Touching me.* Are you still there, caller?'

'I cannot believe it,' I croaked as she closed the phone. 'Vengeance is mine, sayeth the Lord,' she replied, smiling, with a quotation from the Scripture proverbial among Russians because Tolstoy once used it as an epigraph. 'And I will repay. So there, your towelhead's got his comeuppance.'

I couldn't believe what I'd witnessed, but despite the horror and the nausea and the pain I felt, I couldn't help admiring the unrehearsed ease, the effortless elegance, with which Vera had carried out the farcical seduction of my nemesis. In the argot of the Russian criminal world, in which my grandfather's play about the life of thieves was written, such a quick operation on a *friar*, or mark, would be called a *dynamo* or *winding* job, and the girl performing it – *making him* – a *windlass*. In the wake of the admiration, unexpectedly, came the hilarious thought that it was all so easy. Like taking candy from a baby! The whimpering fool whose sleazy and clumsy attentions to the only woman I ever loved have cost me the world has just been wound up like a grandfather clock by somebody behaving like a dollar-a-minute sexline whore. And he hasn't even seen *her* cleavage.

What did that say about the woman so easily taken in by such a snivelling loser of a mark? What did it say about me, so easily taken in – *made*, I ought to be saying – by the woman who ended up as the sucker's sucker? What did it say about us, and was there ever even a single chance for us, one chance in a billion?

That, of course, had been Vera's conscious motive for taking up the multilingual sexline challenge to begin with. She sought to dramatise, as though to the proverbial fly on the wall which at one time or another every frustrated lover wants to become, the paucity of real content in the romance in the pages of which she was now the afterword, and to suggest by implication that it was there, in the powerfully realistic epilogue untrammelled by the exigencies of plot and individual style, that the final tying-up of loose ends would take place, whereby every cowardly weakness in the author's conception of the world would be vindicated.

I saw the motive, and in a certain way I approved. She was there to cure me, wasn't she? That was her role, her function. That was her destiny. She was put on this earth to make me forget.

12

As befits a problematic convalescent, I spent the next two months in bed with Vera. In that same canopied bed.

I never told her I loved her, and Vera was nobody's fool. She knew that although the patient on her hands appeared alive, lucid enough to tell her a funny story and coordinated enough to unzip her favourite dress, he was for all intents and purposes a vegetable, a victim of a trauma so eviscerating it was unlikely that, even with all the libidinous care and sensuous attention she was uniquely qualified to lavish upon him, he would ever feel anything again. She saw that the canopied bed she shared with him was ever in his mind *that same bed*, and that under its baldachin he awoke from nightmares with a face wet from tears, something he claimed he was congenitally incapable of achieving when conscious.

She noticed that he never parted with his mobile, hoping that some news would trickle down to the netherworld from the world of God's light, if only in the form of another telephone call from the *friar* she'd had such a good time winding up, which it did another couple of times, until the poor bastard finally figured it out and realised that it was the *other* number on the card that he had been meant to ring. But she did not notice it when, at half-past seven on New Year's Eve, of special significance to Russians because it is believed that 'as you'll meet it so you'll spend it,' that accursed mobile of his lowed into his hand as if in animal anguish. He never showed her the text message, written in an English that seemed to have improved dramatically over just a few weeks, and he chose not to wonder out loud whether some progress had not been made also with the Arabic. He was feeling particularly vindictive just then. God, what a message.

19:34. Farewell to your first and last love, whom you might have had but lost forever. Happy all your next life! I will never forget our passion. Money, money and sex I wish you, it is all that you can get with your dead heart. I left you in the year that passes. O.

But back to Vera. She was nobody's fool, my little sumptuary Vera, nobody's but love's. Just like the writer *manqué* she was so taken with, just like the homicidal yeggman who was so besotted by her. What, you think it's that easy to dynamo a cold caller? Sure, if you've got the tools and the talent, and the same with writing an intelligible paragraph or cracking a safe, but how good would I be at his job or he at mine? We were all players, all winning losers, only our endowments differed from one another as dramatically as our vulnerabilities and our caprices. Hence the romantic diminuendo. Hence that unbreakable cycle of degeneration, wherein one's weakness is another's strength and everyone is the fool of somebody's else love.

And so, however much it was that she, being nobody's fool, was able to see, her most cynical observations were powerless to reveal to her the truth as it really was, the truth at its harshest, least coloured and most unpleasantly incandescent. She could never see that, to the man she loved, the mere memory, no, the faintest trace – no, the whispered sound of the name – of the woman he loved was a million times more real than her own voice, more significant than all those numberless thighs and nipples and bums. No, but what am I saying, what sound! That the mere sight of the capital letter *O*, in an Italian sport pages headline predicting the promotion of Palermo into the premier league – *O*, peace be upon you, strange cipher, mysterious *O*, *O* as in *awful*, in *omega*, in *zero*, *O* capital of sorrow, *O* dawn breaking over the battlefield, *O* in *if only* and *lost cause* and *you go to hell* – affected him more profoundly than the sight of her nunnery whore tears.

Thus he was able to conceal from her for the better part of those two winter months that he had subscribed to a Russian satellite film channel with the sole secret purpose of scanning the film credits, hoping and dreading that the sacred name would drift past, as of course quite often it did. It is, after all, a common Russian name, as common as Vera. Once, in the credits of a soap opera that was being shown four times a week, he discovered it twinned with his own Christian name, a husband-and-wife team, apparently, responsible for the music arrangement. Another time there was a woman, a rather famous opera singer as it turned out, who had both the name and the surname.

Leafing through magazines like *Vogue* or *Vanity Fair* made him angrier than stories of genocide and reports of natural disasters in the newspapers. There the bodies of strange women crouched in the underbrush of fashion spreads, their faces leapt at him from the urban gloss of the social pages, and his fists would clench, instinctively, as though a white knuckle or two could protect the innocence of love which was his sacred past from the intrusion of unadorned zoology.

How meagre was the beauty of those women! How miserly, how uncomplicated, how empty. How like a greeting card with *Season's Greetings* in gold and a picture of Santa's sleigh. O, to think there were people in the world who mistook that caged, fairground travesty with a domesticated snarl of a smile for the ferocious roar of beauty in the wild, for the untameable beast that comes like a thief in the night, for the act of God which is awful beauty.

13

Their faces were to hers what insurance is to religion. Quite right, too, because insurers do not offer their clients cover for *force majeure*, compulsion acknowledged to be irresistible. For insurers it's a money spinner, not unlike the zero in casino roulette when the house takes half of everything that has been wagered on even chances; while priests haven't the luxury of supposing that Armageddon is more objective than slipping on a banana peel just because it is more likely to be recognised as such in The Hague. Their faces had escape clauses, and the longer one looked the more one understood them, in all their money-grabbing cynicism, like an apparently difficult passage in a legal brief that becomes easier, clearer and more shameless the oftener one reads it, until finally one realises that what it actually says can be expressed in a dozen short words without injury to the overall dastardly meaning.

So at first a face seemed to suggest elegance by elongation, a kind of Modigliani or Tamara de Lempicka conjuring trick, but when one looked at it a minute longer one saw a donkey. Another tried to conjure up Rubens health, or perhaps Victorian prosperity, but a minute later all that remained was the sticky mess of Christmas pudding. A third went in for class and sophistication, but in the end what one saw was a lot like a man, and not the kind of man one wanted for a son-in-law, either. Thus, wherever he looked, he felt cheated, offended, abused. It was as though the women of the world were impostors, false idols placed on cardboard pedestals by some mendacious conspiracy of erotomaniacal impotents.

Then he turned to look at women who passed him in the street, just as he remembered doing in the good old errant days before Lucifer claimed and branded him at the mews house, and again he felt cheated and dejected. He dreamt of seeing just one face, *just the one, please Holy Virgin Mother of God, and I promise I won't ask for another,* to rival hers, a single face that would blind and scald, a single forehead that phosphoresced, a single pair of eyes with damask steel in the iris. If he could just see the one, a point of light attached to a strap in rush-hour traffic, a dynamic silhouette swishing past a busy cafe, he would surely regain his composure. There would be hope. There would be something other than desolation to the prospect of forgetting, for if there was one, there might be another. But there wasn't one.

Then again, he now felt that his judgement had been impaired to the point where he would not have been able to tell an African violet from a cornflower, and not solely in matters concerning a woman's beauty. Who knew, perhaps it was Vera

over there, tending her floral tresses at the dressing table in
the middle distance, who was what she said she was, the
woman for him? No, that couldn't be right. He felt an almost
perverse desire to vacillate, to appear indecisive, to make pronouncements that were indeterminate, and if somebody were
to ask him how he took his tea, he imagined answering that
he liked it hot, cold and tepid, without sugar and with. Everything now seemed equally arbitrary. Even hitherto self-
evident distinctions, such as the one between life and death,
appeared too tangled to bother with in the circumstances, as
in one of those Russian songs of the Civil War.

I was lucky to die of that wound:
The cowards all croaked in detention.

Some of these sentiments he ventilated and some of his
reflections he never bothered to conceal, but Vera's mind
reinterpreted them – just as he had reinterpreted lots of
things, and rationalised them, and turned them upside down
in his mind – as accidental, transitory and irrelative. When
they came back to London in the middle of January, she saw
that a skirt, hanging under non-reflective glass in a black
frame on the white wall, was still the only decorative feature
of his Spartan bedroom. It was a brown tweed skirt with in-
sets of brown velvet, prêt-à-porter from an Italian designer,
but it had been backed with the finest silk moire and the
frame had little hooks on the side by means of which the cap-
tive odalisque could come out and, presumably, take a stroll
in the sultan's garden.

On the bookshelf beneath the Victorian skylight she saw
a pair of black court shoes by Yves Saint Laurent, and with-

out knowing its biography she accepted the blatant fetish as an *objet d'art*. If it could but speak! In all likelihood it would have been asked to deliver a lecture on modern idolatry before the Royal Geographic Society. She saw similar objects in drawers, on kitchen shelves, on the writing desk, wreckage left by a cult so pervasive she would have had to burn the whole place down before beginning to accustom herself to its downfall.

Had she the curiosity or the presence of mind to look in the scuffed leather hatbox, inside the top hat he said he needed to take her racing she would have found a dozen folded squares of pink notepaper, each bearing an identical legend in a Russian schoolgirl scrawl, *undress me except for the frigging topper*, souvenirs of a Sunday prize draw in which no losing tickets had been issued. And in the camcorder case that now lay in a dusty corner, placid and dormant like a sated lemur, she would have found more than twenty videotapes labelled in the same loopy hand.

She did see him reading some long letters, though. Again, in that loopy hand. A number of them, judging by the handwriting on the envelopes, had come in the post during their absence from London, but those he had put away unread in a drawer and said he would never open. Didn't have the courage, he said, and she answered that *that* was courage. It was useful to have an intellectual kind of girl by one's side. Always said the right thing. Too bad there was that song, with the hypnotic refrain.

I was lucky to die of that wound:
The cowards all croaked in detention.

No, what the dead man now clutched at, as he lay there on a pile of rotting straw, were the letters left over from when he was still alive, when he was still a living and breathing coward.

Fallen leaves of autumnal quarrels, those letters were part of him, part of his heritage. They were part of the cult, part of the habitation which he had made a shrine, part of the whole apparatus of idolatry he had set up so laboriously, only to become frightened by the powers he had unleashed and run away like the coward he was from the very thing that gave his life meaning.

14

Let me ask you a question. What is it that you're after? What do you want? What on earth is making you so miserable? And another thing. Why won't you accept me as I am?

Yes, lesbianism is a desire to simplify, but not the way you make it out when you put it down. It reduces everything not to a micro-organism but to a microcosm, which is a very different kind of sim-plification. As for prostitution, it's not based on desire at all, but most of the time on dire need and urgent necessity. The addictive element you talk about can only tumble out of the mind of somebody who does a whole lot of watching from the sidelines: historian, philosopher, writer. The theory doesn't square with the practice, you see.

Take history as an example. How can a young person like myself believe what adults — professors, teachers, parents — would lead me to believe is the truth of history, say about the last world war, when one day somebody like your friend Viktor Suvorov comes out with a complicated hypothesis which overturns the accepted view of the war, and tomorrow somebody else comes out with another complicated hypothesis, which overturns Suvorov? That's why everything's relative for somebody like me, and the only thing that matters is the individual's innate tendency: where we want to go in life, this way or that way or some other way.

I don't want to be typecast as a student, but I do want to spend more time in the society of my contemporaries, people my own age like my makeup artist friend Elena, for one simple reason. I neither want to acquire an inferiority complex, nor do I want to be thought of as stupid. And the adults talk about all those complicated hypotheses of theirs in a way that's way over my head. So all I really feel is that I don't have to believe any of it, that it's boring and that I can't understand it.

But when I had Elena to stay with me the other night, I didn't feel free to ask her to sleep over and I felt like I was doing something terrible. It's your hotel room. And yet it's me, it's my life, it's how I am. You'd think it's a way of distracting me from thinking about what's happening between us, but actually it's a way of keeping me from going to pieces. It's so easy to let oneself go to pieces, you know, but then the question arises, who's going to put me back together again if I do? Because all I have to count on, at the end of the day, is myself and myself alone.

If I were to have a place of my own in London, I think I'd feel freer, freer to think, freer to look at things from other points of view. And one thing I can promise you, if I were to have such a place I wouldn't let anybody else into my bed unless our relationship has broken down irreparably, though of course I must be 100% certain that you'd comport yourself with the same dignity. I can make such a promise because I know that otherwise I wouldn't be able to sleep with you no matter what, and because at this point in my life our relationship is what counts most for me. Why would I let you down?

I write this so soon after we've parted. I don't feel as nervous as before about corresponding with you, now that you've told me you're not mad at me. I'm going to use this time alone to try to understand you, to figure out what you want in life and what's making you so anxious. Meanwhile you're going to love me, be faithful to me and stay away from the casino.

I want to learn to evaluate my own thoughts and actions using your eyes and words, and if by the time my stay here at the hotel is over I've learnt to think a little like you, then it'll be my time and your money well spent, don't you agree? The first problem to address is our relationship. I never said I fell in love with you at first sight. But I've come to love you as I've never loved anyone before, I have totally new feelings and sensations, new experiences, and sometimes I'm so happy I feel I could faint.

But you're right when you say that I haven't thought enough about how to keep you. That I'm not saturated with the idea of you from the top of my head to the tips of my toes. That I haven't leapt into the ice hole or thrown myself into the boiling cauldron. Maybe it's because we spend too much time in bed, which I think is bad for us! It makes everything much too simple, as you would say. But I so like going to bed with you that I cannot deny myself the indulgence, and the thought of putting it off for the sake of some adult theory gets lost in the shuffle. O—O, how I want to get into bed with you now!

15

I'm jealous, do you hear me? I'm jealous of your past, and of who you are. I'm now listening to your wife's favourite tango music, not because I want to torture myself, no, not at all, but because I like it. And you know I like it. In the same way you're jealous of my past, I think, with the difference that all I had to do to rid myself of it was to throw away my old telephone number. Now my past is only in your head.

But I live with the thought of her, which turns to the reality of her whenever you pity her. Just the mention of her name, no, the mere shadow of her name, hurts and frightens me like the sight of a hypodermic needle. But I must live with it and live with it I will, because I'm going to fight for you, my beloved. Yes, I'm going to fight for the man who recites Pasternak, for the man I love. And this is why I'm howling, and screeching, and scratching.

Sometimes I think I need to make a resolution of some kind, something like 'first sort yourself out, disengage, untangle your past, and only then come and ask for my hand in marriage,' yet I want to be with you now – now. The keys to the flat are on my desk, but I will not come. It isn't my home, and I want to be like the man who doesn't return to the house he's left. It feels empty, and there's nothing for me there. What I want is you, but not no matter where or how.

I have never lied to you. I'm not a liar, I swear it on our relationship, which at this moment is the one and only sacred thing I have to swear on. I had been wrong in the past, I had evaded and avoided, I had withheld and economised, I had tried not to admit, not to confess, not to tell, but after our first quarrel it all changed, I promise you. I can write it out in my own blood, my darling, my darling, I love you, my darling.

But you just go on like a broken record, stuck in the same old you're-lying-again groove. When a brilliant psychiatrist tries to cure patients in his ward, that's great, but when he tries so hard that he starts going mad, maybe it's time for him to see a doctor. My diagnosis is: Woe from Wit. Why don't you ask for somebody's advice, talk to a person of your own circle? Or anybody at all you just happen to run into, since anyway you have brains enough for two.

As for me, why don't you allow me to stay exactly where I am. This means: I love you. This means: I like being with you. This means I hate it when we quarrel: darkness, emptiness, fear. It means I don't want to be without your soft skin. It means I love going to bed with you. Because I'm a creature of sex, made for it as a woman, and that's all I am.

O, O—O, I am a beautiful woman. I'm just that, you know? A beautiful woman. Venus, with childbearing hips, with full breasts. Here, watch, I'm going to come for you: O–O–O. How can you not understand this?! It so simple. A woman! And if you're no longer in my life, then I should tell you now that your place will be empty for a long, long time, and even if I get married to somebody else and make him a family, and children, and Katya, it may still be empty then, even when everything looks different from the outside. So don't panic, I love you and will never do anything to hurt us unless you prompt me to act otherwise. Goodbye, my love.

16

I am writing this in the daytime, and feeling a little more lucid for a change. Another thing I want to say is that, with you, I'm now *trying to lead the life of the normal average Western person. You aren't one, you despise, mock and ridicule such people, and the problem is that your loathing, directed at them, ricochets at me. All right, let's say I don't like them either. But I'm trapped in a comic situation, where one of my feet is on their turf and the other on yours, and my feet are sliding apart and I'm going to end up in the water.*

This is something I need to put myself through. I can't just jump over it and avoid the situation, because I want to know about everything and since I'm already here, in this country, I may as well give it a go. It will take patience, though. I need a lot of time to sort myself out before I can take that last step in your direction. I thought so much about life over here when I was living in Russia, when I still didn't know there was somebody like you. (O—O, but I had so perfectly imagined you, and everything about you!) So, please, don't break my back, just direct me, direct me and give me enough time to find myself and to come to you of my own accord.

Now it's eleven past one in the morning and I'm not well. Yes, you have shown me the world and I should thank you. I've seen so much, we've been living so rapidly, so richly. Even the depression I went through in May doesn't seem all that bad when I look back at everything that was happening with us. But at the moment I'm not well, my body is aching all over, it feels like I'm dying inside myself. Why did you make me leave the brown skirt, why, why is it so precious in your mind? Is it burning you, like I used to burn you? With me that wouldn't work, you see. I need your care, your warmth, your arms. I need them more than anything in the world now.

It's starting to rain. This morning I woke up without you and thought it was the first time this ever happened. Can't remember anything of the week before, only hell and fear. What are you doing now, I wonder? It's killing me not to know where you are and with whom. Why do you torture us, me and yourself both? I want to be with you, live with you, care for you. My dove, my kinsman, today it finally dawned on me what you meant by 'Sunday' that Sunday last, forgive me that I'd left you misunderstood, O forgive me, if you only knew how I hate my inexcusable egoism. You'd been left dangling, with question marks in your eyes and on your lips, mis-understood by the person who is closest to you on earth. I myself find it hard to forgive myself. Punish me, you should punish me.

O vanity of vanities! How could I have been so blind, I've been asking myself all day. But now I want to go to sleep, and so I tell myself that everything will yet mend, and all will be well with us, we'll have money and children, we'll even cut a brilliant swathe through society!.. If we're still together, that is. Come back to me because I'm waiting for you, because I love you.

I love you, and if it's not too late I want to be with you, to be your lover, your wife, your mistress. And I do feel sorry for you, be-cause I can see that you've painted yourself into a corner, which makes it so much easier for me to forgive you after a quarrel and to cool off quickly, steadying myself with your love.

Come to me and let us weep together, let's weep with the rain! This afternoon I had a good long cry with my friend Elena, and you know, it helps so much, it gives a person so much more strength to live, and I thought: everything could be worse, everything could really be a whole lot worse. At least I'm looking for the light, at least I still hope to find it, at least I already know what it is, when there are so many people out there in the big world who haven't any idea. And me? I love you, and so I can just ask you to please absolve me of all my sins. Let's live together again, I promise I'll be good, I've al-ready become different from the person I was just a few days ago.

Darling, I want you to know that I haven't unpacked the suitcases

*you've had sent over. I'm afraid to check and find that the pearl neck-
lace isn't there, that you've done something really irreversible and
vindictive, that maybe you've returned the gift to the person who
gave it to me. Afraid, do you understand me? I'm afraid!*

17

The most powerful idol to watch over my childhood idyll was
Pasternak, and by the time I was twelve I knew by heart
every poem in *My Sister Life* and his other early collections:

> Among the lilacs grown wild,
> This awful beauty never dies:
> It cannot help stealing the child.
> And thus suspicions must arise.

I do not adduce this fact of autobiography in order to fur-
nish the reader with a gloss on the obscure *locus* of Olga's
letter where she refers to me as the man who recites Pasternak; as a rule, I provide few such glosses, being of the opinion
that it is more important to capture the overall tenor and
texture of the funereal episodes I describe than to nail up
every last particular like a cheap pine coffin. No, my purpose
here is to suggest that not since my adolescence had I read
any text as closely as I was now reading those letters of
Olga's.

When I arrived in the West as a young man, I spoke and
wrote English. No sooner did I find myself in the English-
speaking milieu than I was seized with the desire to tell my
new interlocutors, in a language that was to me mysterious

and strange, about Pasternak and his universe, about his peers, about the Russia that no longer was. I began translating the poems in those early collections, and can now confess that I remember little of my university years in America apart from the summers, when I was absolutely free to engage in the westward transport of Pasternak's elements. Some years hence the long haul was over when a volume of those versions had been published in England.

As I said, I knew the Russian text of the poems by heart, and among my first insights into the hell that is literary translation – though no more a hell, admittedly, than any other undertaking requiring total immersion in pain or pleasure – was the realisation that while the beauty of the original is, in the translator's mind, immediate and limitless, the beauty of his version of that original in another language is mediated and reflected, limited, as it were, by himself. But then, as the reader may judge, this may or may not be the case with all writing, where what remains on paper is but an impress of the original image glimpsed by the writer:

> In alphabet it strains its sinew
> To glow as a blush within you.

Ruefully I would suggest, moreover, that this may well be the case with all love, where the beauty reflecting in the lover's eyes bears only a faint resemblance to the objective, awful truth of the original. Beauty is no more in the eye of the beholder than Pasternak is in my translations, or than Olga is in this prose version of her. They are but tangible mementos, souvenirs of great illuminations.

As the compelling task of the artist is to describe, and cre-

ation only an egomaniac's excuse or alibi, so too the translator's deepest ambition is to comprehend rather than to render. In order to translate Olga's letters into English, I had
to understand the text. But in order to understand them,
I had to impose my understanding on the text, written, as I
say, in the kind of childish hand called 'chicken scratches' in
Russian schools.

Some passages in those letters from the writer's middle
period were simply illegible, with many of the words
smudged or inked out completely so that only a few charac-
ters remained. Most expletives, much coarser in Russian than
their ostensible English equivalents, could be deleted altogether, on the grounds that they were mere distractions,
while other forays into plain speaking were replaced with
generally accepted circumlocutions, whence the plethora of
sleep-with and go-to-bed-with euphemism. Elsewhere it was
necessary to emend egregious errors of orthography and to
supply punctuation, which in written Russian is as much of
a key to meaning as the syntax it is meant to unlock. Finally,
where some of the longer and more difficult words had obviously been misused, I had to replace them with others.

Thus invested with a meaning that was in some part mine,
the letters were no longer completely Olga's, and no amount
of poring over them – which, as I say, was what I did night
after night in those weeks, with Vera hovering in the background like the anxious wife of a reckless gambler, her eye
to the keyhole as he sits at his desk, in a dressing gown with
frogged lapels, cleaning his old service revolver – could com-
pensate me for the loss of Olga in her letters, yet this was
one of the only few places I could think of where the clue to

the loss of Olga in my life might have been hidden. If there ever was a clue, that is.

I might have completely ignored Vera's view, dismissing it as not even remotely objective – to the effect, basically, that no such clue to the story of Olga could ever exist, not in the illiterate letters, not in the lacerating memories, not in the fetish mementos, for the simple reason that Olga was a void, a nullity, a fiction I had created for my own masochistic amusement – had it not been for the alarming fact that my entire milieu shared this view. I had already fought with Irina, who, like Vera, was an intellectually sophisticated Muscovite and, unlike Vera, a disinterested observer of my doings. I had already alienated and distanced myself from most of my English friends, who saw but comical self-indulgence attendant upon wilful obsession in what I claimed was manifest destiny. Having gone that far, I was not about to yield, even if I could.

But anyway I couldn't. I just couldn't, not in those numbered days and mournful nights, relieved as occasionally they were by indulgent answers to Vera's prayers, because however suicidal it was to persist in what others saw as folly, it was even more suicidal to pull out, to call it a day, to leave the table a loser. Thus the fool who is up will play on, of course, but the wise man who is down has no other choice but to dig himself in deeper and deeper into the hole, or else get lucky and suddenly find himself as though stark naked under a spring shower of gold and banknotes.

In for a kopeck, in for a rouble. If Olga never existed, and hence there was never a solution, then I was a madman to have gone as far as I had. If she did exist, then there had to have been a solution, which, admittedly at the risk of madness, I could yet discover. And so I never stopped reading the letters, interpreting them this way and that, filling in the lacunae of sense and fact, conjecturing, correcting, composing. The clue had to have been in there somewhere, maybe not in the letters, maybe not in the memories and the mementos, but one day it was all going to fall into place with a click, *O* as in *Open, Sesame*. One day I would capture her, tie her down, make her my obedient master and cruel slave, *O* as in *The Story of O*. Yes, one day she would come upon me like the gambler's shower of gold, *O* as in *zero and the neighbours*.

This was my dream, my hope and my prayer. Please Virgin Mary, Mother of God, take my reason from me, but make today the day when at last I understand the letters of Olga. Reveal the meaning of the pentagram. Let me win, just this once.

The name Olga is five letters long in the original, the middle one being a soundless character of the Russian alphabet that softens, with the silent determination of a dripping icicle, the consonant which it succeeds. It looks a little like *khamsa*, the cardinal numeral five in Arabic, and has no value on its own, like zero in mathematics. It is the bud of the name, the part I most wanted to touch with my tongue.

FOUR

A NEIGHBOUR OF ZERO

1

One day in the middle of January I found my decree nisi in the morning post, which meant that my old life was officially over and I was now legally alone. Later that same day, as luck would have it, my naughty nurse left me to my own day-dreaming devices. She said she had to spend the night in a private clinic and went on to evade discussion of the reasons, which suggested that they were cosmetic and hence best left shrouded in the amaranthine coyness with which she approached nearly all practical matters. For the first time since the rupture with Olga I was completely alone, both legally and physically.

It was New Year's Eve for the second time round, because many Russians celebrate the coming of the new year not only by the modern Gregorian, but also by the Julian calendar, still the calendar of the Russian Orthodox Church, which is thirteen days behind Greenwich. As you'll meet it so you'll spend it, remember? *Money, money and sex I wish you, it is all that you can get with your dead heart. I left you in the year that passes.* Here was a second chance. And how often does calculated risk get a second chance?

Christmas is celebrated throughout Europe in the last, shortest, dreariest, most sunless moment of the year because, even as a matter of basic physiology, everyone knows it to be the moment of our lowest, most keenly felt dejection. For those who believe, Christ is born at that hopeless moment, and from that moment onward, for those who believe, all is well. The dealer has been changed, a new, luckier hand is about to spin the wheel. A revolution begins, a new leaf is turned over, a second chance is anyone's for the taking. The thirty-six numbers make a full circle of 360 degrees, *et nunc, et semper et saeculum saeculorum*. What a beautiful dream that is, a new year.

And what a terrible curse that was, the old year. *Money, money and sex I wish you, it is all that you can get with your dead heart. I left you in the year that passes.* I know, I kept saying to myself, I know the old me has been left for dead in the year now past, but what of the coming year? What about my second chance, my new leaf, my new life? I had to open the new letters, the ones that came while I had been away. Maybe they were all about money, the money for the flat, the money she supposed I still owed her, and then that would be a pretty good clue, wouldn't it? No, all *she* ever thinks about is sex and money! No, I left *her* in the year that passes! Then I would see that Vera, and the rest of them, and even the feeblest of my suspicions were right on the money, that no matter how much you feed the wolf he still looks to the forest, that you can lead a horse to water but you can't make a lady out of a whore... And then surely I would forget, and meet the new year having forgotten, and never again remember what it was that I needed to forget. Yes, maybe it was the money.

Still indecisive, I headed for the unopened letters, and then a strange thing happened. From among the books on the bookshelf I had clumsily knocked into rolled out a lost ring of Olga's, a plain band of gold, one of the two I had supplied her with to make sure all the proprieties were observed at the sham wedding. The other was now languishing in Palermo, most probably in a we-buy-gold shop somewhere in the Sette Cannoli quarter. Dutifully she used to wear the ring, but then mislaid it at some point, and it had lain there, an O-shaped symbol of the missing clue to the bride's disappearance, hidden by all those useless books for much of the year. Watching everything. Only now it was deaf and mute, like a Sicilian witness to the kidnapping of the century.

The ring had seen and heard it all. The terrible date of the wedding had been engraved inside the rim, along with the Christian names of my runaway bride and the sham groom. It still smelled of the fugitive's perfume, as gold often does for some reason. Quarrels and reconciliations, acts of love and hateful words, solemn promises and jealous accusations, nothing escaped this curtain-twitcher's attention.

The ring had seen the Arab interloper's card in flames. It had seen the last of the bride's tears. It had seen the other woman arrive and watched the act of betrayal, intentional and premeditated, as it could now testify under oath if it weren't busy silently burning my fingers. And as it lay there in my tightly closed hand, on the last day of that horrible Russian year, as though branding me with the hot-iron thought that there are things in the world one can never forget, I knew that I had to open those letters. Come on, coward. Open them.

2

'Hello?' she answered briskly in English. 'Olya, it's me, I'm calling to wish you a happy Old New Year,' I said in my most officious voice, proffering the Russian greeting customary on the occasion. 'It's only a couple of hours away. The thing is, I just found the ring you'd lost.' *Just say something, Olya. Just one word, I beg you.*

How do people do it, I wonder. How was it possible for a man like myself, a loser in love who had spent interminable weeks and never-ending months in the self-flagellations of anxiety and uncertainty, who had dreamt of the voice that was now on the other end of the line for as long as his pride held out, who had never found the missing clue but compromised on an auspicious portent, grabbing hold of that wedding band as if it were a lifebuoy, how was it possible for me to simulate this sort of detachment, to feign this kind of polite equanimity? I just found the ring, indeed. And a happy, happy to you and yours.

'Look, I know you were really upset when you lost it, and also that you need it for Home Office reasons. So I've put it in an envelope, and what I want to propose is that, since you've still got the front door key and sometimes pass by the house to collect your post, maybe I could just leave it downstairs for you.' *Just say something, Olya, just answer, just one little word, because I'm dying to hear your voice, I've been dying to hear it since the day we parted, and since that day I have known nothing but sorrow. Please, just say something, and may your voice tremble a little when you're saying it, so that I'll know that the year that's past was not some horrible joke, some nightmare filled with vicious clowns in face paint, some desert mirage with an ever receding oasis... So that I'll know that you're real, that you have feelings in your life and not just what seems like feelings, though what do I know, I was never able to find the missing clue and without it I can't understand if those letters are the real you or a cunning facsimile. Please, Olya, I don't want to lose the last of my faith!*

'No, I don't want you to do that,' she said, and her voice did not tremble, not at all, not even slightly. 'What I want you to do is to see me this evening and give it to me in person. I'm at some people's New Year's Eve party, but I'm going to tell them I have to leave, all right? Leaving now. I'll be over in a few minutes.' *Olya, but how can I see you? Even though it's the one thing in the world I want. And how can I see you here in these rooms where I live by the thought of you, yet with the signs of another's presence so heartlessly evident? You're the only woman I've ever loved and the only desire I've ever had, but it looks like I've lacked the faith or the strength to win. I bolted again, I ran for my life, I tried to put you out of my mind and failed at that too, thank God, but the ugly truth is that now I have even less faith than before, less faith and less strength. I never did learn to cry, Olya.*

'I really don't think that's such a good idea,' I said out loud, still speaking with the same nonchalance, same glib detachment. 'It's better if I don't see you, things being the way they are. It's just too difficult for me.' Rationally, lucidly, she began insisting. Calmly, politely, I kept on refusing, and was about to put down the phone on a take it or leave it, this is my final offer, you may now do as you like sort of note, when suddenly her voice trembled. She said my name, and it trembled. Just the way I'd imagined it would.

Olya, my unfallen angel, maybe you did love me once, and maybe

*it isn't over? We mended it once before, remember, we stuck it all
back together with spit. Maybe you love me still. Maybe it's all just
an epic misunderstanding, a comedy of errors, an antic masquerade,
and the moment I see you the clock will strike midnight, and the
masks will come off, and that revelation will be a million candles
more powerful than any clue to the truth, which none of them anyway I was ever able to find, because it will be truth itself. And then
my eyes will open, and I will see you exactly the way you are, and
you will say my name again and your voice will tremble just as it
did a second ago. Happy New Year, my angel.* 'All right, how
about if we meet in the street, say in front of the hotel near
my house?' I named the hotel known for the funkiness of its
swankiness. 'Fine,' she said. 'Be there in ten.'

The plan that had formed itself in my head was as simple
as it was cowardly, an oblique resetting of the drowning test
that first separated us when I fled to Palermo that spring.
We would meet in the street not far from my building; naturally she would suggest that we go up to the flat to talk
things over, but since it really was psychologically impossible
for me to let her intrude on my misericord, I would have the
fortitude to refuse; thus, once I had ascertained that no great
revelation was in the offing, I would be able to resist her,
whereupon life in the new year would be no worse a hell than
it had been. On the other hand, if the revelation did come like
a bolt from the blue, all bets would be off anyway; nothing
would matter then, and I'd happily set fire to the damned flat
with everything in it. Then I'd just have to play it by ear.

Still, just to spread the bet a little, before I went out in the
street I lit a candle before an Orthodox icon, knelt, and then
prayed to Sant'Antonio. He was a Catholic, of course, but I

could think of no Russian hierarch who was the patron saint of lost things and, logically, of lost causes. Besides, by now our saints were sick of lost causes.

3

The various and conflicting news of a possible reprieve terminated in the sound of her steps on the wet pavement that evening. It was so just, so deliberate, so incontrovertible, like the sentencing of a criminal convicted after a lengthy and well-publicised trial in the course of which the defence, as the phrase goes, have tried every trick in the book. It was a summons to a beheading, and only a man deeply sceptical of his own innocence could have harkened it with head bowed.

A light fog was all that remained of the evening's drizzle, and from this fog, as though pumped up into the architecturally undistinguished Victorian street by Pinewood technicians working to costume-dramatise a murder in London's East End, Russian nannygladness came upon her compatriot, erstwhile employer and lover, emerging slowly enough for him to be able to recollect the three distinct stages of its approach for the remainder of his natural life and perhaps beyond. First there was the gait, which would have seemed implausible, like the thunder that, in animated cartoons, is not obliged to follow on the heels of lightning, without the persuasive *obbligato* of headstrong stilettos on the damp asphalt; then the posture, just the dynamic silhouette that all that time I had been vainly seeking to glimpse in another form; then the face, angelically luminous in the distance, but glowing more minacious with every advancing step and finally exploding before me the phosphorous charge of its beauty.

She had on a winter coat of brown cashmere with a sable collar, 'tightly belted,' as a 1950s *vendeuse* might have explained to James Stewart, 'to emphasise the waist,' which I'd bought her but never had the chance to see her wear. There is that famous scene in *Vertigo*, when the heroine emerges from the dressing room as though in a radiant cloud of mist; mist in the eyes of her fetishist beloved, who has persuaded her to assume the form of the woman she was in another life. All I can say is that the terror I felt matched Hitchcock frame for frame. How well would that coat have gone with the brown skirt under glass on my bedroom wall.

'Well, there it is,' I said, in the gruff voice of a schoolboy responding for the first time in his life to a concierge's dulcimer query about exactly what kind of fun he had in mind. Silently she extended a gloved hand, took the envelope containing the ring and slipped it into her coat pocket. I recognised the glove. From Hermès in Sloane Street, with a gold clasp, in chocolate brown. She had me buy these gloves for her to go with a riding crop she wanted in the same colour. Just to have it, she said, and smiled. Then, still without saying a word, she put her arm through mine.

Even when it is tied with the silk ribbons of wordy peace treaties and wrapped in the marbled verbiage of assured sovereignty, capitulation, in war or in politics, is still accepted as such. Submission, whether in the case of a nation unlucky in war or of a party trounced at the election, is no less sweet in the mouth of the victor when the dignity of the vanquished is upheld by hollow proclamations. *It ain't so in love* was the point, I think, so eloquently made by her silence. Not so in love in any real or meaningful sense, at least. Not so in sado-masochism, certainly. Not so in the case of any other compulsion that preys on exalted emotion, where not one stone is left standing upon another once what little resistance there lingers has been suffocated in the irresistible grip of the conquering hand.

'Olya, those gloves are perfect on you. But where are we going?' I felt I had to say something, and that's what I said. The ensuing pause, though in real time no longer than a few seconds, was apparently just long enough for the steel point of silence to prize open the walnut shell of her walking companion's meandrine brain. 'Thank you,' she said slowly, turning toward me as though in slow motion and pressing the meretricious slowness of the Russian word of gratitude so close to my ear I thought I was going to faint. Her mouth. Her lips. Her face, her forehead. Her hair, tied back like always with a velvet cord. It was all there, as the wonders of Medici Florence may all be there for a housewife under hypnosis somewhere in suburban New Jersey. 'And... as for... where we are going... that... I don't really know. Yet.'

And so in silence we walked, arm in attentive arm, through a midnight London that was comically unaware it was New Year's Eve, and it seemed to me that it was our feet that were taking us, like a horse heedful of the stable, in the direction of the Chelsea hotel where everything had begun; where, at Olga's slowly uttered suggestion, I asked for and was given the key to the room where she had become my life; so that we could go up there, have some tea and just sit and talk, as she said. Or maybe it was I who said it, and she nodded.

4

I should like to note in passing that 315 is a room number quite impossible to mistake for another, because 3 and 26 to the east, with 32 and 15 to the west, are the neighbours of zero, 'neighbours' being casino terminology for the two pairs of numbers flanking a number on the roulette wheel. Remember, gamblers are sometimes in a great hurry to place their bets. Once the ball is in motion, belated resolve may get a hunch about it landing in a particular section of the wheel, so instead of putting chips on the layout, some wiseguy will pretend to be a real player, acting on impulse, by calling a neighbour bet to the croupier. Losers weepers, however, for as luck would have it the ball has already dropped.

Three-fifteen was always my favourite call bet, covering as it did the whole topmost quadrant of the wheel, with the true north of zero like a green star at its centre. If zero came out, you'd be paid double for the two neighbours overlapping, and that was seventy times your stake, or seven times your whole bet covering nine different numbers. And if another of the nine came out instead, you'd still be all right, still in the game, having more than tripled your money.

So quite a lucky room this 315 was, no doubt about that. But then again, as some people would argue, a neighbour bet is a sucker bet. 'If you think zero's going to come out,' they'd splutter, 'why don't you just put the lot on zero?' Well, there are two kinds of people who are likely to say that, and one is different from the other as night is from day. One kind isn't gamblers at all. They probably think roulette is a sucker's game to begin with, what with the lousy odds and it all just being down to chance. They know nothing and are nothing. The other kind is gamblers. The real players. They are the elect, God's chosen ones. They are what I've tried so hard to become, men of stout heart and blind faith. One day they too must lose, of course, but only in the sense that there comes a day when even a saints leaves behind this life of illuminations and miracles.

Just sit and talk, as one of us had said, and this is what we did, all night long, in the lucky hotel room where I once hit zero. This was all we did, because to do more – though, as a matter of literary fact, is there anything *more* that two Russians can do in a room together? – would have been a travesty of reconciliation, a greedy, furtive snatching at the purse of fate, an insult to our century-long past of romantic debauchery and a smear on the immemorial innocence of idolatry which I ever longed to regain:

> O benefit of ill! Now I find true
> That better is by evil still made better;
> And ruin'd love, when it is built anew,
> Grows fairer than at first, more strong, far greater.

How I wanted to clutch to this worm-eaten fragment of Shakespeare, to that fragment of ruined love.

It had foundered on money, but money wasn't what we talked about, not till the very end, when, at dawn, we said our goodbyes and returned the room key to the sleepy lad at the desk. I told Olga of what I had been through in those months, of how I had looked for a woman to rival her beauty, and of how I had been watching Russian satellite television to see her name flicker past on the screen. I told her that the woman I was with did not matter, that it was only my pique, my jealousy and my murderous resentment that had settled her, like an indulgence that wanted remitting, in my misericord of a flat, and that henceforth a general amnesty, covering every evil thing that either of us had done until then, would come into effect.

Olechka, if you only pretended to believe what I told you then, believe it now. I've scanned every face, I've thought every thought, I've scrutinised every motive. There's no woman on earth to rival your beauty, there's no thought as complex as the curve of your forehead, there's no motive more pure than the eyes with which I watched you that night as you lay on the bed. It sounds like a fulsome compliment, but I swear by my love that it is nothing of the kind. You were at once magnificent and modest, condescending and gentle, imperious and penitent.

I sat in the armchair opposite, feeling scruffy, unkempt, confused. I remember that I was shaking with rage while telling you of the despair I felt at the sight of women who weren't you, and all you kept saying in reply was 'It's all right, it's all right, it will all be alright somehow, don't worry, we'll fix everything, 't will heal ere you marry, what's confessed is half redressed,' and stroking my hair. And although I was careful not to mention Vera by name so as not to offend your ears, it was her I was talking about, and from your shudder I knew that you understood what I meant, when I told you that one little finger of yours has more Christ in it than a whole confession of those pious women, and let them go on being hypocrites with their God while Mary the harlot prays to Mary the mother.

O pity me, Olya, pity the coward in me, I said. Can it really be that this is forever, and that I can never have you? Never have you the way I want you, completely and without residue, dissolving in myself like an ignoble metal? Can it be that I can never have you, full stop, in the same absolute sense in which I will never be offered the presidency of an international bank or win a medal in the next Olympics? In the same sense in which I cannot become twenty-six, or a male model, or even rich? In the same sense in which no woman can ever rival you in my eyes, or possess my soul with the same terrifying completeness? You're so near I could touch you, Olya, but even now I'm afraid. You're so beautiful I'd sooner die than touch you. Tell me if it's ever possible for a man like me to become worthy of such beauty.

At these words you reached out to embrace me, and the second great miracle of our love occurred. Tears began pouring down my face, large and round like the pearls in that accursed necklace, just as I had always imagined them, so large and so round they seemed artificial, like the crystal drops used to represent tears in a famous Dadaist photomontage of the 1930s. Then I knew you were right, that all would be well, that somehow it could still be fixed, that lost causes have a way of finding themselves in our hearts, and that it could not be that the son of these tears, as St Augustine has his mother say in the Confessions, *would be lost forever. Was I wrong again, darling? Was I blinded by these tears, so long in coming? Was it because I hadn't been born a saint?*

You know, long before I met you, at university, I used to edit a magazine, and one of the authors I had writing for us was an old Romanian called E. M. Cioran. He's dead now, but his was the voice most reminiscent of our Rozanov. Vasily Rozanov, so unhappily married to Dostoevsky's mistress, remember the story I was telling you? Well, Cioran had this book, published in English as Tears and Saints, *and there he says that if it weren't for their tears, saints would be of no more interest to us than anything else that went on in those little backwater towns all those moons ago. Tears, wrote Cioran, are the searing joy of ignorance, the ecstasy of the mind overwhelmed by the heart, the bliss of submission newly experienced by reason. Like music, they are a surrender.*

Olya, you can't have forgotten that night. You can't have forgotten those tears, you just can't. A little later we found ourselves talking about the money. I said I would send everything to the solicitor's account first thing in the morning. No good, she said. The flat originally agreed had gone to another buyer in the interim, and a new one she'd found, in the good part of Earls Court just behind the Boltons, was £30,000 more. That was all the cash she had, but she was prepared to part with it. The mortgage lender had agreed to the change of property.

All right, I said, I'll transfer the lot in the morning and take the cash off her later. This was, to the penny, all the money I had left, and I knew I would need the neat little bundles from her suitcase to finance what the tabloid papers might call our *life of Riley*, unless they were envious enough to call it *an empty and meaningless sex, drugs and alcohol fuelled existence.*

5

In the early hours of the following day I gathered together all of Vera's personal effects and sent them off to her in a taxi without so much as a *billet-doux* of regret. Then, having faxed the relevant instruction to the bank, I set off in search of Olga to present her with a copy of the date-stamped transmission.

She had been living with Elena and her husband, whom the *makeup artist* had married for his British passport but then, seeing that at the moment her opportunities were few and far between, thought better of it and decided to become at least a selectively dutiful wife until something better came along. At any rate, this is how he himself chose to explain it to me on our first meeting, adding that he regarded himself as the last of the realists, a view I chose not to contest. 'She's a blonde, a stunna,' he said, 'I hann't seen real-life tits like that at close range since college, so tha's goo on me, an' soon's the bitch *misbehaves* she's out on 'er dumb li'l butt, an' don't you worry, I'm ready for it.' And I thought to myself, yes, of course, real-life tits, but what does this realist know of real-life tears, said by some long-forgotten English dreamer to be liquid pearls pure enough for angels to bathe in?

He was a Turk, born in Islington and wily as a coyote, stealing cars, dealing drugs, swindling old ladies out of their pension money in his spare time. He was handsome, vain about his appearance, and for all that as sharp as a blade, what the Italians call *sveglio*. For some reason he took a liking to me from the start. I think that, having heard the story of my love affair second-hand, initially from his wife's but later from Olga's lips as well, he pitied me the way convicts in *Notes from the House of the Dead* pitied Dostoevsky. 'What are we going to do with you,' his eyes seemed to say, 'you're too innocent for this world, but it would take more than killing you to put you out of your misery and just at the moment I can't think of what that is.'

The first thing the innocent noticed, after descending into the Turk's one-bedroom basement flat that morning, was a ballpoint pen. It lay on a little table by the telephone, next to the couch in the sitting room where Olga was staying, and

I saw that emblazoned on its side, in a nasty kind of gold, was the name *Hotel Raphael.* What a lapse of security.

That Olga was always secretive, a trigger for many an explosion in our past, was beyond doubt ever since those weeks of life with the Finn called Valerie. When challenged, she would justify it with any number of ready banalities, privacy, space, mood and the like, though the trouble with banalities, as every writer knows, is that they do not convince. When, speaking with somebody, she would jot down a number on the notepad next to the telephone, she automatically wrote it in a secret code, whereby the digits were paired up, punctuated with commas, and transposed into a sequence to which she alone held the key. Equally instinctively, whenever she would write some perfectly innocuous note with a biro, or even a hard pencil, she would tear out and dispose of the sheet immediately underneath, not so much for the fear that the message might fall into the wrong hands, but for no special reason at all, just to be neat, as a good business practice. She learnt lock combinations by heart, removed designer and size labels from her clothes and underwear, and memorised new English words all in the same way, intuitive and unthinking. And yet here it was, material evidence of a visit to the Paris hotel where the Arab *porcone* had proposed to billet Vera's embonpoint. One might almost think it was left out there on purpose.

If I could have been confident at that point that this was mere oversight on Olga's part – that she had not intended to impress on me, like so many hot nails, the realisation that jealousy is prophecy – I would have taken care to suppress the pain. A general amnesty was in effect, after all, since the night before. I had been living with Vera. What right had I to question her doings? Hadn't I thought, as I ran for my life, that if it isn't this one, it'll be another? Well, it was this one.

Then again, far from concealing my liaison, I had made every effort to advertise it, because I wanted Olga to understand that she was out of my life for good and to receive the parting gift of my honesty. But, in the circumstances, what was her understanding if not sheer despair at the prospect of destitution? And what was my honesty if not spite? Still, not twelve hours after the watershed at the Chelsea hotel the anxious question that had been haunting me from the very beginning was again uppermost in my thoughts. Why lie? Why conceal? Why not make a clean breast of everything?

Here's a modern fairytale with just the sort of happy ending I had in mind. A boy and a girl, who have recently met and become lovers, agree to meet somewhere, say in Geneva. The night before they speak on the telephone. The girl, who lives in Geneva, is in what they call a funny mood, sad and a bit tetchy, and she tells the boy that she may have to fly to London to look after a former boyfriend of hers, who is in hospital. The boy, trying hard as he does to be understanding and a good Christian, gets his back up a little, and asks whether he should not change his plans. She is evasive, which he takes as a sign of assent and a tacit dismissal.

The following day, instead of arriving in Geneva by the evening train, due there at six, he flies off to another destination. He feels angry and bitter. She waits for him at the station until midnight, writing all the while in her diary. She is distraught, because she realises that all she wanted to do was to test his mettle, his will, his resolve to love. He has misunderstood, and now she may have lost him forever. But at length they speak, and the ensuing reconciliation cleanses and strengthens their affection for one another. Like de Musset's Brigitte offering her journal to Octave, she reads out to him the diary entry from that unlucky evening at the railway station, and the entries from the day before, and from the night before that. Another few moments, and all becomes clear as crystal, sweet as honey, straight as the Aristotelian line of reasoning.

O hypocrite! I should have said to myself. What about all those epistolary admonitions on the evil of progressive rationalisation and the manifold virtues of complexity? *Now* all of a sudden you want everything to be simple, eh? Now you want her to confess all to you as you have to her, to snivel on your breast as you have done on hers, to dissolve in you as you claim to have dissolved in her? *Why, you old goat?* So that everything can become fairytale-neat, textbook-symmetrical, crystal-clear and honey-sweet? And what about the beauty of life, which you say is all asymmetry and paradox? What about love, which is courage and tears?

But I couldn't keep down the pain, and so I asked her about it. She said she had no idea where the stupid biro had come from.

6

Amnesty, amnesty, general amnesty, that was the byword of those newly mistrustful days. I began a campaign of persuasion intended to prize Olga loose from the Turk's basement, and in the process, quite unintentionally, became his friend and confidant.

I must admit that it was instructive for me to observe the home life of this couple, which, as in one of those fairground funhouse mirrors, reflected some of the essential contradictions of my own life with Olga. Her friend Elena, tall, blond, buxom, something of a stunna not merely in her husband's view, had only *worked* for a couple of months before being taken on by him as his mistress. Unlike Olga, who had been a *professional* in St Petersburg before coming to London, she was only nineteen and a rank amateur. And yet, unlike Olga, apparently in that short time she had managed to acquire all the music-hall traits of a Weimar prostitute. She was so lazy that she wouldn't get out of bed to stub out a cigarette, slipping the butts under the bed where they continued to smoulder, but since anyway she was terribly untidy, with clothes, pizza boxes, hairbrushes and other articles pertinent to the nominal vocation of *makeup artist* bestrewn all over the bedroom like Milton's leaves of Vallombrosa, and since anyway she never liked to leave the bed before three in the afternoon, to her admirers her laziness seemed less an unattractive trait than a component of an intriguingly bohemian personality.

She was also stupid to the point of appearing inanimate, like the jackass of a workman who, after putting up a bathroom cabinet and noticing that it's upside down, scratches his head in genuine disbelief, but here, once again, many men found this quality of her character useful and admirable. If the owner of a pizzeria – I'm not speaking wholly hypothetically, as there was a favourite one in Knightsbridge, in fact, where all Russian hookers congregated – were to tell her that his friend was a famous producer, who would get her into films in exchange for her showing him the way to the men's lavatory, she would believe him as naturally as my maternal grandmother used to believe that unless you made a triple sign of the cross over your mouth while yawning, demons would get inside, demons so tenacious, she left me free to surmise, that even repeated application of menthol ointment to my lower back would be powerless to exorcise them. Yet in reality the friend might be little more than an unsuccessful singer, or an accountant moderately well-connected in the world of Brazilian television, or simply a pizzaiolo from Caserta spending his holidays in the city of Piccadilly.

The Turk watched the proceedings out of a jaundiced corner of the eye. If she weren't such a slob, he reasoned, a girl so objectively in demand all over the place wouldn't have agreed to live with him, and the same if she were motivated enough to get herself a regular day job. But her gullibility got to him, despite the fairly obvious point that it was part of the same mutually advantageous deal, and a few times I was gratified to see him hovering on the brink of physical violence.

Russian thieves have a saying, which their molls often learn the hard way: 'When I screw a woman, we both of us screw her. When you screw a man, we both of us get screwed.' Islington is a long way away from Odessa, of course, and the Turk, a self-proclaimed realist for whom the concept of fidelity was anyway an abstraction, did not espouse this kind of chauvinist maximalism, but he obviously felt humiliated at the prospect of being played for a sucker by a woman who could not tell the difference between Harvey Weinstein and a pizzaiolo from the environs of Naples.

And, slight as that actual difference might be in purely intellectual or physical terms, he was quite prepared to beat up his wife for her inability to recognise it, something he would never have contemplated if faced with the fait accompli of ordinary, impulsive, gratuitous infidelity.

How odd, I reflected, watching him squirm at the approach of the owner of Pizza Puttanesca, a corpulent dwarf with many more tattoos than Hollywood connections, that he should fancy himself a hardnosed realist. For despite all his macho posturing he was in love with the girl; in love, strange to say, with her soul, her personality, and even with the inscrutable titbit of her personality that was her mind. He didn't so much object to another man having it off with her, so long as it was just for fun and she enjoyed it; but he didn't like people taking advantage, that is to say, using their arguably superior intellect to subdue her will and bend it to their liking. It was the dumb blonde's soul of which, unbeknown to him, he was feeling protective to the point of physical violence; for what is the soul, as he ought to have asked himself, if not freedom of the will?

The Turk liked having me round. As I uncovered and marvelled at certain parallels in our respective situations, so he too felt flattered by the idea that I, no thug, but to the contrary, a man of exalted learning and independent means, as he saw it, should have ended up in the same gutter as him. So it is not uncommon for two people, playing wildly different stakes at the same table, to bond with each other when both start losing, though one of them stands to lose a thousand and the other a million. I would even argue that some of the pity, or sympathy, that the Turk felt for me stemmed from the same source, because of course to the richer man the million he is risking may mean a good deal more than the thousand does to his light-hearted neighbour; but when the reverse is the case, and he's out there desperately losing the very shirt on his back, it is a rare pauper who can suppress the thought that a million's a million, and that's just something you can't put in relative terms.

Still, at the bottom of it all, for him as for me, there was something that just wouldn't compute. He inferred, from the sheer fact of my high-rolling presence alongside him in the same leaky boat, that Olga was *way different* from his wife and all the other hopefuls in the subterranean demimonde of Pizza Puttanesca, but I saw that he was at a loss when it came to quantifying that difference; they each of them had two legs, after all, they were friends, they all chatted in Russian to one another as social equals, they had had their implants done at the same clinic, they all were or had been hookers. What other essentials were there? And yet his chips were £5, while I, it looked like, was betting the house limit.

Just think of it, this guy was going to *buy* her a flat. He'd bought her a car, and a passport, and clothes, and jewellery, and what only not. He'd put her up in hotels, at a whim, whenever she happened to be feeling *claustrophobic.* He was coming round, with zinc buckets of tulips and lilac in his arms, to *convince* her to move back in with him, up and out of the dreary, poor man's basement, and guess what, she was refusing! 'Now, have some loyalty, girl! You just can't treat people like that. It's the real world out there, honey, or has nobody told you? If I been him, if I could throw money around like that, hell, I'd have you on the straight and narrow in no time, or else back in "Peter" or wha'ever you call the place where all you russki devils seem to be from. So he comes round here, with these monster bouquets that don't fit in the door, and shows you a fax that says he's done what you wanted. Now you listen here, *I'm British*, I'm not from St Petersburg or wherever, and I know what's a fax and what's a cod, and if I were you, I'd take one little look at it and I'd say thank you, baby, now what can I do for *y-o-o-o-u?* Friendly, like. And what do you do? You turn up your nose, and tell 'im you'll believe it when you see it. Now what kind of way to behave is that, I ask?'

The next day I finally managed to persuade Olga to move to the Chelsea hotel. She couldn't move back in with me, obviously, because the flat had been polluted by my infidelity. But what of her infidelity? And what about the general amnesty? The Turk felt sorry for me.

And I felt sorry for myself, in part to test my newfound aptitude for tears and in part because, like a newly acquired clumsy item of furniture, or even a new pair of slippers, that plays havoc with a confirmed bachelor's mode of life, the truth now seemed to intrude on the dream in a way that, despite the intellectual prowess with which the Turk so generously credited me, I found too awkward to philosophise away. When I wasn't in the same room with Olga, doubt would begin devouring me in a succession of ghoulish scenes from Dürer, their incubi and succubi only more frightening for being more recognisably human than the German artist's. Then I would turn to her letters for a breath of bottled ozone, letters that only days earlier I had been swearing I would never touch. She was alive, those contradictory letters

229

of the writer's final period, panicked and vituperative, said to me. Alive, alive. If she was alive, then it was really true that I wasn't dead.

A salient feature of those letters was that they were all perfectly legible and, by and large, quite literate. It was as though a tardy pupil had suddenly been motivated, that is to say, acquired a motive. She wanted to be understood. But whether this incontestable novelty could have been accounted for by the monetary disincentive with which I had booby-trapped my escape, was a thought too cynical, perhaps, even for my friend the Turk.

7

My soul, my dove, now I say my farewell as I begin distancing you from my heart. I am so sorry that during this time with me you have not been able to change. You must suffer, my beloved, suffer for the rest of your life. Our love broke because it was not right of the man to ask a young decent Russian girl to bear the burden of sin for them both. She couldn't, and in his turn he had to admit defeat. By then he was useless to her, as useless as a sixth finger on a person's hand.

You've been defeated, beloved, not by me but by yourself, and this is why you're ever so intolerant of my failings. You cannot admit to yourself that in your heart there is no longer room for genuine feeling, that I was your last attempt to become a man, that I was your last chance. I grieve with you. Cry, cry, cry now, if ever you can manage to shed a single tear, but better still if you cry your heart out with those hot, heavy blobs that one can almost hear as they fall to the ground. If you can, there's hope. O–O, how cold and shrewd and calculating you are, like a reptile. Goodbye forever, my beloved. We've had everything, we could've had everything. But we've lost it all, and now may the devil help you to live with yourself, the same devil whom I have always loved in you, the devil who is your minister and confessor.

So cry well, my beloved, and don't worry about the money, it's only a trifle. O–O, I don't think you'll make it this time, I really don't, but I do pray to the devil that he helps you to organise yourself, to rearrange things, to adjust as you've always managed to do in each of your nine lives. I'm not going to lecture you on morality, because you've always said that this is something that only immoral people do, and how I worshiped you for saying that! No, I wish you to survive, that's all, and to keep on living in a way that you will convince yourself is happiness, without love, with only books to supply what is hidden from you in life, the only kind of happiness you have known and are used to mastering.

I cannot sleep tonight. O—O, because it's tonight. Yes, tonight my fate is going to be decided.

I accept your failure so easily because it is only now that I see with my own eyes just how weak you are. But still I cry, if only because I can. And still I cry, if only because I was so wrong about you. I thought that apart from being a great charmer you were a nobleman, a man of character, a man with an unstoppable will. But you're not even a weakling, you're like the inside of the bread that in prison they'd shape into any kind of little figurine they wanted. You've run away, you're afraid to meet with me, to see me, to answer me. You're probably not even reading this letter.

Son of man, find the courage to look the woman in the eye. Why do you want to suffer? I know how you're torturing yourself now, how terribly unhappy you are, how tormented by your own twisted and sadistic conscience. Meet with me, spend a few minutes in your ideal world, be honest with yourself. Writer, you need this more than I do!

Writer, stop using your cold and slippery brains for tying up your heart into knots, stop drowning your emotions like newborn kittens. Allow yourself just another few moments of life, who knows, maybe you'll always look back on it as the most precious gift you've ever received, and follow the dictates of your inner world, the world I alone have seen in you, because you know something? Nobody besides me gives a damn. And so I'm waiting to hear from you, your Olga is waiting, beloved!

Forgive us, forgive me, forgive yourself. Let mercy be my redemption.

8

Good morning, my once stern taskmaster, my once gentle maidservant. I write with the news that my mortgage has been approved by the bank. I enclose copies of everything that's been sent over by the broker. My life is now in your hands. If you only knew how I long to meet the new year in a place of my own, you wouldn't think of dashing this dream, you'd want to see it come true because you love me still.

I know that you do, I can feel it for all the distance between us. I know that you fantasise about my bed and all my enticements, about my indulgences and reprisals. You see, I can freely admit that there are still moments when I think I'm going crazy at the thought of all that. And you shouldn't deny your love either, but should tell yourself that not a year will pass before I drag you back into my bed, which is where you belong. — The customer(s) must read all of their valuation report, particularly any sections relating to repairs to the property, and should give a copy of the report to the legal conveyancers. Funds sent by telegraphic transfer will normally be sent one working day before completion, providing sufficient notice has been given by the customers' conveyancer. This offer is valid for six months from the date of the valuation. If the customer(s) do not complete their mortgage within this time, updated references and a new inspection of the property — *sorry, I started writing on one of those papers. So I beg you, don't destroy our marriage bed, as neither of us can live apart from the other. Or maybe I'm wrong? I probably am.*

Meet with me. See me. I refuse to believe that when you took my blood money from me you were secretly laughing. I don't believe it, I just can't believe it, I'm not going to believe that you're like that. My dove, don't smother your soul, I beg you! Call me. At the very worst, another six months or a year will go by and we'll be good friends. But I don't want to end it the way it seems to be ending.

At least let's behave like adults and part from one another in a better way. Let's wind up our relationship and be done with it without bitterness on both sides, with a light heart and even a goodbye kiss. I'm an adult, and you too have become more mature since we've met, so why can't we behave like ladies and gentlemen? I know how you value your honour, your dignity and your name, so why don't you break up with me honourably? You'll still have your pride, and I'll have mine. Don't be a coward. Meet with me, look me in the eye.

We parted badly, it was morning, we weren't ourselves. Meet me in the day, speak with me soberly and calmly, sort us out. I know you're on the run, twisting yourself this way and that, trying to wriggle out of the truth I'm telling you by every means at your disposal, both moral and immoral. But unless you come and see me before it's too late, that truth will keep coming back to you, like a restless ghost, no matter with whom or where you are. I'm not afraid of ghosts any more. Show me that you aren't either.

O—O, I was your love. You've tried to love and couldn't, just like you kept trying to cry and couldn't, like you wanted to be sincere and couldn't. Nothing could ever have changed you, I don't think. But now you've really put the nail into your soul's coffin, by throwing yourself again, as you have, into the debauchery of easy money and heartless pleasure, and by extinguishing within yourself the one little spark that glowed when you first knew me. So I know that nothing I write here will change your mind, because your soul isn't there to make you listen.

Yet, knowing this though I do, I believe that you're suffering none the less, especially if or when you're alone, at the terrible thought of how little of me you've been able to have and to hold. Having lost your soul, and with it your faith in love, you probably suffer from having only yourself to torture with your lovelessness. I, on the other hand, am both a painful reminder of your present poverty and a glimpse of the future luxury that is forever denied you, a young, beautiful woman who has defeated you fair and square. This is why you can't bring yourself to meet with me. The hallmark of your character is weakness.

When you finally read this letter, and when you read it again a second time, I want you to ask yourself if there's any point living the way you used to live before we met, which is again how you're living now. Haven't you had enough of those pitiful attempts at sensuality, each of whose trivial plots you've long known by rote?

234

Yet everything real is closed to you, and has been closed to you since adolescence.

Ask yourself why. You've always been afraid of being alone, you fly from solitude as if it were a contagion, and you're perfectly willing to trade the rare, priceless moments of true sentiment and sensuousness for a lifetime in the company of any number of mendacious and ineffectual people, who, instead of enriching your world view, merely pull you farther along on the road to decadence and dissipation.

The one sincere thing you've ever had inside you is your desire to love, to love unreasoningly and unrestrainedly, because you learnt by reading books that such a love existed. You daydreamed of this love, you lived in the hope of falling under its spell. How's your body doing these days, does it demand more sustenance to have the energy for obliterating this hope? But then, calculating venality is never in short supply in the circles you move in.

In life there is but one choice, love or money. Money is always useful, but love has nothing to do with any of its uses. I feel deeply that you're ignorant of this distinction, in so far as you cannot grasp it with all your heart. You're a Westerner. But still I implore you to meet with me, if only to relieve your sense of anxiety, to salvage your honour, to assuage your feelings of failure and guilt, and to take away the terrible aftertaste of our parting. Just try to act human this once. Not so that we can be friends, I now remember you've always hated this phrase, but so that the gnawing of conscience in your breast can give way to even a kind of peace.

Your first and last attempt at love.

9

The month Olga spent in the Chelsea hotel, before she allowed herself to feel sufficiently placated to move back in with me around the middle of February, felt like a repetition of a roulette sequence, one of those crazy straight runs that gamblers get to ride every so often, when the numbers we fought like demons less than an hour ago come back, in virtually the same order, to restore our faith and replenish our pockets. All of a sudden the sequence, which seemed oblique and made a mockery of our judgement, acquires, by the sheer trick of literal repetition on the part of fate, a meaning that is little short of self-evident, unless, at the crucial juncture when our stakes have just about caught up with our hopes – and our winnings with our anxieties – fate gets tired of watching history repeat itself, deciding to dazzle her pupils once more with a *varia lectio* to puzzle out before closing time.

So the smoothing of the discord between lovers proceeded, as though a copy of the musical score in an earlier version had been taken from the library and the relevant passages perused before each lesson, until one day it transpired that the money I had transferred to Olga's solicitors had been lost somewhere on the way from the Bahamas. Had I made the transfer on the 22nd, or if it had been £22,000 that I'd wired, or even if the bank had had the number 22 somewhere in its street address, the superstitious gambler in me would have breathed a bitter sigh of relief and said, well, you can't go against fate. But nothing of the kind had come to my attention. It was a regular night at the tables.

Every week we checked on the bank's efforts to locate the

missing wire, and every week the answers to our queries grew more ambiguous. Olga's mood, meanwhile, was worsening. I had had some dealings with banks before, and had money lost by them on many occasions, often just when it was most needed to cover up some hazardous indiscretion. Olga, by contrast, had had no experience of banking whatever, and the very idea that a *bank*, a bank *in the West*, couldn't account for a client's funds at any given moment seemed inconceivable to her. If Westerners didn't know about money, what did they know about? It was obviously foul play. I had to use all my worldly wise ingenuity to keep her temper from boiling over, yet as the days passed I felt myself infected by her suspicions. Her attitude of *credat Judaeus* no longer seemed an absurd Grandmother Nadia peppermint anodyne, her village stubbornness had been vindicated and now looked like prudence. Maybe we *were* all of us actors in a private theatre, manipulated by an unwashed demiurge from somewhere just west of the Urals. What worried me, obviously, was not so much the temporary, or even permanent, material loss, but the consequential loss, in one apparently inevitable fell swoop, of all of the woman's confidence in me and in my future by her side.

When at last the transfer had turned up, Olga moved out of the hotel and into my flat. It is possible that the gesture had been intended as something of a quid pro quo, a reward for all the prurient curiosity I had been able to suppress since the reconciliation, as well as an acknowledgement of the fact that the embarrassment caused by the jinxed transfer and the consequent delay had been the result of a genuine cock-up. Her mood, however, suggested otherwise, and the reasons

I read into it were fairly straightforward.

It is well known that buying property in Britain is often a confusing and debilitating affair, certainly for people who, if not on the actual margins of society, have little hope of seeing their names on the printed page. After a month of fighting disbelief caused by a simple bank error, Olga now found herself in a maze of pedantry that led her from signing officially condoned, yet fraudulent, financial undertakings to having other people sign equally official and equally mendacious statements concerning her employment, character and prospects. It was just like being back in Russia, with the vital difference that there was no *authority* to bribe and nobody at all to guarantee the outcome.

Small wonder that her splendid sangfroid began to wear a little thin. And that was just the beginning.

10

By the third month of the ordeal by Western routine, her mood turned distinctly paranoid. It was now the beginning of April, and she seemed no closer to possessing the room of one's own than she had been in November, as estate agents prevaricated, solicitors made excuses and bank managers demurred. In some strange way I saw myself in her present anguish, with the flat as the great unattainable that was Olga, and I pitied and comforted her all the more when I saw it that way.

The key to the flat, for her, was a key to the West. Together with all the legal and banking arcana that went with its acquisition, it represented the frustrating mystery of a text in an unknown language, a cryptic cipher, a conundrum, a code. The solution was so close she could hear the sound of the door opening, yet this brought her no nearer to the state of unqualified possession than the lingering of her scent in the bedroom brought her to me. By this juncture she was wanting to *complete* with a kind of aggressive uncertainty that bordered on manic lust; her fear of failure bore all the marks of a lover's fear; and her resentment at being messed about by the various functionaries, united in a conspiracy aimed at separating her from the object of her affections, was something like jealous rage.

Her nascent paranoia, oddly enough, brought us closer together in those months, closer than we had been since the course of tender care in sunny Palermo. She saw me as the only person about who fully understood her problems, who worried about the eventual outcome, who knew all her bureaucratic enemies by name. She threw herself into housework, at first ironing ironically, in nothing but a stripy blue-and-white apron and a pair of high-heeled shoes, then seriously, *alla contadina*, cooking and cleaning with a peasant vengeance and hair in a decisive knot worthy of a mother of three. She stopped seeing most of her friends, embarrassed by their questions about the unaccountable delay which seemed to imply that the flat might be a figment of her imagination, carefully planted there by the unscrupulous and manipulative varmint she had for a lover. Finally she took to calling me *Mapa*, uniting the syllables of 'mother' and 'father' into a humorous sobriquet that was in reality, I felt, a muffled cry for help.

I wanted to deepen the source of Olga's new confidence in me, to bind her newfound reliance with fresh emotional complications. It was at that point that I took what was for many reasons a tremendously difficult decision and asked my aged parents to fly over from New York to meet her. They came, put themselves up in a hotel and stayed in London for a few days, scattering the money they did not have with a carelessness that would have given pause to a spoilt teenager. As it ought to be evident by now from even the most basic impression of my character, my parents had never criticised any of my life's ambitions or solutions. My declared love for Olga was no exception. My father recited Blok, my mother sat and looked at her with the liquid eyes of a village woman waiting by the window for her soldier son to come home. She passed no judgement, but once, when she said to Olga 'My son loves you,' and Olga replied 'Yes, I know,' I thought that a flicker of something like the recollection of a witnessed injustice swept across her brow.

On the eve of their departure a terrible thing happened. I was with both my parents in their hotel room when Olga telephoned, choking on tears, to say that her father had died. He was an alcoholic. He died in his sleep. I rushed home to hold her in my arms, but by the time I arrived the fit had subsided. She was now an orphan, though unfortunately the orphan I found was morose, withdrawn, distant, deep in her shell.

I knew that Olga had not been on good terms with her hard-drinking father at least since her mother's death, when she was sixteen, and that more than a year had passed before she sent him word that she was living in England. There was bad blood between them, I realised, yet just how bad the blood was I never dared to ask, suspecting the worst. It had all the signs of a classic scenario, and her subsequent flight to St Petersburg from her small home town half way out in Karelia, her maniacal self-reliance and secretiveness, and her distrust of men, only exacerbated by her subsequent choice of profession, all owed something, I guessed, to that initial breach of trust some ten years earlier. Still, there was going to be a funeral and she might want to attend.

It was, of course, an unignorable irony of fate that my own parents – so pathetically permissive, so naively tolerant, so ridiculously loving – should have been present at the very moment of the suspected malfeasant's death. Why do these things happen? Why is it that no sooner does the man who's been playing zero and the neighbours for the last six hours, with nothing to show for it but a full bladder, leave the table to at least have himself a tranquil wee, than the electronic display in the gaming room, neon red on lacquer black, explodes like fireworks with his heart's desire: *32! 3! 3! 26! 15! 0! 0! 0!*

Needless to say I felt like a loser again. The two worlds, Olga's and mine, as irreconcilable as Petersburg and Moscow – as Russia and the Russian emigration, as corrupt patriarchy and veiled anarchy, as bleak monochrome and instamatic colour – could not have collided at a moment less opportune.

11

My sentimental improvisation having backfired, in the days following my parents' departure I had little success in luring

Olga out of the shell into which she had withdrawn, and one fiasco in particular, as symbolic as it is mysterious, goads the memory. The Sunday on which the Russian Orthodox celebration of Easter fell that year was everybody else's Easter Sunday, a coincidence which, due to the vagaries of astronomy used to calculate the timing of the moveable feast, happens no more than a few times in a generation. I would not go as far as saying that I took it as an omen, but there was certainly *something* auspicious about the coincidence as far as the union of the two worlds was concerned.

I had not been to the Russian church in Chiswick, with the colourful name of Cathedral of the Dormition of the Most Holy Mother of God and the Holy Royal Martyrs, since the day my son had been christened there, though I admired the wise, plain-speaking priest and, whenever I felt flush, sent him money for the needs of the parish. Easter being the highest point of the Orthodox calendar – far more important than Christmas, certainly, for the good reason that anybody can be born and even wangle a whole bunch of presents from the magi, but just go ahead and try raising yourself from the dead – I thought that bringing Olga to hear the splendid liturgy might somehow begin to fill the hole in her heart.

It was about seven in the evening. We didn't need to leave for another few hours to get to Chiswick in time for at least a part of the service. Even if we got there by eleven, we'd still be all right. The high point of the ceremony was the procession of the Cross, which began at midnight.

She said no, she wouldn't come. 'Olya,' I began begging, 'I ask this of you as a favour. That means, something that's done without thinking, just because another person's asked you and said pretty please. In fact, don't you agree that in this most basic sense I've never asked a favour of you in all the time we've known each other?' This was true, and I'd only realised it at that moment. 'And I wouldn't think of spoiling this amazing record if I thought that my wish was something just for myself. But look, I'm asking you to come to church, not to a football game. How egotistic is that?'

She said she loathed the smell of incense. My heart sank. I've never been much of a church goer, and don't regard myself as excessively pious, but there are certain things that, in Russian, one simply does not say lightly. There is a set phrase, *shying away like the devil from incense*, which is used to describe a mortal fear of something. Olga's unsmiling appropriation of it *en clair* to excuse herself was, to say the least, unsettling.

'It would only be for an hour,' I pleaded. She withdrew into one of her interminable silences.

At length she came back with a different stratagem. Slamming the bedroom door, she shouted that she would never come because *she* would be there, and that I knew it. It took me awhile to understand what she meant, but then I remembered the night in the Chelsea hotel, and *although I was careful not to mention Vera by name so as not to offend your ears, it was her I was talking about, and from your shudder I knew that you understood what I meant, when I told you that one little finger of yours has more Christ in it than a whole confession of those pious women, and let them go on being hypocrites with their God while Mary the harlot prays to Mary the mother.*

She had taken good aim. What could I say in rebuttal? To say that Vera attended a different Russian church, the one in Ennismore Gardens in Knightsbridge, would have recap-

tured my past with her in a far more gross and tactless admission of intimacy than the mere mention of her name. All
of a sudden I felt old, used and weak. 'Olya,' I said, on the
verge of tears, 'I implore you to come, and I promise that if
there is anybody there you want me to spit on, anybody at
all, I will obey you and spit in *his* or *her* face.' Fine, she said
unexpectedly. And began to dress.

How amazing she looked that evening in her churchgoing
costume, in a long dark dress and under the white scarf that
always made her look like Grace Kelly at the wheel. But she
kept biting her lip, and we drove to Chiswick in silence. The
church, dedicated to the Dormition of the Immaculate Virgin, was bedecked with white flowers and drowning in candles, and the smell of incense had come upon us even as we
were leaving the car in Harvard Road. She was pale as death
and seemed unsteady on her feet.

I held her arm with one hand and crossed myself with the
other as we entered, but then she veered left to the women's
side and I took a step to the right to stand with the men. Not
five minutes later, I turned round and saw she had gone. Hur-
riedly I crossed myself again and backed out of the crush into
the churchyard. She was nowhere to be seen. New worshippers kept arriving, streaming past me as I walked all the way
back to the street corner where we had parked.

She was sitting in the car, smoking a Marlboro Light, with
the radio on. I had never seen a face so deathly pale, like the
chalky, pergameneous kind of drafting paper used by archi-
tects. 'Why?' I said. 'Why can't you do this for me?' 'I just
can't,' she said. 'The smell is too strong. Makes me sick. You
stay, but I'm not going back in there.' The procession of the

Cross was beginning, and from where I stood by the car window I could see hundreds of glow-worm sparks pouring out of the church and into the churchyard, milling about by the doors and swarming round the stuccoed edifice, as white in the candlelight as that beloved suffering face. Of course I didn't stay. We drove home just as we came, in unbroken silence.

12

Completion was all I had left to pin my hopes on, right alongside hers it seemed, and then at last the miraculous happened. On the morning of 21st April my beloved collected her keys to the West from the estate agent's in Old Brompton Road. Together we gave the new flat a quick clean and moved her things there. Her clothes, her books, her stereo, her video camera, her precious suitcase of silvery aluminium, all it took was a couple of trips.

The following evening we went to drink champagne in a restaurant nearby. The place was crowded, throbbing like a drainpipe with the spending power of Chelsea youth, gurgling and spluttering with the usual amiable inanity one can hardly avoid in these pointedly democratic places. A bunch of Italians were at the next table, with their gregarious *ma sai, mia madre, cio è, io non so* drifting toward me every few seconds above the general pandemonium.

Olga was now free of me. Our mutual friend the Turk, whom I had seen a few times in those weeks, had told me to watch out for this moment when it came. As a man in love and a man of the West, he understood all along that I was playing it straight; as a man of the East and a cheap crook, he understood that I was buying Olga freedom. He didn't think she was ready for it, any more than his own wife was. More important, he thought that I wasn't ready for it. But then, what did the realist know? He hadn't even read *The Idiot*. 'By Tolstoy?' he said, with a knowing nod.

And yet, and yet. I started feeling unwell after the first glass of champagne. There is between people who have been together for some length of time a tightly stretched spider's web of mutually recognised signals, and the lightest tugging at the bit of gossamer at its centre has all the dramatic and sinister import of a midnight telegram. It was at the centre that Olga kept tugging, as though on purpose, and it was the sense that she was doing it on purpose, of course, that made the purpose seem as sinister as it did.

She was going to Russia, she said. Oh, just for a few weeks. 'What on earth for?' I asked, more hurt than incredulous. She knew that so long as we remained together it was the thing I feared most, the raw nerve for which I thought no salve strong enough, the card I believed no other card in my deck could trump. I didn't want to, I couldn't go back to Russia. It had been the defining distinction of my consciousness as an émigré since the day I became one. *The Return* was the title of my grandfather's play. Once an outlaw, always an out-law. Good men never went back to beg Cain for clemency. I would never return, not for anything in the world, not even if I were given the Stalin Prize, like Brecht, or whatever non-communist-sounding handful of tinsel it was that they bribed writers with these days, maybe the Dostoevsky Prize, or the Tsar Nicholas Prize. Not even for her? Not even for the love of my life? O, but she would never demand such a sacrifice.

This meant I had to let her go on her own, and that meant I was going to lose her. Maybe not to a sudden reversal of consular benevolence, or to an unforeseen problem at immigration, or to a change of mind on the part of her old keepers, but to something for sure, something dark and dank and without a name, something out there in the unreachable loneliness that was the very soul of that grotesquely made-up political fiction. To a man. To a woman. To an idea. I felt it in my racing pulse, and in my temples. I felt it in my groin. I felt I was seeing her for the last time.

'You're returning to Leningrad?' I asked helplessly, because I had never been able to bring myself to say *Petersburg* with a straight face. Petersburg?!

I've returned to my city, familiar to tears,
To inflamed glands, to childhood's veins and fears.

For Osip Mandelstam, even seventy years ago there was no more Petersburg.

You've returned, now see that the dose is right:
The cod liver oil of Leningrad's quayside light.

And she? She, who had been my nostalgia and my redemption? *Now listen, for God's sake, Olga, just listen, this is not just a matter of nomenclature what I tell you,*

Petersburg! I don't want this to end:
I still have your telephone numbers to hand.
Petersburg, I still have the addresses
To locate all the corpses for parting caresses.

247

'Yes, first to Petersburg,' she said coolly, 'then home to visit my father's grave and what's left of the family, but then I'm planning to stay on for a few weeks, maybe a month. Maybe go to Moscow. You remember the photographer I used to work with? Well, I think I'm going to stay with him for awhile.'

She had, in fact, once showed me a portfolio of photographs, of the sort that the girls in London needed to have done whenever they joined a new *escort service*, which often kept the pictures on its website long after the girls themselves were gone, off to a new life, a new photographer, a new madam. And so I asked the question I'd taken care never to ask before. 'Yes, of course I have. And what of it? He's nice. Listen, I was living in his studio, what do you expect? Half of my stuff is still there.'

Anybody may judge me now. God knows I've judged myself ever since.

13

I ran out of the restaurant, and ran past Battersea Bridge along the Embankment until I could run no more. Then I sat down on the front steps of somebody's house, to catch my breath and to think. No, not to think. Thinking was out of the question, an impossible proposition, as unnatural a manoeuvre as riding a bicycle backwards. What had I to think about? About a life wrecked for the sake of a mirage? It had been that before Olga. About the frailty whose name was woman? That too had been in the air for quite some time before the young lady made her appearance. About the fact that I was a jealous maniac? But I had never known jealousy until I met Olga and fell in love with her, so obviously one feeling was part of the other. On the face of it I was no maniac at all, except that it was perfectly clear to me that I was. But trying to think about why this might be the case seemed useless.

I began walking, with hardly a thought to where my legs were taking me this time. The last time they took me to the Chelsea hotel, where Olga taught me to cry. I might have reflected that while my two previous attempts at flight, the first one an eternity and a half ago and the more recent one – November, December, January, that's three, then February, March, April, naturally, today is April bloody twenty-second – exactly six months earlier, had ended in thinly veiled ignominy, this third could be the lucky one. Russians do just about everything in threes, kissing, crossing, and even forgiving, as witness the popular nursery rhyme:

First time forgiven,
Second time forbidden,
Third time, for all time,
We latch the gate shut.

Sooner or later, it had to end. The gate of the Baumann Garden had to slam shut as suddenly as it had opened. There was no future there, only darkness and fear and banks of violet snow.

Besides, what kind of future did I ever envision? Did I imagine her as a school teacher, in one corner of the room softly lit by a table lamp, marking up examination papers, while I, a Decembrist in exile, sat in another corner in my old dressing-gown, composing an angry feuilleton at a penny a line and, once every so often, looking up to launch a tender obeisance in the general direction of the table lamp?

Or did I imagine her as a modelling agency executive, prostituting her willowy charges since before breakfast, lunching with pimps, totting up columns of figures before calling it a day, and then coming home to kiss her beloved, at work on the greatest Russian novel written in English since *Lolita*? No, I'd only ever imagined her as my wife and as the mother of our daughter, though *mother* and *daughter*, as I should have known even from my own life's scant experience, were merely words, not realities, and giving them tender names, like *Olya* or *Katya*, did not render them any more immanent. So really it was all just a kind of madness.

I realised that I had been walking towards Earl's Court Road, in the direction of her new house. A minute later I was leaning on the bell. Was she home? Was she alone? 'I won't let you in,' she said through the intercom, with matronly dignity in her voice. 'You're angry, and I'm afraid of you.' I lost my temper, lending fresh substance to the charge of disorderly conduct, and shouted something unintelligible into the little prison grille. But this was the West now. The gate had been shut. Her home was her castle.

As the rest of that feverish night passed, I began to think. I remember asking myself some hard questions that I'd never dared to answer before, and this time I answered them to the prosecutor's satisfaction. The whole subject of general amnesty was reopened, and I was even able to introduce into evidence the Turk's testimony of some Spanish boy's *freebie* visits to the basement over Christmas, as well as his sworn statement that the controversial sojourn in Paris had *paid off*. Furthermore, she had *really linked up* with the star-making owner of Pizza Puttanesca, who did not neglect to tell her that he would find the right job for her *in fashion*. There was no way out of the shabby dialectic, it seemed, either for her or for me.

While thinking all those horrible thoughts and juxtaposing pieces of evidence, one more gruesome than the next, I was calmer, oddly enough, than I had been in months. I felt that an organ, or an extremity, had finally been amputated successfully, and though I still sought its presence with my heart, at least I could see with my own eyes that it wasn't there. By and by my mind began to turn to more mundane issues, as I reassured myself with sadistic glee that *life is practical*. She still owed me money for the flat. Far from being unable to spend it on a life with her, I would now be unable to spend it on a life without her, which, while being cheaper, was probably longer. Apart from that, speaking of gangrene, there were those damn videotapes of hers.

The thought of Olga's experiments in blue-movie making falling into a stranger's hands made me squirm with a pain like no other I had known, though on rational reflection much of it was as invented as the pain of parting from one's beloved. For, once this emotional Rubicon had been crossed, was there anything out there that was not invented? Surely not shame, humiliation, embarrassment? Surely not honour, dignity, reputation? *Having lost the head*, goes the Russian proverb, *no sense crying about the hair*. Having thrown away the love of my life, to say nothing of having discarded my family like an empty matchbox, was I going to be such a niggling little Philistine as to strain at a tiny gnat of blackmail?

In the morning I spoke with Olga by telephone. I said nothing about the money, asking only that she return the videotapes and the spare set of keys to my flat. But when she came to see me, late in the afternoon, instead of bringing back those unlucky souvenirs – twenty-two of them, comically enough, when counted last – she handed me a box of smashed plastic and loose tape, an artful deconstruction that, notwithstanding the inconvenience of her having had to drive to a shop earlier in the day to buy blank Sony cassettes, had been intended to put my mind at rest. When I objected, she said that she obviously didn't want the tapes in my possession either. I said that it would've been more fair if we'd destroyed them together. With this, automatically I took the house keys from her, and apparently just as automatically she turned to go.

'Olya, wait,' I said. This time I knew this was the last time. My voice broke, but the broken fragments I now found on my lips were as familiar as any of the images one happens upon in a recurring dream. 'Olya, I just want. To say one thing. If ever you decide that you really want to have Katya. I mean, if ever you decide you want me. Specifically, you see? Even if I'm with somebody else. Even if I'm married. I swear to you. You understand?'

She was standing by the open front door, her face almost in profile. She never turned to look at me. Over the half-mouth that I could see there hovered a distracted, Archaic half-smile. An amiable half-nod, and she was out the door. *Olya, wait! I just want to tell you one last thing. If ever you think you really want to have our Katya, if you decide you want me, specifically me, I promise you it will never be too late. Even if I'm with somebody else, even if married or on my deathbed, I swear by what's left of my life that you're its only love.*

14

And yet all of that made for incontrovertible proof of her duplicity. She would keep the money just as she had kept the videotapes, and there was nothing I would be able to do about it. For the last three months, since January, I had been living on borrowed time. I had done no work since I left Venice. My bank account was overdrawn, my credit cards over the limit, my mortgage in arrears. Christ, I hadn't even played roulette since November.

Would she come back? In the afternoons the stillness was unbearable. The gaping bath was dry as a boiled ox tongue. A tap dripped poison over the kitchen sink. Music? I couldn't be bothered, it was all the same, a million variations on the same gypsy tune:

You say there's no love?
Then live without love!

Books? It was all lies, lies. Apart from the perfection that was Nastasya Filippovna, of course. Films? I did watch Hitchcock's *Vertigo*, about thirty times in one month, and eventually even located an English version of the unobtainable French novel on which the screenplay was based. *Why couldn't Flavires simply love this woman and leave it at that, instead of poisoning their relations by his ceaseless probing... If you carry logic to its uttermost extreme, isn't that the same thing as madness... What he loved in her was not that she was Madeleine, but that she was alive... There always remained a confused feeling of enormous injustice, but no alcohol on earth would ever quite remove that.*

Ah, yes, there was alcohol, which I now drank in enormous quantities, two, sometimes three bottles of cognac in the space of a tearful day and a sleepless night. It made the waiting easier. That, and the book of Russian poems I began one day when I was sad and sober:

> Graft your weak seed onto a healthy vine
> Before the salt is made to lose its taste:
> In kohl self-adoration draws the line
> As poppy-lips tell lies to your face.

But waiting, in the words of Giancarlo Menotti's heroine with eyes the colour of tears, was my main occupation. It was like praying, really, with the Russian words and their consonant rhymes like the beads of a rosary of I knew not how many strands, and the book that came into being in those summer months was all the more perfect for being a kind of accident, a collision with time's chariot that had recklessly stopped on green.

One day the Turk came to give his condolences. It was the merry month of May, I was quite drunk, and he brought me a gram of cocaine. I wanted cheering up, he said. We sat up all night, and he told me that Olga never went to Russia to visit her father's grave. She went back to Paris instead, and was now again in London, but only for a couple of days, as she was planning to join the owner of Pizza Puttanesca and the girls in Cannes for the film festival. The Arab, he said, had been treating her nicely, gave her lots of jewellery and paid off her car loan. But it wouldn't last, he said. This girl will screw it up every time, you mark my word.

Then she was going to the Grand Prix in Monaco. He did not know with whom, because she wouldn't tell him. 'She's a real fruitcake these days,' he said. 'She's been telling everybody that she thinks you're going to kill her. Are you?' Of course not, I said. 'Are you going to set fire to her flat? Because she says she's afraid to sleep there.' No, I said, I wouldn't know how to set fire to somebody else's flat. My own was all that I could probably manage. 'Well, I wouldn't envy her. Shouldn't surprise me if she goes off the deep end.'

A few days later Alex, the Russian photographer who had walked off with the real Italian princess at Olga's sham wedding and was a mutual friend of mine and Irina's, telephoned with a piece of staggering news. Irina *urgently* wanted to make peace with me, he said, but that wasn't all. Olga had been to see Irina. Olga had tried to seduce Irina! Olga had left her car in Irina's underground garage. Olga had left her *suitcase* with Irina for safekeeping!

That evening I went with Alex to make peace with Irina, an episode which may be of passing interest to people who, in their idle moments, find themselves wondering how peace is made among Russians. 'Just get the suitcase, first make the peace then get the suitcase, just get it from her, then you can always come back and make as much peace as you want,' Alex was coaching me on the way. We headed for Kensington, where Irina lived in guarded splendour in one of those fortified enclaves of foreign wealth that allow embassies to nestle in their midst because facades overhung with national flags make them look less conspicuous. An electronic gate opened begrudgingly, and the tallest in the row of three dangerously tall doormen, who seemed even taller in the uniforms of the imaginary Hussars regiment that had been designed for them by their employer's anachronistic whimsy, lazily reached for the phone to announce our arrival.

'Ah, there's our incorrigible young Werther!' yelled Irina from somewhere within an enfilade of dimly lit rooms, 'Your milkmaid's just been here!' Irina's eccentricity, nurtured by the wealth of the Russian *biznesmen* of a husband from whom she was separated, was a London legend. She was a perfectly sane, clever woman in her thirties who outwardly resembled a Dresden figurine, but her Moscow upbringing had infected her with the notion that sanity and even cleverness were the purlieus of the vulgar; consequently, she shuttled between the morning role of a psychotic recluse, when she was quite sober, and that of an expansive extrovert, when she got a little tipsy in the evenings. The incongruity was not unpleasant, and the spectacle of a diminutive blonde with a porcelain complexion reciting by heart a long passage from Kant's *Critique of Pure Reason* would have been amusing enough, had it not been for one concomitant feature of her character. She never seemed to listen to anything anyone said, not even for a few seconds, and I often imagined myself marooned on a desert island, dying of exposure and dehydration in her presence while she raved on about Kant's appalling naivety.

The story I heard was this. Convinced that the break in my friendship with Irina was permanent, Olga came over to ask Irina to keep her personal effects for her while she was abroad, explaining that I was sure to break into her flat in her absence. She then presented Irina with the official version of her life which I had invented – nice girl, poor family, university years, odd jobs, flight to England – and a sombre account of our final quarrel, which led on seamlessly to her removing her clothes to illustrate what I had lost and what Irina had to gain.

'I hate seeing people naked, don't you?' said Irina, and went on talking without waiting for me to answer. Eventually Olga was coaxed into a pair of pyjamas, stayed the night, and left the following evening with one of Irina's drivers, allegedly for the airport, to visit a girlfriend in Ibiza. But the driver later reported that no sooner were they out of the gate than Olga changed the destination to Waterloo Station, where she took the train to Paris. One of Irina's Hussar doormen, moreover, recognised her as a nocturnal visitor to the hotel in Park Lane where he used to work.

Despite all this, and despite the fact that I had originally fallen out with Irina because she *wouldn't* accept the version of Olga's life I'd invented, she was now resolutely on her side, while I couldn't get a word in edgewise as usual. Olga was terrified of me, Olga was confused, Olga was hurt. I was a stupid bastard and a dangerous lunatic.

Hours passed. We were becoming more and more drunk, as Irina took turns bemoaning Kant's naivety and my failure as Olga's saviour, my shortcomings as a man and my lack of talent as a writer. By four in the morning I found myself on top of her, my fingers closing around her porcelain, Dresden shepherdess throat, strangling the living daylights out of her as Alex tried to pull me off with cries of 'This is how you make peace?!' After a short exchange of expletives, Irina threatened to call security unless we cleared out of her life for good. We left. I walked home alone through the Kensington dawn of shutting casinos and piles of newspaper returns outside Indian corner shops.

At seven in the morning my telephone rang. It was Irina. 'You know, you may be right,' she said. 'Come and get the goddamned suitcase.'

15

A friendly Pakistani locksmith in Old Brompton Road had the suitcase opened in the time it had taken me to produce a £50 note. The videotapes were there, all twenty-two of them and another, unlabelled one, nearly an hour of running time. The footage was of Olga, seated in front of a mirror.

She was heavily made up, almost to resemble a circus clown, and the atmospheric neuroticism of the footage owed much to expressionist pioneers of silent cinematography. The lipstick alone was worth the price of admission, Chanel's most vitreous magenta applied with all the slashing nihilism of a film heroine's suicide note. She was trying on the new jewellery she had been given over Christmas, which was also in the suitcase. I remembered the Turk, his cynical words and his disgust at the thought of people taking advantage. This was the diamond pavé from Dubai's duty free, the braided gold from the malls of downtown Beirut, the pale and cloudy rubies from Bombay's shopping arcades. And she was trying it all on in front of the mirror, intoxicated, excited, guilty, disgusted even, but triumphant all the same, a huntress bloodied with the still-warm blood of the quarry.

I found the good stuff, which I had given her, and packets of cash in four different currencies, much more than she had ever admitted to having. I took back all the jewellery, leaving only the Arab's gifts, and all the money she owed me for the flat. I took the mobile phone bills, which she had always kept locked, and copies of her expired passports, which I had never seen. I also took a bunch of keys, and some bank deposit receipts, and a few unsent letters addressed to me.

THE DORCHESTER

9th January, 4:22 AM

Are you sleeping? I'm not. I've been out all night, but I cannot sleep. And you? How are you? Still as cynical and acerbic as always? Still as condescending as ever, my little fool? What am I to do with you, my child… My defenceless, vulnerable child.

Speak to me, my unhappy manikin. Talk to me now. I am your hope, your dream. Your love isn't sleeping. Are you? Are you sleeping? Are you really sleeping? Sleeping… But how can you be?! Goodbye, my child.

The money I took to the casino and lost in a single night. The jewellery I gave away, piece by piece, in the course of four consecutive evenings, to women I scarcely knew, including a waitress in an Italian restaurant where the owner used to let me drink at the bar for hours after closing. Then I lugged home a case of Hine's Rare & Delicate and started in on the mobile phone bills. I may have believed that, without art, truth is invisible, but *seeing* is not what a drunk man is after. Now that the last ethical bridge had been well and truly crossed, I wanted to roll in literal, direct, undifferentiated truth as if it were the gutter. I can only say that reading those bills confirmed every cynical opinion the Turk ever vented, though obviously what mattered at this point was not who was right about Olga's moral character but the morning clarity with which I now knew that she would never come back.

But that unlabelled videocassette, where was that from? It must have been made just after Christmas, maybe on New Year's Eve. The histrionic mood of the footage suggested that on her part, too, an ethical barrier had been crossed, a new leaf turned and an old one burned. How unhappy she looked in those frames, only slightly drunk but coked up to her ears, making come-hither faces in the glass like a child playing with her mother's makeup, camping up the dilemma now behind her. A lighted candle stood to her right on the dressing table, symbolising what I couldn't decide. That her days were numbered? Remorse? Faith?

The bunch of keys must have been to the Arab's apartment. There were some receipts for bank payments, and blank letterheads of the horrid hotel in Park Lane. I remembered the desperate words of her letter, which must have been written just after Christmas, *I cannot sleep tonight. O—O, because it's tonight. Yes, tonight my fate is going to be decided.* Yes, it rang a bell. This is what the heroine of Ostrovsky's play *The Dowerless Bride* says just before she accepts a face-saving proposal of marriage from the loser of a suitor whom she loathes. Olga knew the play in Nikita Mikhalkov's film version, *A Cruel Romance*, which she often watched on video at my house.

That marriage never takes place. The town beauty, the portionless bride of the title, is seduced and abandoned by the local grandee, a ship owner who himself marries an heiress to shore up his fortune. 'I love you,' says her pathetic eleventh-hour suitor, a postal clerk, in the final scene, 'just tell me how I can deserve your love.' 'You lie,' she stammers. 'I've searched high and low for a man's love, but I've never found it. They all look on me as a plaything. There is no love in this world, and no point looking. I haven't found the love, but now at last I shall begin to look for the gold.'

'No, now you must be mine,' he exclaims. 'Anybody's, but not yours!' is all she has the time to say before he fires a pistol at her. 'Darling,' she says, dying. 'What a blessing.'

16

Later all sorts of terrible rumours started, and began flowing towards me through various channels, of whom the Turk was as ever the most reliable and Irina the most convoluted. Olga had been to the Cannes film festival, and to the Monaco Grand Prix. She had been seen there with several men of Eastern physiognomy and spending habits, and though the owner of Pizza Puttanesca never found her a job, it appeared that in the end she did not want one anyway.

On her return to London, she immediately reclaimed the car, with the unlocked suitcase back in the boot, from Irina's garage. Her home might or might not be a castle, but as to whether Irina's was there had never been much doubt. The tall doormen in Magyar guise were strict, and never allowed her to go up and meet her treacherous friend face to face; more angry than tearful, apparently, she phoned Irina that same evening to tell her that what she had done was not unlike murder in cold blood. Irina countered by telling her that one ought to not tell lies to those on whom one relies; except that in the original Russian what she said was less like a proverb and more like a curse.

The Turk said she had gone back to work. She had no way of paying the mortgage on her flat unless she began *seeing people* again, and since doing this without an intermediary was enervating and possibly unsafe, she had had to find a flatmate to keep her company. This was Anya, her friend and colleague from Vita's days in the mews house. They would share the same bed, drink tea in the kitchen as they talked shop, sometimes get called out together. Anyhow, it was better than ending up back in Peter.

Then again, it appeared that she was not averse to the idea of an intermediary either. Gala, a lifelong friend of the famous London madam whose name I had used as a bugaboo when trying to dissuade Olga from a career in fashion, rang up to say that my ex had been in touch, asking for work. Aware of what she regarded as Olga's unprofessional conduct in my case, Gala gave the applicant a bad recommendation, and the golden door closed. 'There's honour among thieves, don't you know?' said Gala. 'Anyway, she doesn't want clients falling in love with the girls. All kinds of nasty stuff can start.'

One evening my telephone beeped and I saw Olga's number on a text message that read as follows: 'Do you want to see me and talk?' She was addressing me by my Christian name, which she had unaccountably misspelled, in a message written in English. 'To see you and talk?' I texted back in English. 'Why? To tell you that I love a liar, a cheat and a thief? We both know that you are, and that I do.' All I remember feeling was a slight tremor of satisfaction at the slimy thought that if I couldn't defeat her in any other way at least she'd be left feeling defeated by my syntax.

A liar, a cheat and a thief. Was that really what she was? No more so than I ever was, to be sure, or anyone else for that matter in a set of circumstances that encouraged erratic and unconventional behaviour, such as love or war. But the more I kept thinking about it, washing my brain like the hands of Lady Macbeth of Kensington and Chelsea with French brandy, the more some inexpressible realisation tugged at a corner of the mind, and I hardly knew anymore whether I kept drinking to tease it out of myself or to suppress it like the memory of a crime.

Could she really have been so naive as to feel that she was doing a clever thing when she went to park that precious suitcase of hers at Irina's? Could she have been stupid enough not to have reflected that Irina and I were old friends, two people of the same milieu, and that what we had in common made for a social bond far less elastic than the pity one blonde feels for another, even when the other's a homeless orphan? Could she have so badly underestimated, on this one occasion, the power of society, its conventions and rules, the invisible power she had so often chided me for acknowledging as real, yet one she herself had so often felt with her very own skin? *Or had she done it on purpose?*

The trouble was, I could just see it. I could easily see her doing it on purpose. I could imagine her, in a self-destructive mood veiled by rational platitudes, in a fit of self-loathing camouflaged as practicality, even as common sense, convincing herself that she needed to leave her life in somebody else's safe hands, yet knowing equally well all the while that what she really craved was not security but betrayal.

I could easily imagine her planning the whole episode as a histrionic trap, never really sure whether it was intended for herself or for me, leaving the aluminium suitcase with Irina in the divided hope that I would abase myself to reclaim my due and punish her in the process. It was a schizophrenic's idea of catharsis, and the suitcase represented the material substance of life that had been tearing us apart since the day we met.

As a gambler I knew all about catharsis, but one really didn't need to be much of an Aristotle to figure out why, after having reclaimed my due just as Olga had hoped and feared, I wanted to rid myself of every last trace of that material substance as if it had been the weapon used in a double murder. This is why I knew I had to throw those packets of money back into the casino maw, and why I gave away her jewellery to nameless strangers. We deserved one another, Olga and I, and all the cognac in France could not fill the enormity of the emptiness I saw in the love we had lost.

17

Did she ever exist, or did I invent her? Was she a mirage, a kind of apparition designated by the Sanskrit word *maya* in the Vedas, a thirst quenching source that I had wished into being by the spasm of a desiccated and loveless heart? Was the awfulness of her beauty merely a reflection of my latent fears? Was her personality simply a suitable vessel, an aluminium suitcase with a number lock, for my nostalgia? Was it all just a gambler's terrible dream?

These questions are deeply offensive, of course, but this is not why I flinch. I flinch because anybody who would ask these questions has misunderstood what I have meant to say in this book, which in turn suggests that my failure is now complete. For in love it is indeed the privilege of the *weaker* to invent the *stronger*, not the other way round. And thus I may not have invented my wife, nor poor Vera, nor any of the other women whose manicured fingernails ever grazed the surface of my skin; but to have invented Olga, who was more real than I ever was, is the portion I have in consolation.

To claim otherwise is to deny the awful truth we stare at in the street every blessed chance we get, which is that it is the loved one who is stronger than the one who loves. To claim otherwise is to follow the absurd logic of the vulgar argument that beauty is in the eye of the beholder, when in fact the very substance of our pupils becomes softer than white Carrara under the master's chisel when objectivity reaches down to straighten a stocking seam.

What in the world isn't invented this way, I ask. Science, art, religion are all formed by the affection, the expectation and the fortitude of their practitioners, who blow fantasy after restive fantasy, like so many glassblower's bubbles, into those recognisable and workable shapes which the world eventually comes to regard as beautiful or useful. Given everything that we now know about the epistemology of science, for instance, it is downright foolish to say that Newton discovered gravity. No, he wished it into being; wished it in the teeth of common sense and accepted logic with the maniacal obstinacy of a lover who wants to see wisdom where the inanimate others observe sheer cupidity; wished it with the blind faith of an artist determined to see a flying machine where the rest of the world sees merely a mess of wooden planks resembling an incomplete skeleton of a plywood pterodactyl. Yet each and every thing obeyed, conformed and came into being.

And hasn't the world itself, our whole fierce and beautiful world, been invented and made this way by God's love? A maniacal love, a masochist's dream, a compelling obsession for the sake of which no sacrifice seemed too great or too gruesome? *For God so loved the world* that he has been made by it: as mad scientists are made by their discoveries, as village tinkers are made by their inventions, and as I have been *made* by Olga.

And wasn't the almighty father in that terrible story, in turn, invented by his dreamer of a son, the carpenter *manqué* whom he allowed to suffer and die on the cross and perhaps never loved, or loved only in a way, as Olga loved me? '*Eli, Eli, lama sabachthani?* that is, My God, my God, why hast thou forsaken me?' Wasn't he, this God in Christ's story, *made* in that farewell spasm of betrayed love, in those last seven words, in all his blind faith that he had been put on earth for a purpose, though the soldiers laughed and a mocking voice in the crowd said, 'Let us see whether Elijah cometh to save him.' And wasn't he, Christ himself, made in this same way by the suffering love of his natural mother, which, as I say, must have been absolute, objective and indubitable, by the real, uninvented love with which everything ended and began? 'Woman, behold, thy son!'

Yes, she has *made* me, this windlass made me by the life-saving and crucifying power of her beauty. The unscrupulous dynamo has made the poor slob of a mark, she has made him into a man capable of feeling, of weeping and praying, and then, like the great confidence artist she was, she has returned home to the notional heaven whence all beauty comes and where it lives. Like the great artist, she took in her hands common clay and breathed life into it with her painted lips and her eyes like two dying stars, and the lump of clay moved, and wrote a sad poem, and stood up like a man to confess his pitiful commonness.

Oh sure, she's used him. The maker has every right to use whatever material suits his aims, clay, marble, bronze, or paper, and has even newsprint ever complained? But has he not used her more than she's used him, because in Moscow as in London a ream of blank writing paper can be bought from any stationer's with a few small coins, and there are always plenty of paper reams, and all are more or less alike, but a writer's invention is always unique, even when what he aims to write is not entirely fiction. *Without you,* she said to me once, *I lose the sense of my uniqueness.* Oh, how thrilled I was then, I remember, at the sound of those words! *But without you I would never have had that sense to lose.*

Goodbye, Olya. Goodbye, my maker, my avenging angel, my first and last love. I wish I knew where that awful heaven was, whence beauty like yours comes every thousand years or so and whither it goes when its time on earth has been done. How lucky I am to have been chosen by chance as your mark.

I promise to pray to the Virgin to the end of my days — for only a mother's love is immaculate — and to keep confessing my folly and weakness to her in my prayers. I have been proven unworthy of this visitation by beauty, which is a face and a moment whose memory is all that remains of life as a man sits alone in a room, and the light goes out, and he is left darkling.

And so I must now live. This, as they say, is my cross. And so you must ever remain, my love, beautiful as unfulfilled desire, eternal as human vanity, awful as winter twilight.

Olya, where are you?